Cat the Vamp

Cat the Vamp

Christina Martine

By Light Unseen Media
Pepperell, Massachusetts

Cat the Vamp

Copyright © 2009 by Christina Martine. All rights reserved. No part of this publication may be reproduced, stored in a retrieval system or transmitted in any form or by any means, electronic, mechanical, photocopying, recording, or otherwise without the prior written permission of the copyright holder, except for brief quotations in reviews and for academic purposes in accordance with copyright law and principles of Fair Use.

Cover and interior design by Vyrdolak, By Light Unseen Media.

This is a work of fiction. Names, characters, places and incidents are either the products of the author's imagination or are used fictitiously, and any resemblance to actual persons, living or dead, business establishments, events or locales is entirely coincidental.

Perfect Paperback Edition

ISBN-10: 1-935303-01-5
ISBN-13: 978-1-935303-01-5
LCCN: 2009933297

Published by
By Light Unseen Media
PO Box 1233
Pepperell, Massachusetts 01463-3233

Our Mission:
By Light Unseen Media presents the best of quality fiction and non-fiction on the theme of vampires and vampirism. We offer fictional works with original imagination and style, as well as non-fiction of academic calibre.

For additional information, visit:
http://bylightunseenmedia.com/

Printed in the United States of America

0 9 8 7 6 5 4 3 2 1

Thank you, Inanna, for giving me the chance of a lifetime and many thanks to you, the reader.

Catherine drank and immediately was filled with a warmth she had never known before. For a moment, it seemed that everyone else in the room had vanished. She was alone with Morgan, tingling with excitement and elation. She could feel every particle in her body changing, fulfilled and content at last. She traced Morgan's sides with her fingers until she came to his hands. She held them and felt his energy pass into her. Never before had she felt so satisfied, so happy, so perfectly complete.

Cat the Vamp

1

Catherine Taylor had lived in the small cottage in Stoneysea ever since she first came into the world. It was a charmingly simple home furnished with pieces made from the forest surrounding it. The large fireplace in the living room came alive with brilliant flames every night. A red and white chequered cloth covered the oak table in the kitchen, and curtains of the same fabric draped the large window. Catherine's bedroom was next to the kitchen, with her antique four poster bed, and shelves filled with her dolls and books. Catherine's parents, John and Aneese, slept in the master bedroom. Catherine knew that her parents' room had a bed, but there were many other things in there that Catherine didn't know about.

John and Aneese were hard workers, constantly away on business trips. When Catherine asked her parents where they went, they always told her that their absence had something to do with work, and that was all. Catherine knew that Aneese was a nurse and John was a carpenter, but she couldn't understand why they left her alone so often.

But it wasn't so bad when her parents left, because then Catherine's grandmother Alice came to watch over her. Alice was an amazing baker and she spent hours mixing ingredients in large silver bowls. She always let Catherine lick the batter off the spoon she'd used to mix the cookies. It had become a kind of tradition, a good luck charm, to make the cookies turn out delicious. Alice arranged her cakes and biscuits on pretty plates with delicate roses painted on them, while Catherine boiled water and got out two fragile white teacups with hand painted flowers on their fluted sides. Then Alice and Catherine would sit down to an afternoon tea. As they ate their cookies they talked about the weather and how wonderfully the flowers were growing in the small wooden boxes outside the window.

Many careless afternoons passed by like that when Catherine was young and innocent, when little things amused her and nothing could rob her of her happiness.

As Catherine grew into a young woman, Alice became an old one, and with age, her body started to fail. She grew progressively weaker, and Catherine's eyes swelled with tears when she visited her grandmother. Catherine told her tears to go away. She told them that they weren't needed, but they still tried to break free from her eyes. Eventually, the tears gave up and stopped coming at all. Catherine could not cry, not ever. She wouldn't let herself become upset at what was happening to her grandmother. It was natural, after all. But crying was natural too, and because Catherine stopped crying entirely, a part of her became cold and numb.

The night Alice died, Catherine was sipping tea in her kitchen, studying the wilted flowers in the boxes outside the window. She heard Alice call her from the living room and went to her immediately. Alice took Catherine's hand and stared at her granddaughter with her weak, pale eyes that held so many memories.

"My dear Cat, I want you to know that I love you. You've always been there for me. You've always shared your heart with me. I cherish the moments we've spent together." She took in a slow deep breath. "You've been like a second daughter to me. It's your love that has kept me alive for so long." She took another deep breath of air and trembled slightly. "In time, you will know where they go. You will know the secrets."

"What secrets, grandmother?"

But Alice didn't answer. Her body was limp and her eyes stared blankly at the wall. Death filled the air and Catherine breathed it in.

Catherine gently let her grandmother's hand fall to the side of the sofa. She stood staring at the corpse on her couch for a few minutes, not knowing what to do or how to react. She tried to cry, but the tears were trained and did not come.

A few days later, after a rather depressing funeral, Alice's ashes were scattered over the cottage garden where they seeped into the ground and made the pale pink roses turn deep crimson.

For the next week, Catherine stayed in her bedroom alone. She didn't go to work. She refused to join her parents at the kitchen table for meals and only nibbled at bits of food that Aneese brought to her. She spent the first few days sleeping and thinking. The twinkling eyes of the dolls on her shelves seemed to follow her around the room.

How did grandmother know she was going to die? Where does who go? Mom and dad? What secrets was she talking about? Nothing makes sense!

After this dark period of silent contemplation, Catherine was frustrated, and even angry, that Alice had died and left her alone.

As a young girl, Catherine would sit playing with her dolls for hours, dressing them up in frilly pink dresses. She would sit painting colourful pictures of rabbits in sunny fields and be content. But now, nothing seemed to please her. She had lost her innocence and her passion for life.

On her seventh morning of solitude, Catherine stared at herself in her bathroom mirror. She gazed numbly at her long, sandy hair and the emerald green eyes that lately seemed more expressive than her mouth. When Catherine was upset, sometimes she couldn't find the strength to speak. She tucked a strand of hair behind her right ear, licked her lips unhappily and sighed. She knew she had to face her parents.

John and Aneese were in the kitchen talking quietly. When

Catherine entered the room, they became silent. They glanced at each other and then at Catherine, who was pouring herself a bowl of cereal.

"Cat, can you sit down for a moment?" Aneese's voice was quieter than usual.

Catherine continued to pour her cereal. She closed the cardboard box, put it back in the cupboard, and went to the fridge for milk.

"Catherine, please sit down. We need to talk," said John. "I know your grandmother's death has been very hard on you, and we want you to know that we're here for you."

Catherine sat down at the kitchen table and dug her spoon into her cereal. She heaved a lump of flakes onto the spoon and stared at them for a while. Then she tilted the spoon from side to side and watched as droplets of milk fell and splashed on the mound of flakes like drops of rain on a hilltop.

"Catherine, look at me." Aneese's voice had risen slightly.

"Why should I look at you?" Catherine shouted suddenly. "You're never here. You're not parents. Don't tell me to look at you. The one person in this world who cared for me is dead."

As John and Aneese stared at Catherine, she stood abruptly, pushed back her chair, and left the room.

Catherine didn't look back at the cottage as she marched down the dirt path, her worn black boots kicking up dust and rocks. Finally, she came to a small house painted robin's egg blue with vines twisting up the walls. Catherine sighed as she knocked on the front door. A brown-haired girl, quite a bit shorter than Catherine, opened the door.

"Hi Rose."

"Hey Cat. Just let me get a sweater." Rose returned wearing a brown sweater that matched her hair. Catherine was silent as she and Rose started walking along the dirt path. "How have you been?"

Catherine shrugged. "Okay, I guess."

"I missed you. It's been a whole week since I've seen you. That must be a record!"

Catherine laughed. Still laughing, she let Rose pull her into a hug. With the laughter finally came the tears that had been waiting for so long. Catherine pulled free of Rose's hug and put her hands to her wet eyes. Salty tears flowed down her cheeks and into her mouth.

"It's okay, Catherine, it's good to cry, it's not healthy to hold it all in."

"You always make me laugh." Catherine wiped her eyes with her sleeve. "I'm so glad I have you as a friend."

Rose hugged Catherine again, and the girls stood with the wind whipping at their backs until Catherine was ready to continue.

Rose and Catherine had known each other since they first began school. They had bonded instantly and been inseparable ever since. If Catherine was not at home, she was likely to be at Rose's house. Rose was such a frequent visitor in Catherine's home that she often went unnoticed as a guest. Rose could walk into the cottage, grab a bite to eat from the fridge, and then go rest in the living room and no one would question it.

"You need to get your mind off all the sad things that have been happening recently." Rose kicked a smooth grey rock off the side of the path as they walked. "You need to focus on something else. Let's go to The Cove."

Catherine just nodded, sliding her hands into her jeans pockets.

The girls hiked up the dirt path through the forest, the trees swaying in the wind. Catherine watched the dappled sunlight dancing along the earth floor, and listened to dry leaves crunch beneath her boots. She smelled the fresh autumn air and smiled, glad to be outdoors again.

The Cove, a cozy little coffee shop, was in a clearing just outside the forest, on a cliff with a large lake beneath it. Rose walked in first with Catherine following a few feet behind, scanning the place for people she knew.

"What would you like, Cat? I'll get it for you."

Catherine brushed her hair out of her eyes and studied the menu written in white chalk on a blackboard. "I'll get a hot chocolate."

"Great. I'll get the same, please."

Rose paid the lady behind the counter and the girls shifted over to the side to wait for their drinks. Catherine surveyed the room. There were a few kids sitting with their parents whose faces she knew, but she couldn't recall their names. A man sat in the corner staring out at the sun while he tapped a pencil on a crossword puzzle grid in a newspaper. A woman who Catherine had sometimes seen shopping in town was curled up in a large chair with a book in her lap. She was sipping from a large black mug and every so often she hummed part of a tune that seemed to calm Catherine.

When the girls received their drinks, they slipped out the back door to the patio overlooking the lake. Catherine licked some of the whipped cream off the top of her steaming cocoa as she leaned against the railing, focusing on the water below. "The lake is beautiful today."

The sun was sitting low in the sky, casting a calm orange sheen over the land and water. The air was cool but refreshing and Catherine took in deep breaths of it.

"Hey Rose! Hey Cat!"

"Hey Jake." Rose's lips formed a wry grin as Jake walked toward the girls. "What are you doing here?"

"I'm just taking a walk, having a smoke, you know."

Catherine smiled at Jake and he smiled back, but he didn't say anything about Alice. When it came to talking about death, most people didn't know how to begin.

"The wind is really starting to pick up." Jake took out a cigarette and lighter.

He lit up, and took a deep drag, then turned to the girls to offer them a smoke. Rose and Catherine took cigarettes and Jake gave them both a light. Catherine inhaled and felt the poison seep down her throat. She exhaled and watched the smoke travel in swirls to the sky.

"Are you okay?" Jake asked Catherine.

"Yeah. I'm okay."

She was okay, but not great, and she wasn't happy. She felt a constant yearning inside, like a part of her was missing. Catherine knew it had nothing to do with the death of her grandmother. That had hurt, but in a different way. The aching within her had been there long before, but now it seemed stronger than ever. It was a hunger for something she couldn't name because she didn't know what could possibly fill her, complete her, and make her whole.

Rose and Catherine walked back to Rose's home to rest and talk. It had begun to rain, and with that and the wind, it was no longer very pleasant to be outside.

"Jake looked really good today," Rose said. "He looked so cool and confident. He looks great in red. But I'm sure I didn't appreciate it as much as you did."

Catherine giggled as she looked out at the rain. Large crystal drops were falling hard and splashing against the ground. Puddles were beginning to form on the uneven grass, and in the places where animals liked to hide. Worms were starting to wiggle their way up to the surface, and the crows watched from high treetops with eager eyes.

The rain stopped after dark and took the clouds with it. Catherine had always imagined a scene in which a painter of night flicked his brush at the vast, black canvas of sky, causing millions of stars to become nightlights for children all over the world who feared darkness.

Catherine and Rose decided to camp out in front of the fireplace with sleeping bags. They made s'mores and told stories and talked about who they liked and the problems they had and what they were going to do with their lives. They had always questioned and learned from each other and basked in one another's light.

"That's why we get along," Rose told Catherine. "You're kind of like a child who daydreams and fantasizes about things and I'm the one who's organized. We balance each other out."

Rose fell asleep long before Catherine did. Catherine had always been a night owl. Her body craved the darkness. She felt her best at night, always wide awake and excited. No matter how many hours of sleep she got, she would be lethargic during the day. It was just one of those things she was born with. Her parents liked the night, as well.

When Catherine finally slept, she had a strange and vivid dream. She was walking along a hall in an unfamiliar house and she felt the presence of someone else very near to her. She turned on the spot, her eyes scanning the place for the other person, but no one was there. She continued to walk, but the feeling lingered. When she couldn't take it any longer, she said, "Who are you?"

A man's calm voice answered. "You tell me first. Why do you always follow me?"

Jolted, Catherine awoke. She was still in Rose's house, camping on Rose's living room floor. *But the voice was so real.*

When Rose woke up, she insisted on making pancakes, so Catherine stumbled over to the kitchen table, still groggy. She rubbed her eyes, her attention drifting off to the outdoors. Sun streamed in through the open window, its rays warming Catherine's back.

The girls put maple syrup and strawberries on their hot fluffy pancakes. Catherine tried a strawberry, delighted at how the sweet yet tart juice tickled her taste buds and made her mouth tingle. "Do you ever have dreams that almost seem too real to be dreams?"

Rose was now plopping a berry into her own mouth. "Well," she began and paused to swallow, "sometimes you know you're dreaming and can control dreams."

"No, that's not what I mean. I had this dream last night and someone talked to me. He asked me why I always follow him, but it's strange because he was the one following me."

"What did he look like?"

"I didn't see him, but I know he was there. He seems familiar, too."

"Do you think he was trying to contact you telepathically?" Rose was grinning.

Catherine grinned back and took a bite of her pancake before she answered. "Who knows? It's possible."

When the girls were done eating, they got dressed and went outside to take advantage of the glorious sunshine. Catherine felt better after spending some time with Rose. The day seemed brighter and Catherine felt renewed and energetic.

When Catherine returned home, John and Aneese were sitting quietly in the living room.

"Cat, honey, we've packed your bags with everything that you'll need. We're all going on a trip together," Aneese said.

Catherine, feeling much more accepting than the day before, took a seat opposite her parents. "To where?"

"It's a surprise," said John. "You're a smart girl, Catherine, and you're old enough now to be informed."

Confused, Catherine frowned and crossed her arms. She felt frustrated at how secretive her parents were being, yet at the same time part of her was eager for adventure and the unknown. She had spent most of her life in Stoneysea, only taking short trips to neighbouring cities.

"When are we leaving?"

"Tomorrow morning," Aneese said.

"Just like that? What about work? What about my friends? I have to tell Rose! Where are we going?"

"You'll see," said John calmly. "Everything has been taken care of. I spoke to your boss at the market and he's completely fine with you taking some time off. Business has been a little slow lately."

Catherine shrugged and walked to her bedroom. She flopped down on her bed and reached over to her side table for her phone, and called Rose.

"My parents just told me that I'm leaving tomorrow with them. They won't tell me where I'm going or what we're doing. They even packed my stuff, which I'm a bit upset about. I mean, it's my stuff!"

"Why won't they tell you where you're going?"

"I don't know. Maybe they think I'm upset because of Alice and they're taking me on vacation to make me happy."

"That would be sweet."

Catherine's eyes were searching her room as they talked and she noticed that some of her possessions were missing. She got off her bed and tripped on a large black suitcase, causing the phone to go flying. Half laughing at herself, Catherine crawled over and retrieved the phone. "I'll call you later."

Catherine placed her phone back on the cradle and then bent down to look at her new suitcase. She could tell it was full, but with what?

After considering a few moments, Catherine unzipped the zipper that ran all around the outer edge of the suitcase, lifted up the top flap and peered inside. A few pairs of pants and shirts were folded neatly along with her underwear, socks, notebook, and another book that she had never seen before. She pulled it out and held it up to look at. It was a clean black book with Catherine's name printed on the front cover in gold lettering. She opened the book to find that the pages were blank and smelled fresh. Catherine smiled—a nice, new journal. She closed the book and slipped it back into its original place. She ruffled through the layers of clothes and came to a silky black dress. She let the smooth fabric, like fine satin sheets, slide between her fingers. Catherine folded the dress and tucked it back into the suitcase. She searched for more new and exciting treasures, but there were none, so she zipped and buckled the suitcase closed and sat on her floor thinking. She felt quite confused and called Rose again.

"I just found a suitcase full of my clothes. And there was also a journal in there and this beautiful black dress."

"Do you think they're gifts from your parents?"

"I really don't know. My parents are so weird. You're lucky you have sane ones. I'll call you tomorrow before I leave, okay?"

Rose agreed and the girls said good night. Catherine went to bed with her head full of unanswered questions.

In her dreams, Catherine walked down the same hall that night and once again someone she felt she knew was there with her.

"Who are you?"

"I'm right behind you," the man's voice said.

Catherine turned around and found herself facing a young man who seemed to be her age. He was tall and thin with dark hair and pale skin, but his figure was blurry. Catherine tried to focus on his face so she would remember his features, but it was no use.

Daylight came and Catherine returned to the waking world. Her dream seemed so real that she pinched herself several times before she was convinced she was truly awake.

John poked his head into the room. "I've made breakfast, Catherine. You'd better get up, we'll be leaving soon." Catherine nodded and rolled out of bed.

After some toast and tea, John and Aneese rushed Catherine out of the cottage with her suitcase.

"But I didn't call Rose!"

"You'll have time for that later," Aneese said.

Catherine sat silently in the back of the car while John loaded the trunk with luggage. Aneese sat up front looking over a map of some sort. When Catherine leaned forward to see what the map had on it, Aneese quickly folded it up and placed it into her coat pocket. Catherine sighed loudly as John returned to the front seat and started the car.

There wasn't really anything Catherine could do. She had just turned eighteen, after all. She closed her eyes and prayed that they were taking her somewhere exciting, somewhere she would like.

The trip seemed to take forever and after a while, Catherine stopped trying to decipher where she was and where she was going. Every tree they passed looked the same. Every house they went by was plain, dull and boring. Catherine closed her eyes and let sleep come to her. A mass of green was the last thing she saw before nightfall.

2

The car had stopped and everything was still when Catherine awoke. John and Aneese were nowhere in sight. It was dark, Catherine was alone, and she had no idea where she was. The scenery was not even vaguely familiar.

"Catherine," a voice whispered, "we're here."

Catherine turned to the partly open window and saw a figure standing just outside of the car. "Who's there?"

"Your mother, of course."

Catherine let out a sigh of relief and climbed out of the car to greet her parents. That was when she saw it: a great, stone castle looming above her, standing alone in the night. There were no other houses around, only trees.

"What is that?" Catherine shivered in the chilly breeze.

"We are in Meadowshell and that is Blacklune, your new home for a little while," John said.

"My new home? But what about the cottage?"

"You'll stay here to learn our ways," said Aneese. "You'll learn to harness your talents."

They all took their bags and walked toward the castle along a stone paved path. Catherine's eyes were adjusted to the darkness now. She looked up at the sky overhead, her heart beating quickly. She didn't know the exact time, only that it was night. The sun had set hours ago, and from the woods, Catherine could hear the calls of creatures hidden amidst the swaying fronds of plants. Their voices echoed off a body of water somewhere, which made sounds travel strangely. Howling surrounded Catherine like an unknown force. She was shivering again when she reached the castle doors.

Catherine watched her father inquisitively as he carefully inserted an ancient looking metal key into one of the large wooden doors. Everything was silent as the family entered the foyer. Catherine's mouth opened in awe and a gasp escaped her lips. She gazed around at the dark red walls lined with candles in sconces that made shadows dance about the room. The ceiling was painted to resemble a black sky with glistening white stars dotted over it. In the centre a large crystal chandelier hung delicately from an image of the full moon. Rays of light reflected off the chandelier's surface, causing luminescent streaks to glide over the entire room, creating an enchanting and ethereal entranceway.

Catherine spun slowly around to take it all in. "This is beautiful!"

"Come upstairs," John said, eyeing his daughter with a smile on his face.

Catherine followed her parents up a set of stairs carpeted in scarlet to another hall alight with the glow of candles. John stopped at a door with Catherine's name on it and placed a different key into the lock. It was a silver key and at the top of it there was an intricate metal design. The door opened and all three stepped inside. This room was brighter, lit with electric lamps. The walls were covered with green, white, and blue flowers, and at first the colourful wallpaper shocked Catherine. After her eyes had adjusted to the pattern, however, she found it to be rather soothing. It was so different from the rest of the castle she'd seen. It reminded her of home. There were luxurious green chairs to match as well. A fire roared and crackled in the small gas fireplace surrounded by bricks.

"Cat, sit down by the fire and warm yourself. We have a lot of explaining to do," Aneese said.

Catherine ensconced herself in one of the soft welcoming chairs by the fireplace and watched her parents take the seats opposite her.

"By now, you must be filled with questions," John said, his eyes flickering from the fire to Catherine. "Your mother and I have been extremely secretive throughout your life, but for good reason." He stroked his chin for a few moments, as the fire cast ominous shadows across his face. "You see, we wanted to tell you, but we assumed you wouldn't understand. But now that you've grown up and become wise, we agreed that it was time." He paused again and cleared his throat. His eyebrows furled and he closed his eyes, taking in a deep breath before speaking. "Catherine, your mother and I are vampires, and so are you."

Catherine closed her eyes and let darkness encompass her. She told herself over and over again that she was not dreaming. For a while she just sat there, silent, thinking. Finally she opened her eyes and studied her parents' expressions. "What are you talking about? I go out in the sun all the time and I don't burn to a crisp."

Aneese chuckled softly and then sighed. She smiled lovingly at her daughter, her gaze concentrated and serious. "You may have read about vampires that fear the light, but real vampires can exist perfectly in sunlight. The vampires that you have come to know from fairy tales and stories are dissimilar to us. Real vampires live normal lives like any other human, but there are several differences that define them.

"Vampires are born with a lesser amount of life energy than other humans. Because of this deficiency, vampires become unhappy, upset and depressed if they don't receive the extra life energy they need in order to live a happy life. Some say it is a flaw, but we choose to believe it is a blessing. Being a vampire gives you a unique way of viewing life, but to achieve that view, there are a few steps that have to be taken.

"First of all, life energy is something we all are born with. It keeps us alive, keeps us thinking, and keeps us happy. It feeds us and helps us to grow and learn. It's found in the air, in sunlight, in the food we eat, in the earth, and in blood. Yes, vampires drink blood to acquire the energy they need to sustain themselves. Whereas normal humans can satisfy themselves with food alone, most vampires choose to drink the blood of others along with eating. Do you understand?"

Catherine nodded. "Are we immortal?"

"We are not immortal," said John, "but we do live longer than most humans. Like them, we seek passion and adventure and make the most of our time here. You must have more questions, sweetheart. Don't be afraid to ask."

"Will a cross or garlic hurt me?" Catherine felt slightly embarrassed at herself for asking this.

"Of course not," said Aneese. "You'll die the same way any other human does, as you age."

Catherine smiled suddenly at her parents. "So that's why I like the night, and that's why I'm so pale."

"Not every vampire is pale," said John. "Most of them tend to be because they prefer to be active at night."

"So, what exactly am I doing here?"

"Tonight there will be a ceremony held in your honour," Aneese said. "It's to celebrate your entering our select society. A party will be held afterwards, and the guests will be arriving shortly."

"So this is where you go all the time? Do you come here to have vampire meetings?"

"Yes," said John. "We come together as a group, to learn and study, to talk about events, and to celebrate. Most vampires in this area know each other quite well, but some choose to keep to themselves. You, however, are here for your ceremony, and beginning tomorrow, your classes. You'll learn our way of life, how to achieve happiness, and how to live as a vampire. This is your room."

"How long am I going to be staying here?"

"You'll be home for Christmas." John looked at a clock on the mantle above the fireplace. "It's getting late. We must leave you now and go to our own room." He handed Catherine the same metal room key he had used to open the door before and kissed her head. "Good luck. We know you'll do perfectly fine here."

"Change into the black dress in your suitcase and come to the entranceway at midnight." Aneese kissed her daughter on the cheek. She reached into her pocket and took out some money. "Keep this somewhere safe and spend it wisely. And before I forget, take this." She reached into her other pocket and pulled out a beautiful silver chain with a small crescent moon dangling from it.

"Thank you," said Catherine, putting the necklace on. "What's this for?"

Aneese grinned. "This is a special time for you and this is a very special necklace. I've had it for a long time now. It's very old and one of the most precious gifts I could give you. Take care of it."

When her parents were gone, Catherine explored her suite of rooms. A door from the sitting room opened into a bedroom with light blue walls and a large window draped in sheer white fabric. A wide bed with a white comforter took up most of the floor space. A small table stood to the left of the bed, next to a sliding-door closet. Catherine carried her suitcase into the bedroom and opened the bathroom door. An ivory toilet, sink, and bathtub greeted her eyes. White shelves filled with towels lined butter yellow walls. There was a skylight in the ceiling with a window that could be opened. The suite even had a kitchenette complete with a fridge, stove, square table, and chairs. A counter with a sink stood beneath a set of cupboards. Catherine smiled at the thought of having her very own place for the first time in her life. She went to her bedroom to get settled.

She unpacked her clothes and rested on her new bed, letting her body sink into the deep puffy comforter. She felt comfortable and content, gazing out the window at the sky.

By eleven-thirty, Catherine could hear voices outside her door. She sat in her silky black dress by the fire, waiting for the clock to strike midnight.

I'm a vampire. She tried to let that fact sink in. *My parents drink blood.* She shook her head and laughed. *This seems mental...but it is exciting.*

She left her room to see if anyone else was in the hall. Effulgent candle flames licked the air as Catherine walked along the dimly lit corridor, passing door after door, each with a different name on it. She didn't know where she was going and she didn't know where the hall led to, but she had a feeling she was going in the right direction. Something inside of her was telling her to go on. She stopped suddenly when she heard a familiar voice.

"Who's there?" Her eyes jumped from one door to another.

A man's voice replied. "You tell me first."

Catherine grinned and slowly turned around to see a tall, slender young man with dark brown hair, standing beside the door to his own suite. "You're the boy from my dream!"

"And you're the girl that I keep dreaming about."

Catherine took a few steps closer to the boy. "What's your name?"

He smiled and gestured at his door. "Come and find out, Catherine."

Still grinning, Catherine walked over to the door to read the boy's name on it. "Morgan Silverwood," she said quietly, her eyes returning to the young man's face. "You know, most people call me Cat."

"When did you first arrive here, Cat?" Morgan's eyes were studying Catherine's face.

"Today. My parents just told me why I'm here. I suppose you're here for the same reason?"

Morgan put his hands into the pockets of his sleek black pants and gracefully leaned back against his door, smiling at Catherine. "Yes. We're vampires. I was just informed as well. I've been searching for something like this for so long...something that would finally make me feel complete."

Catherine nodded, her eyes still locked with Morgan's enticing dark stare. Her heart was beating fast and she could feel her blood warming.

"Are you here with your parents?" asked Morgan.

Catherine nodded again. "But I don't know where they've gone off to."

"My parents disappeared, too. They said they'd see me later."

"I know I'm supposed to wear this black dress for some ceremony."

"I was told to dress in this for the same reason." Morgan brushed his hand over his tailored black shirt. "It's almost midnight. We should probably go down and greet the others now."

Catherine agreed and they walked together down the stairs into the entranceway. A sea of black-clad vampires all turned their attention to Catherine and Morgan, and the sound of subdued applause rose around them. Catherine paused and shot a glance at Morgan. Morgan smiled back at her and nodded in the direction of the crowd. Catherine walked forward, Morgan at her side, and scanned the room for her parents.

As the applause died down, a man with greying hair stepped out of the mass of vampires to greet Catherine and Morgan.

"Welcome, both of you, to Blacklune. I am River. We are so pleased to be welcoming two new members into our society." He turned to the group and placed one arm around Catherine and the other around Morgan. "This is Catherine, daughter of John and Aneese Taylor." Clapping started again. "This is Morgan, son of Wolf and Marie Silverwood." The clapping continued and finally died down when River raised his hands. "Everyone follow me to the ballroom."

River walked off, his dark cape billowing behind him, to a set of open doors. Catherine and Morgan followed him into a large elegant room with windows that stretched from floor to ceiling. The floor, chequered in black and white, was shiny and glowed under the light of what appeared to be hundreds of candles that lined the walls. The guests filed silently in behind them like swift spirits and positioned themselves in a circle around River, Morgan, and Catherine. It was time for the ceremony to begin.

"Creatures of the darkness," River said, "tonight we honour Catherine and Morgan and wish them well on their path to knowledge, not only at Blacklune, but throughout their lives. Tonight we watch as Catherine and Morgan become one with the night."

River turned to Morgan and Catherine and stared silently at them, his eyes filled with an emotion Catherine couldn't place. She couldn't seem to take her eyes off him. She felt drawn to his presence, his power, his very being. No one spoke a word. There wasn't a sound in the great room.

"Catherine." River's voice was smooth and deep. "Are you ready to taste the crimson life force that flows through every person in this room, the energy that you have been yearning for?"

Catherine nodded slowly, shivering slightly.

"And Morgan, are you ready to finally fill the void within you, to drink what you crave?"

Morgan glanced at Catherine and then nodded.

"Let the veil of darkness consume you."

Without warning, a group of vampires stepped forward out of the circle that surrounded Catherine, Morgan, and River. They held a large dark piece of fabric, and they began to run with it. Catherine watched as the vampires ran in a circle around her and Morgan. River had moved back into the outer circle. The vampires continued to run, with the fabric billowing in the air like the waves of the ocean. As the runners moved in closer, the fabric began to wrap Catherine and Morgan tightly from shoulders to knees, like a shroud. Catherine and Morgan's bodies were pushed together, and Catherine took a quick gasp of air as the fabric grew tighter. Her nose grazed the side of Morgan's face, and she could feel the young man's warmth through her silky dress.

River raised his hands to the ceiling and the runners stopped, still holding the edges of the fabric in their hands. River slowly walked up to Morgan and Catherine, now entirely bound together in black cloth.

"Catherine, you must tilt your head back and to the right. I'm going to make a small incision on your neck. Don't make a sound. This will only hurt for a moment."

Catherine's heart was pounding so loudly she could almost imagine it outside her body, thumping somewhere on the floor beside her. She glanced about the room, her eyes flitting from one black figure to the next. She drew in a deep breath, closed her eyes, and hesitantly, tilted her head back and waited. She could feel Morgan's heart speed up as River drew a small silver dagger from a sheath and held it up to the crowd.

"Hold still and breathe slowly," said River, raising the dagger to Catherine's neck.

Catherine didn't dare to move. Everything was happening so quickly, she could barely collect her thoughts. She breathed in deeply when she felt the cold blade touch her neck. She bit her lip as River quickly cut a small slit in her flesh.

"Morgan," whispered River, "you must drink Catherine's blood to become one of us. You must do it now."

Morgan nodded and inched his head closer to Catherine's fresh wound. He looked terrified. Catherine could feel Morgan's hot breath against her skin. Her body trembled as Morgan's lips touched her neck. When he began to drink, something inside of him changed. Catherine felt his body tingle and get warmer. When he finally came up for air, he exhaled with a long moan of pleasure. Catherine opened her eyes and carefully turned her head to face Morgan. She saw his lips wet with her blood, but she was most drawn to his eyes, now filled with the same emotion that River's eyes had held.

"Calm yourself, Morgan. Don't speak." River said. Morgan was grinning, but he tilted his head back and waited for River's blade, suddenly eager. Catherine's eyes widened with anticipation.

When River had made the incision Morgan squeezed Catherine's sides and pulled her close. Catherine drank and immediately was filled with a warmth she had never known before. For a moment, it seemed that everyone else in the room had vanished. She was alone with Morgan, tingling with excitement and elation. She could feel every particle in her body changing, fulfilled and content at last. She traced Morgan's sides with her fingers until she came to his hands. She held them and felt his energy pass into her. Never before had she felt so satisfied, so happy, so perfectly complete.

Then the moment ended and Catherine and Morgan stood face to face once again, their lips stained with each other's blood. Catherine stared into Morgan's eyes and felt vulnerable and empowered at the same time. She laughed aloud at how ridiculous this was, but it was all real. It was happening. Her knees grazed the soft fabric of Morgan's pants and her body tingled with electric prickles. Morgan tightened his grip on Catherine's hands and they interlaced their fingers, still staring intensely at one another as the colours around them became more vibrant and sounds more alluring.

The runners began moving again and slowly the dark fabric began to loosen. No one spoke, so Catherine and Morgan obeyed their hearts, which told them to stand still and bask in their happiness.

When they were free of the cloth and all the vampires were back in place in the circle, River returned to the centre. Almost in a trance, Catherine and Morgan didn't move. With a crooked smile, River placed a hand on each of their heads. "Well done."

Catherine and Morgan both took in a deep breath. Catherine couldn't stop staring at Morgan's skin. It seemed brighter, softer, and smoother. He was still grinning and his eyes were wide. Catherine pulled free from Morgan and felt her own flushed face. She was warm. She blinked hard. It seemed as if she couldn't close her eyes. She turned to River and saw that his robes seemed darker and his grey hair appeared silver. She felt both completely at ease and overwhelmed with amazement by her surroundings. She wanted to dance off and explore with her newly awakened senses. But she stayed where she was and waited for River to speak.

❦ Cat the Vamp ❧

"You might be feeling a tad strange at the moment," said River, "but you will get used these feelings and soon will be able to use them to your advantage. Let us all now applaud and celebrate!"

The circle of vampires clapped vigorously and slowly began to disperse. Some headed over to a table illuminated with red candles where glasses of blood were being served in tall crystal flutes along with rich chocolate desserts.

River took Morgan and Catherine to a corner and explained to them that it was best if they rested for the remaining portion of the night, even if they felt energetic. "Sit out the effects of your first blood feast as you become accustomed to what you are experiencing. You may take whatever you please from the table if you're hungry, but abstain from more blood for tonight. You might also feel a slight pressure as your teeth push out."

River moved off gracefully toward his guests and left Catherine and Morgan sitting, dazed, on an antique velvet couch.

"That was one of the most amazing experiences of my life," Catherine said. "Now I know what I've been missing out on, what I've been searching for."

Morgan slid his hand on top of Catherine's and sighed. "I've never felt so close to someone so quickly before. It's like we were one person, like the same blood flowed between us. My heart was your heart."

Catherine smiled and felt a flake of dried blood fall from her lips to the floor. She stared out at the gathering of vampires, flitting gracefully about the room. She closed her eyes and curled up on Morgan's lap to dream.

She was in her new bed. Everything was dark, but something strange was happening. Something was hurting her mouth. She got up and walked over to a mirror and saw two long knives being inserted into her gums.

She awoke from her startling dream, but the excruciating pain was still there in her mouth. When she climbed out of bed she found that she was still wearing her black dress. She couldn't remember how she ended up in her room. Someone must have brought her here and put her to bed. She pulled aside the gauzy drapes from her bedroom window and saw that thick grey clouds were hiding the sun. She walked over to the bathroom mirror and inspected her mouth, to find out why it hurt so much. She ran the tips of her fingers along her teeth and laughed aloud in surprise. Two small but sharp fangs were protruding from her gums. She pressed them slightly and pain spread through her face. She snarled at her reflection and felt powerful and dangerous. Then she started to laugh again, still shocked at what she was going through. She rubbed at her cheeks and left the bathroom to find out the time.

The clock on the mantle ticked softly as Catherine turned on a lamp. She winced as light flooded the room. It was ten o' clock. Catherine sat down in a chair and stared at the bright bulb. Her stomach grumbled with hunger, but she yearned for something else.

She thought of Morgan's charming face and his long strides. She giggled quietly when she thought back to the previous night when Morgan had been pressed against her. She touched the cut on her neck and found that the blood had dried and formed a delightful scab. She had an immediate urge to pick at the scab, and she firmly put her hand down onto the table to stop herself. Her fingers touched something wonderfully smooth that wasn't wood, but fine paper. It was a letter, addressed to her in a swirling script.

She unfolded the letter and began to read it aloud.

"Dear Catherine, your parents left last night and send you their love. You may be feeling slightly confused, but there is no need to worry. You are in good care here, and you'll adjust in time. I've listed your class schedule below. Don't be late, as you have lots to learn." Catherine sighed at the prospect of school and read over the schedule. "Class begins at noon and ends at three every day. There will be frequent trips out of Blacklune. Weekends are free. You may roam off campus when you choose. A map will be handed out shortly. Breakfast is served at ten, lunch at three, and dinner at six in the ballroom. Monday night dinners come with a serving of blood. The castle doors will be locked from ten at night to seven in the morning. Enjoy your stay."

Catherine set the letter down and went to the bedroom to change into jeans and a long-sleeved black shirt. She brushed her hair, carefully brushed her teeth, and then filled a bag with her notebook, a pen and some lip gloss. She left her suite to get some breakfast, hoping to see Morgan.

The ballroom was less crowded than the day before. Now that morning had cast a soft glow over everything, it seemed more relaxing and inviting. Circular tables were set up all about the large space. One long rectangular table held an enticing array of breakfast foods, juices, and two large pots of freshly-brewed coffee.

Catherine caught a whiff of the coffee and sighed with relief. She poured herself a steaming hot mug full to the brim and added a tiny bit of cream to it. She surveyed the ballroom and noticed there were only a few students sitting and chatting at various tables. She felt a rush of excitement flood her as her gaze fell on Morgan, his eyes dreamy, lost in thought. Catherine gripped her mug tightly, forgetting about how hot it was, and walked over to greet him.

"Hi," she said, taking a gulp of her coffee. "Ouch, my teeth."

Morgan looked up from his book and smiled brightly as he watched Catherine settle into a chair. "How are you holding up?"

"Excluding the fact that my teeth are killing me, I'm pretty good, actually. I'm just...overwhelmed."

Morgan took a sip from his mug and nodded in agreement. "This seems surreal," he said, his eyes travelling to the windows. "For the longest time when I was growing up I would think to myself, there has to be something more than this. I couldn't stand getting up every day and feeling this ache inside of me."

"I know exactly how you feel. People always called me selfish. They told me I shouldn't have been sad because I had everything going for me: a home, a family, a good life...but none of that mattered because I couldn't appreciate it in the state I was in. I didn't even know I was in a state until now…now that I know I don't have to feel like that."

"I'm finally realizing what true happiness is. I used to try to find it in others, in material possessions, but I could never find it in myself."

Catherine giggled suddenly. "You sound like my friend Rose. She kept telling me that I needed to feel okay with myself before I could feel okay at all."

"You know what?" Morgan bent forward so his face was closer to Catherine's. "We're basically two very unhappy individuals who have found a reason to be happy, and now we're coming together to celebrate it. And you know what else? I don't feel bad at all about celebrating it. I used to feel embarrassed to show that I was happy, because I was so used to feeling bad. Now, I feel like I can do anything."

Catherine took a gulp of coffee, her heart beating faster with anticipation. Her eyes rested on Morgan's lips, and she smiled. "Me, too."

Morgan smiled back and flashed his newly-formed fangs at Catherine. Catherine felt an impulse to reach out and touch Morgan. Somehow, she knew he felt the same way about her.

"Hey, I overheard your conversation. You sounded a lot like I did when I first came here." A girl with flaming red hair took a seat next to Catherine. "My name is Amber. Just thought I'd welcome you both to Blacklune, since we're going to run into each other eventually and all."

As she and Morgan introduced themselves, Catherine studied Amber's attire in amazement. Amber was wearing a tight black shirt with rainbow hearts streaked across it, a blue plaid skirt, fishnet stockings, and large black combat boots. Her wrists were adorned with colourful beaded bracelets and her hair was decorated with sparkly clips.

"Anyway, see you two in class." Amber hurried off to meet her friends.

"Quite a sight to behold," Catherine said. "I like her."

"Quite a talker. I like her too."

"By the way, do you know where the library is? Class begins there at noon."

Morgan smiled, tapping his fingers on the table. "Yes, I do. But first I want to show you something."

Catherine followed Morgan as he led the way out of the ballroom. She admired the way Morgan was dressed. He wore jeans that were fitted, but not tight, and he had on a loose black shirt. Their outfits matched. Catherine giggled to herself. "Where are we going?"

Morgan didn't reply. They climbed the stairs and finally stopped at a large door at the end of the upper hall. Morgan opened the door and led Catherine up another set of stairs and out onto the balcony of the tallest tower.

Catherine gasped with astonishment at how high up she was. She and Morgan edged closer to the railing and peered down at the earth below where a large colourful courtyard was laid out beautifully. Patches of lavender and herbs of all sorts were scattered beneath them, creating winding paths. Vines with golden flowers that hung like shooting stars climbed up trellises. Benches were placed here and there, along with stone gargoyles and dragons. At the far end, there was a small pond with a few glittery fish swimming about in it.

"You know, dreaming about someone over and over again is one thing," said Morgan, taking in a deep breath, "but meeting them in real life...it's just so amazing."

Catherine turned to face Morgan. He was looking at her with a seductive smile. Catherine bit down on her lip and turned away, trying to conceal her excitement.

They were interrupted by a steady beeping. Morgan looked down at his left wrist and switched off his alarm. "We better get to class. The library is just to the right of the staircase in the entrance hall."

3

A middle-aged woman with hair pulled back into a neat bun sat at the library counter reading. She had deep red lipstick and was tapping her long purple fingernails on the countertop. She smiled at Catherine and Morgan over the top of her horn-rimmed glasses. "Hi, I'm Maggie. Welcome to the library. Your classmates are sitting at the back tables. Feel free to look around and if you'd like to check out a book, you know who to come to."

Catherine glanced at Morgan, who was grinning wryly. "Thanks, Maggie."

The library was quite large. Tall wooden shelves packed full of books on religion, magic, healing, history, and of course, vampires, divided most of the room into long straight aisles. The windows near the front of the library had ornate wooden frames with Celtic designs. Bay windows lined the back wall. The window seats had red cushions with golden tassels. It was a calm and quiet place. Only one bookshelf stood against the back wall of the library. Four large rectangular tables were surrounded by chairs to seat students. To the left of them was a carpeted area, empty aside from a smaller table that supported a few unlit candles.

As soon as Catherine and Morgan reached the back tables, they heard Amber calling to them. "Over here."

All the students sat at the same table. A rather handsome boy with spiky blond hair sat next to Amber. He smiled at Catherine and Morgan as they took their seats.

"I'm Zach. Nice to meet you finally." He put both hands out for Morgan and Catherine to shake. "I was at the ceremony yesterday. You two did amazing."

"And you're so cute too," said another boy, whose hair was dyed hot pink. "I'm Kevin, by the way." He pointed to a girl sitting across from him. "That's Emily." Emily looked up from her book and smiled, her eyes darting from Catherine to Morgan and back to Kevin. She said nothing and went back to reading. "Then there's Tyler." Tyler waved and said hello. "And finally, Alex." Alex smirked and wriggled her fingers in the air. She kept her eyes locked on Morgan. Morgan grinned as he and Catherine glanced at each other. "You two are seriously sweet." Kevin gave a long drawn out, overly-dramatic sigh. "If only I could find my prince charming."

"Just ignore him if he starts to bother you," said Zach. He ran his fingers through his hair and Catherine noticed that both his wrists were cuffed with spikes. He had an eccentric charm about him that Catherine found rather enticing.

"So, we're having a little get-together and we'd love it if you guys could come," said Amber, quickly glancing from Zach to Catherine and Morgan. "Come to the door with my name on it at nine o'clock tonight. No need to bring anything...well, aside from an open heart and mind."

River stepped into view and everyone went silent. He was wearing a long, dark knee-length coat. He walked over to Catherine and Morgan and handed them each a key. "This is the master key to the castle, so don't lose it. It's yours to keep from now on." He stepped back to the open area in front of the tables.

"Good afternoon. I hope you all slept well. By now you all have met our newcomers, Catherine and Morgan. Let's begin with a little lecture on energy.

"Everyone has energy in them. Vampires lack the necessary energy to sustain themselves and therefore need to retrieve it from outside sources. Some are talented enough to feed off the energy people hold by simply being near them. Others have to use physical contact. Someone right now might be feeding off you." He paused, looking at the students, and twitched his eyebrows. "Today you're going to practice taking in energy, and shielding yourself from others trying to obtain that energy. I want everyone to find a partner."

Catherine's and Morgan's eyes met and they nodded silently.

"You better be my partner," Amber told Zach.

"Fine," he said, grinning.

"Emily, would you like to partner with me?" Tyler said, and Emily smiled and nodded.

"Looks like we're stuck together," Kevin said, taking a seat next to Alex.

"Fantastic." Alex rolled her eyes.

"Turn to your partner. Decide which person will be doing the taking first. Before we begin, I want to point out that this is not to be abused. You may have noticed in the past that you get juiced up, or empowered, when you are around people. You might have even noticed that when others are around you, they can't seem to keep up with you. This is because you have been draining them. Now that we all know that we can use our gifts to take the energy of others, we have to make sure not to be too greedy. You don't want to end up relying on the rush that energy gives you.

"There is energy in everything, including nature, but we'll talk about that later. There are activities like meditation and yoga which help focus energy. We'll be practicing these later on, but for now, I want everyone to close their eyes. Clear your mind of any worries or thoughts. Imagine a dark screen. Allow your eyes to focus the way they would if they were open, but keep them shut. Kevin, I see you peeking. Now, the one being taken from, I want you to imagine yourself being completely open and relaxed. Allow your energy to flow from you. You may want to imagine your energy as a stream of white or blue. The taker, I want you to focus on your breathing. In and out. In and out. Slow down. You are open for receiving energy.

Tell yourself this in your mind. Concentrate. Take your partner's hand and feel energy rushing into you. Imagine it flowing through you, warming you."

Catherine felt her hand prickle as she slid it into Morgan's. She imagined his energy travelling into her arm and all through her body. Her head spun, but she continued to take.

"Ah," Morgan said suddenly, pulling his hand away from Catherine. "I can feel it."

"Now switch places," said River. "Focus and breathe."

Catherine let herself relax. She concentrated on pushing her energy into Morgan's palm and felt it leave her as Morgan drained it away.

"Ha! Got it back," said Morgan, his eyes opening wide.

"Good job," River said. "Now we're going to shield. Close your eyes. The person who took first, I want you to take again, but this time, I want the one being taken from to imagine a white circle of protection around them, blocking out any forces trying to take from you. Some of us do this naturally when we're angry or uncomfortable. Concentrate. No one can break your shield."

This time, even before Catherine could place her hand on Morgan, she felt something pushing her away. She didn't want to touch him, but she did anyway, and felt her hand tingle with a repelling force that hurt her slightly.

When it was Morgan's turn to take, he inched his hand close to Catherine and hesitated, grimacing as if from pain. He winced, but forced himself to touch her. He gave up on focusing, jerked his hand away and opened his eyes. "I couldn't get anything from you. My hand felt so cold, it burned."

Catherine focused on clearing her mind. She opened her eyes slowly, smiled, and took Morgan's hands in her own. Morgan sighed, relieved that Catherine had returned to normal, and leaned forward until they were almost nose to nose. Catherine saw herself reflected in his dark eyes.

"Witches often call upon the elements for power. You may

choose to do the same," River said as he paced back and forth slowly, his hands behind his back. "With time and practice, energy transfer will become second nature and quite enjoyable.

"Now I'm going to talk a little bit about something that originated in ancient India: chakras. You will be given a book on them shortly so there's no need to take notes. Just listen. Chakras are energy centres located in your body. Chakra one is located at the base of the spine, where all your raw energy sits. It represents the earth element and grounds us. This chakra brings health and security. Chakra two is related to the water element and is located in the lower back and sexual organs. This chakra brings depth of feeling, among other things. Chakra three, the power chakra, is located in the solar plexus and is related to the fire element. It rules our metabolism and personal power. Chakra four represents the air element and is called the Heart Chakra. It is related to love and brings together opposites, such as mind and body. Chakra five relates to creative energy and is located in the throat. Chakra six relates to light and is known as the Third Eye Centre. It opens our psychic abilities and allows us to see clearly. Chakra seven is related to thought and is known as the Crown Chakra. It connects us to a timeless place of all knowing and brings us knowledge and bliss.

"In chakra meditation, we start with focusing on the third chakra, activating the first three chakras. Then we focus on the fourth one, activating both the fourth and fifth. Lastly, we focus on the sixth chakra for wisdom and psychic seeing. In advanced meditation, energy from the third eye will jump to the seventh chakra and a state called Samadhi occurs in which one is merged with the worlds of light. But that is enough for now. Next class we'll be practicing our meditation skills, but for now, I want you to skim through the book I'm going to hand out."

River went to a nearby shelf, collected eight thin books, and handed one to each student. "Read through chapter one for the remaining portion of the class, and be sure to wear comfortable clothes to class tomorrow."

Cat the Vamp

After Catherine had finished reading the chapter, which she found quite interesting, she allowed herself to drift off and daydream. Her insides squirmed with joy at the thought of having a new love.

Before class ended, River handed out a map of the grounds and told the students they were free to go off school boundaries if they wished.

Morgan, Catherine, Amber, and Zach all left the castle together, venturing down an old road that ran through the forest. Zach led the way, his map held out in front of him. A cool breeze swept by, making the trees shake and shed a cascade of leaves.

"If we keep walking east we'll come to the town," Zach said. "Sweet. There's a great view of the ocean there. Too bad it's too cold to go swimming."

When Catherine shivered, Morgan hesitantly wrapped an arm around her. She huddled against him and walked on happily, wind whipping at her face and turning her cheeks rosy.

"Who wants ice cream because I seriously want ice cream," said Zach when the group came in sight of Café Crème. "I'm buying."

As soon as he opened the door to the shop, the sweet smells of baking cookies and cinnamon buns filled their noses. There were spicy soups being ladled into bowls, creamy milkshakes being poured into glasses, and enormous scoops of ice cream being served in cones.

"Can I help you?" asked a cheerful woman behind the counter wearing a flowered apron.

"I'll have a scoop of double chocolate, please," Zach said. He turned to the group. "Anybody else?" The other three called out their orders. Morgan asked for mocha and Catherine had decided on mint chocolate chip.

The woman eyed the students as she handed Amber her cone of bright blue bubblegum ice cream. "You must be from the castle. Well, you're always welcome here."

Amber smiled sweetly. "Thanks." She joined Zach, who was

studying his map.

With Zach navigating, they left the sweet shop and roamed through the town, stopping to browse through stores that interested them. Tourists with cameras wandered the streets. Local residents of Meadowshell went about their daily business, stopping at markets for fresh seafood and vegetables.

"Let's go to the dock to get a better view of the sea," Catherine said.

They all walked down to the dock and looked out at the water where anchored fishing boats could be seen gently rocking back and forth. A couple were quietly enjoying dinner on their yacht off in the far distance.

Catherine finished the last bit of her cone, ignoring the pain it caused her teeth, and gazed out at a light house that stood on a rocky, jagged-edged outcropping. She heard the steady crash of waves and the faint echo of seagulls crying out. She took in a deep breath of salty air and felt renewed. "It's so beautiful here."

"It's also kind of boring," said Amber. "I could really use some gum."

Morgan brushed the hair from his eyes and leaned against Catherine. Catherine felt energy surge into her and she began to laugh.

Zach pulled a small black radio out of his bag and pushed the power button. Loud guitar music blasted from the speakers. Amber, Catherine, and Morgan winced and glowered at Zach.

"Way to ruin the peaceful atmosphere," Amber said. "Come on. Let's go hang out on the sand."

When they were relaxing on the sandy beach, Zach pulled a joint out of his pocket. "Does anyone mind if I smoke?"

"As long as you're sharing," said Amber.

"Oh, of course," Zach said as he lit up.

They took turns puffing as music played on in the background. Catherine inhaled and kept the smoke inside her for as long as she could before she released it to dissipate into the atmosphere. She stretched out on the sand and her body seemed to melt into the earth.

"Cigarette, anyone?" Zach offered the pack. Everyone gladly took a cigarette and lit it with Zach's lighter.

"What else have you got in that bag of goodies?" Morgan asked Zach.

"Some candy, a sweater, a pack of gum—"

Amber eagerly cut him off. "Did you say gum?"

Zach tossed her a pack of peppermint gum.

"Thanks." A moment later she was leaning back and blowing enormous gum bubbles.

Catherine took a deep drag of her cigarette and watched the smoke travel to the sky. Her thoughts drifted back to the last cigarette she'd shared with Jake and Rose, and her home.

They rested on the sand, letting the music course through them, until the sky was a deep, inky blue. Catherine stood up, took off her shoes and socks and ran into the ocean, letting waves splash against her feet. Morgan, Amber, and Zach joined her and soon everyone was screaming and splashing each other with water. They dried off their feet with Zach's extra sweater and walked back up to where the shops were.

They stopped at a restaurant decorated with nets and anchors to get warm and grab some dinner. Morgan and Catherine shared a hot bowl of soup while Amber and Zach split a platter of fish and chips. They bought candy to munch on as they walked back to Blacklune.

"Catherine," Amber said, giggling, "truth or dare?"

"Truth."

"What's one of the most embarrassing things you've ever done?"

Catherine took a moment to consider. "Once I went swimming and I forgot to bring a pair of underwear to change into. The problem was that I had a dress on that day...and it was a windy day. You get the picture."

Everyone squealed. It wasn't terribly hilarious, but they were all still too high to notice.

"Okay," said Catherine. "Zach, truth or dare?"

He stopped with his hands on his hips and his chest thrust out. "Dare."

"I dare you to kiss Amber," Catherine said, suddenly embarrassed at herself for being so childish.

"If you say so," Zach said, pulling Amber toward him.

Amber started to giggle as Zach placed his lips on her own. She closed her eyes and her knees wobbled. She followed Zach's lead as his fangs tickled her lips. When the kiss finally ended, all she could say was, "Wow."

Catherine and Morgan chuckled. Zach grinned and snapped the gum Amber had passed to him during their lip lock.

Back at the castle, they all went up to Amber's suite to help her set up for the little party she was throwing. Amber's sitting room had wallpaper with flecks of orange, yellow, and red on it. Catherine was amused at the way it matched Amber's hair.

"Okay people," Amber said, hurrying to a dresser, "we have one hour."

She began by placing candles of various colours all about the room. Then she halted abruptly and circled on the spot. "You," Amber pointed at Morgan, "light all the candles and turn on the fire." She turned to Catherine. "Take the CD player from my bedroom, bring it out, and press play. Then—"

"Whoa, somebody likes to boss people around." Zach was sprawled out on the floor.

"You can help by finding my flashlight," Amber said, then quickly added, "please."

Zach rolled over onto his back and let out a groan. "Found it." He pulled out a black flashlight from beneath him. Amber took hold of the flashlight, but instead of letting go, Zach wrapped his arm around her back and pulled her on top of him. Amber smiled, expecting to be kissed, but Zach merely grinned and whispered, "Here," as he placed the flashlight in her palm.

Amber rolled her eyes and climbed to her feet. She hurried to her bedroom and came back carrying a medium-sized scarlet book.

Morgan, who had turned on the fire and finished lighting the candles, joined Zach on the floor and watched as Catherine fiddled with the volume on the CD player. "Meow," he sang playfully. "Here kitty, kitty Cat."

Catherine turned to look at Morgan, her eyes glistening in the candlelight. The flames of the fire danced on her porcelain skin. She walked over to sit next to Morgan, snuggled against him and purred softly.

Zach shook his head partly from confusion, and partly from amazement at Catherine and Morgan. "Woof?" he said to Amber.

Amber smiled and then growled seductively. Catherine hissed and Morgan clawed the floor. Zach got on his hands and knees and howled long and loud.

"Okay, what are we doing?" Amber suddenly asked, settling into a cross-legged position on the floor. There was a moment of silence before everyone burst out laughing, including Amber.

"What the hell was that?" asked Morgan, his cheeks red and sore.

"Whatever it was, it was fun," Catherine said, choking on her words. She lay back on the floor, soaking up the heat from the fire.

Someone knocked on the door and Amber jumped up to answer it. It was Alex, wearing a tight red dress, her blonde hair falling in curls.

She walked confidently into the suite, followed by a very eager-looking Kevin, and two very nervous-looking vampires, Tyler and Emily.

Amber herded everyone to sit in a semi-circle in front of the fire. She took a deep breath to collect her thoughts before she began her speech.

"So, I've called all of you here today because I want to start a club. I know this maybe sounds a little lame, but come on, we're all here together and we can make it fun. So I was thinking, we should make it like, a party club, like for hanging out and playing games and stuff."

"Why don't we go on missions," Catherine said, "like in the castle."

"Why don't we play pranks on people? Sometimes there are more vampires here than just us," said Tyler. "People come stay here like a hotel, like lost witches and stuff."

"Okay," said Amber. "Good input, people. Now, let's take the oath." She reached over to a table, picked up a shiny razor, and grinned as she held it up. She turned on her flashlight. "Who wants to go first?"

"What exactly are we doing?" asked Emily, her eyes widening.

"Good. A volunteer." Amber turned her flashlight on Emily like a stage spotlight. She set the flashlight down and took Emily's wrist. "Hold still while I cut you."

Amber opened her red book to the first blank page and placed it on the floor beneath Emily's wrist. Then she carefully made a tiny incision. Little droplets of blood rose, creating a beautiful contrast to Emily's creamy skin. Amber turned the bleeding wrist so it faced the book and everyone watched as Emily's blood dripped slowly onto the page.

"That wasn't so bad, I guess," said Emily, "but I'm going to need a bandage later."

Amber let Emily go and raised her hands to the ceiling. "What should we name our first member of the club?" She reached into her bag for a pen.

"Mouse," Tyler said quickly. "She's quiet and sweet and cute... like a mouse."

"No objections, then?" Amber looked around at the group. "Good. Well done, Mouse."

Amber wrote Emily's name and her new nickname next to her blood drops. She pulled Zach's wrist over the book next. Zach breathed out a moaning sigh and looked Amber directly in the eyes.

Amber wiped clean her blade and swiftly swiped it across Zach's tanned wrist. His blood rose quickly and he let it flow out in thick drops onto the page, trying not to let any splatter onto Emily's portion.

"We should call him Wolf," said Morgan. "He howls like one."

Kevin volunteered to go next and thrust his arm into Amber's hand. Amber smiled as she watched red ooze from the clean cut she made. Kevin watched, eyes agog, as his blood dripped onto the book.

"We should name him after a bird because he's colourful," Emily said, trying to make sure her blood didn't spill onto the carpet. "You know, because of his hair and well, his chipper attitude. How about Robin?"

"Sounds good," Amber said, jotting it down. "So who's next?"

Tyler inched his hand forward and raised his eyebrows as he waited for Amber to work her magic. He started to laugh as his skin parted, and before his blood even hit the page, Alex called out, "Hyena!"

Alex crawled over to Amber with her hand out. Amber grinned and cut carefully along Alex's shimmery smooth skin. "Ouch!" Alex yelped. She winced as a few drops of blood landed on the page.

"Let's call her Poodle," said Zach and everyone agreed.

Morgan slid back his sleeve and bared his ivory wrist to Amber. Amber took it and cut with care. His blood rose in large drops and splattered onto the page.

"Whoa, that's a lot of blood," said Kevin. "It flowed from you like mad! What flows? Fish flow! What fish are you? No! You're a shark! And sharks like blood! Damn I'm good."

Catherine giggled and then let her hand fall into Amber's. She bit her lower lip as the razor slid through her skin, then gave a little cry at the rush she felt when she saw her blood well up and settle on her flesh. She let her drops plop onto the page and grinned when one of them merged with Morgan's patch of red.

"We can't call you Cat even if you sound like one, so Tiger will have to do," said Amber, handing the blade over to Catherine. "Cut me."

Catherine laid her bleeding hand on her lap and steadied her other hand over Amber's wrist. She had to move some beaded bracelets out of the way before she could find a suitable cutting place, but once she did, she dove in with force and speed.

"Shit! Not so hard."

"Oh, sorry."

At Amber's roar of pain, Tyler said, "Lion. Definitely Lion."

Amber nodded in agreement, took up her pen, and jotted it down next to her blood smear.

"Now our club needs a name," she said, her pen hovering near the top of the page.

Zach turned to Morgan. "That howling thing we did before everyone came was like foreshadowing the club."

"You're right," Morgan said, laughing.

They high-fived each other. Amber and Catherine started to chuckle and high-fived too. Alex, Kevin, Emily, and Tyler looked puzzled for a moment.

"Okay, so why not Animal Kingdom?" asked Tyler.

"Like it," said Zach.

"Me, too," said Emily. "So now can we please do something about our wrists?"

"Let's not waste fresh blood," said Alex. She turned to her right, picked up Morgan's bleeding wrist and began to suck. Morgan, instantly excited, turned to Catherine to feed off her wrist. Catherine turned to her right and fed off Tyler, who fed off Emily, who fed off Zach, who fed off Amber, who closed the blood circle by feeding off Alex.

Energy rose and passed like a strong electric current around the circle. Their heads were dizzy with an overwhelming sense of power and passion as the room around them became clearer, yet more surreal.

Tyler straightened up first and kissed Emily's wrist before he released it. Emily sat up, breathing hard, and smiled at Tyler.

Once everyone had raised their heads and sat upright again, Amber wiped her lips and sighed with satisfaction. "Well, I'd say that was a *great* first meeting of Animal Kingdom."

She got up, turned up the music and went to the bathroom to fetch some gauze and bandages to hand out to her guests.

Catherine gazed out the window, distracted by how brightly the stars appeared to be shining. She stood up, taking Morgan by the hand, and together they walked to the window to look out at the night sky.

"Do you ever wonder if someone on the other side of the world is looking at the exact same star as you, wishing for the exact same thing?" Catherine said. Her skin and hair were luminescent under the moonlight.

"Yeah, I have wondered that actually," said Morgan, pulling Catherine's hand toward him. "What do you wish for?"

"If I tell you," Catherine said, tilting her head slightly, "it won't come true. But I know for a fact that some of my wishes have already been granted."

"Mine too," Morgan whispered into her hair.

Catherine raised her face to Morgan's and she started to laugh. "Your pupils are like craters."

"So are yours. It's like we're high on blood."

"Well, we are." She wrapped her arm tightly around his waist. "I love the way it makes me feel. I don't even mind the taste anymore. I feel fantastic right now."

Morgan's eyes widened eagerly, and he whispered, "We should drink more, now."

"From where?"

"Each other."

Catherine gasped, and she followed Morgan as he led her away from the window to Amber's bedroom.

As soon as they were inside, Catherine leaped onto the comfortable bed and sank down into the warm comforter. Morgan jumped from two feet away and landed beside her. They both started to crack up as the bed creaked and bounced madly.

"Someone's getting it on in Amber's bedroom," Kevin shouted from the sitting room.

Catherine faintly heard Amber reply with, "Shut up."

The lights were off in the bedroom, but the window let in a little starlight. The room was painted blue, like Catherine's bedroom, but a much darker blue like the night sky itself.

Morgan turned to face Catherine. She could feel his breath on her lips.

"From the moment I saw you, I've wanted to kiss you," Morgan said. "I've never wanted someone more than I want you. Even when we're silent, I don't mind because I'm still around you."

Catherine's heart melted. "It feels okay when we don't speak. I feel like we have this connection. I can't explain it, but I can feel it all the time. It's freaking me out a little." She was slightly shocked at her own words, but everything she said came from her heart.

They lay there for a moment, staring into one another's eyes. Catherine knew what was coming. When Morgan dove into her lips she felt that same tingling energy spread into her body. She gripped Morgan's chin and sucked at his lips, tasting and savouring every moment. She was being carried on a wave of bliss and she never wanted to return to the shore.

Morgan took in a deep breath of air and ran his hands through Catherine's hair. He stroked her cheeks, her lips, her chin, her neck. He felt her arms, her waist. He pulled her close.

Catherine slipped her fingers between Morgan's. She felt Morgan's moist lips moving over her own and she kissed back, allowing her eyes to relax and take in the tranquil darkness. She felt the curves of his back as she traced her fingers along his spine.

Morgan suddenly moved so he was sitting on top of Catherine's knees. He leaned forward and raised the hem of her shirt a few inches above her navel, first feeling her silky skin with his fingers and then tasting it with his lips.

Catherine sighed as Morgan's kisses washed over her like a soft breeze. Everything was happening so quickly, but she liked it. She opened her eyes and slid her hands under Morgan's shirt and pulled it up off of him. He smirked and inched Catherine's shirt higher. Catherine lifted her arms for Morgan to slip the shirt over her head.

Shirtless and energized, they wrapped their arms around each other. With her bare skin against his, Catherine could feel every texture of Morgan's chest. Morgan nibbled at Catherine's lips, and she started to feel dizzy.

"I want," Morgan said, kissing Catherine's collar bone, "to kiss," he kissed the upper curve of her breast, "every part of you." He kissed her all the way past her navel, down to the top edge of her jeans. Panting heavily, he quickly unfastened Catherine's jeans and slid them off, leaving her in only her lacy black underwear. He lowered his head to her thigh and slid his tongue over his teeth. Catherine felt his hot breath against her skin.

"Bite me," she said.

Morgan placed his lips on the smooth skin of Catherine's thigh and dug in with his fangs. Immediately, his head was filled with a tingling sensation and his heart started to pound. He could hear it beating in his eardrums. Every other sound faded away. He felt Catherine's warmth passing into him, filling him with life and energy. He sucked harder, letting the blood overflow his lips and flood into his mouth. He was filled with a satisfaction so powerful that he didn't even hear the screams coming from Catherine. He drank until his brain started to ache. He raised his face to the ceiling to steady himself, and saw only bright, white light. He fell backwards off the bed and onto the floor.

Catherine's eyes began to water. Her lips trembled as she stared down at her bloody thigh. She cried out for help, her entire body weak, her blood still flowing.

Amber shouted from the open door. "Zach!"

Zach ran to the doorway and stopped to stare at Morgan sprawled motionless on the floor and Catherine whimpering on the bed.

"You take care of Morgan and I'll deal with Cat," said Amber. She rushed out of the bedroom to get emergency supplies. She came back holding a wet cloth, a dry cloth, a box of bandages, and a cup of water.

"Well he's not dead," Zach said, poking at Morgan. "He just overloaded on blood and fainted."

"Let him rest and come help me then."

Zach stood and walked over to where Catherine lay like a helpless doll on Amber's bed. His eyes travelled to her black bra and he smiled, his expression distant.

"Pass me the dry cloth," Amber said to Zach.

Zach snapped back to reality and handed the cloth to Amber. After the wound was clean, Amber stuck a large bandage on it and sighed.

"What the hell?" Alex said from the doorway. She, Kevin, Tyler and Emily had all gathered to see what the commotion was.

"Looks like someone was having a bit too much fun," Kevin said, walking into the bedroom to get a better look at Morgan, who was lying spread-eagled on his stomach with his mouth half open and his eyes closed.

Catherine moaned as her fingers groped to feel her bandaged bite.

"Don't touch it," Amber said.

Catherine's eyes widened as she realized that a room full of people was staring at her in her underwear. She pulled some of the comforter over herself.

"How are you feeling?" Zach asked.

"Dizzy and drained," Catherine said weakly.

"Drink some water." Amber handed her a cup.

As Catherine drank, she looked down at Morgan, more concerned than amused. The way he had been so keen on drinking her blood that he ignored her pleas to stop frightened her.

"You're going to be weak." Emily pushed forward to the bed.

"Drink some of my blood."

Catherine held Emily's wrist and sucked where Amber's cut was barely sealed. Emily's blood rose and flowed into her mouth, awakening her senses. She came up for air feeling alert and energized, but not totally satisfied.

"Okay, show's over," said Amber. "Cat, you and Morgan can stay here for the night. The rest of you have to leave. The first official meeting of Animal Kingdom is closed as of now."

The Animal Kingdom members all shuffled awkwardly out of the room. Catherine drifted off to sleep, too exhausted to think about the pain she was in.

4

Catherine awoke to the scent of coffee waiting for her on Amber's nightstand. She rubbed her eyes, sat up in bed, and took the warm mug in her hands. She smiled as she breathed in the fragrant steam, then took a sip and sighed.

"Good morning." Morgan appeared in the doorway. "I hope you like the coffee."

Catherine just took another sip and nodded as she looked at him soberly.

"Look, I didn't mean to do what I did. Amber told me the whole story. I don't even remember what happened, really. I just know I felt great, so great I couldn't handle myself and I just sort of...collapsed with joy."

"You practically overdosed on me," Catherine said, gripping the mug tightly.

"I know." Morgan slowly sat on the bed beside Catherine. "I'm sorry. You're just really hard to resist." He leaned close, grinning slightly, and whispered, "I do remember kissing you."

The corners of Catherine's lips curled into a reluctant smile and she felt her cheeks flush. There was a moment of silence before Catherine leaned forward, closed her eyes, and allowed her lips to meet Morgan's.

Catherine kept her eyes shut after the kiss ended. She wanted to keep the memory of Morgan's lips locked in her mind forever. When she opened her eyes she saw that Morgan had a broad smile on his face.

"You're forgiven," said Catherine, taking a sip of her coffee. She looked away from him, trying to find the right words. "I felt really... alive last night."

"Me, too," said Morgan, placing his hand in Catherine's.

She set her cup down and wrapped her arms around Morgan. They let their bodies ease back onto the soft mattress, swept up in the electric charm of one another's touch.

Catherine pulled back the blankets and showed Morgan her bandage. Morgan sighed, unsure what to say. They relaxed, fingers intertwined, focused on each other's scent and heartbeat as their bodies seemed to melt into one.

Amber, wearing a white apron covered in tiny pink hearts, knocked once before she entered the bedroom.

"Good. You've kissed and made up," she said rather loudly. "Now you can both get up and face the day. I've made some breakfast for you." She waved a spoon in the direction of the kitchen and smirked as she walked off.

Catherine told Morgan to leave while she searched the room for her clothes. She dressed slowly, daydreaming. *I wonder what Rose is doing now. I'll have to give her a call soon. She'll never believe what I have to tell her.*

She was smiling when she joined Morgan and Amber at the table. Her leg throbbed slightly when Morgan slid a hand over her thigh.

"You should have seen your face," Amber told Morgan, handing out bowls. "You looked like a happy child after a Thanksgiving feast."

Morgan shrugged and helped himself to cereal. "I really don't even remember passing out. I didn't hear Catherine screaming at all." He looked a tad guilty.

"We just have to be more careful. It's probably a good idea if

River doesn't find out about the club or the...incident." Amber wiped milk off her chin. "We should all probably cover up our wrists too."

Catherine nodded, her attention fixed on the time. It was eleven o' clock. She had one hour to get ready and make a very important phone call. "I have to go now."

"I'll walk you back to your room," said Morgan, taking one last bite of breakfast. He slid his hand into Catherine's and they walked out the door waving goodbye.

"Thanks for everything...Lion," Catherine told Amber. "I owe you."

"No problem, Tiger. And as for you, Shark, you take care of her."

"I will," Morgan said, smiling.

Once Morgan had left for his own room, Catherine raced to her bedroom to change into fresh clothes. She made sure to wear a long-sleeved shirt to cover her wrist. She tied her hair back, grabbed her bag, and headed down to the library.

Maggie greeted Catherine with a wave of her long fingernails. She put down a cup of steaming hot jasmine tea and smiled.

"I was wondering if there was a phone I could use somewhere," Catherine said.

"Keep walking down the history aisle until you get to the far wall. There's a phone there you can use. It's between two windows."

Catherine thanked her and found the history section. She felt weak and her head spun slightly, but she pushed on until she reached the phone. She took the receiver off the cradle, dialled the number, and collapsed onto the floor with her back against the wall. She took deep breaths, waiting for Rose to pick up.

"Hello?" Rose sounded like she had just woken up.

"Rose!"

"Catherine?"

"Yes! It's me! Oh, I have so much to tell you. So, okay, my parents took me to this castle and they explained to me that I was a...

vampire."

"Okay, I'll humour you," Rose said, laughing. She let out a scream of mock fright.

"I'm serious," Catherine said, lowering her voice. "I even have fangs now. I went though this initiation ceremony and I met this really cute guy named Morgan. We had to drink each other's blood and then I was a vampire. And we like each other now. Well, we made out. Oh, my God. This probably sounds so stupid to you, but I'm not lying. I'm stuck here, too. My parents just left me here and I have to take classes now to like...better myself. It's strange, but really exciting at the same time."

"Okay...I believe you."

"Always with the sarcasm."

"Well, at least it sounds like you're having fun, even if you should be committed."

"Hey! Not funny. Gosh, I miss you. How's everyone doing?"

"Everyone's fine. I haven't seen your parents around, though."

"Nothing new." Catherine rolled her eyes. "God, Morgan is amazing. I can't even explain it. I want you to meet him when I get back."

"When *are* you getting back?"

"I'll be home for Christmas."

"I'm going to miss you so much."

"Me, too," said Catherine, "But I have to go now, so I'll talk to you later. Bye."

"Peace out," Rose said before Catherine hung up.

Catherine hugged her knees and sat thinking for a few moments. When she opened her eyes she spotted a slender black cat strolling toward her.

"Hey kitty," Catherine whispered, patting the floor to get the cat to come closer to her. The cat meowed softly and rubbed up against Catherine, weaving in and out around her legs. Catherine lovingly stroked the cat as it purred loudly.

"I see you've met Midnight." Maggie came walking down the

aisle toward Catherine.

"Oh, is this your cat?" Maggie nodded and looked down at Catherine thoughtfully.

"You seem tired. Come with me and I'll fix you some tea." Maggie helped Catherine to her feet.

Catherine and Midnight followed Maggie behind the checkout desk to a tall mirror mounted on the wall. Maggie took out a long wooden stick and tapped the mirror once. Immediately, it slid to the side, revealing an opening in the wall, which Maggie stepped through. "Come inside."

Cautious but curious, Catherine walked through the opening and found herself in an entirely new room. She walked over to a soft, blue couch and settled into it. Midnight jumped up onto her lap and began to purr once again. Catherine scratched his back while she took in her surroundings.

Maggie hurried to the kitchen where a kettle was whistling, steam pouring from its spout. The sink was strewn with dishes and all different sizes of pots and pans hung from the ceiling. Something spicy was bubbling in a large, black pot on the stove. Dried flowers hung all about the rooms and jars full of herbs sat on shelves along with books and candles. The relaxing scent of vanilla incense wafted through the air.

Maggie walked over with a tray holding two cups of peppermint tea and a plate of cookies. Catherine took her cup and a cookie and thanked Maggie, who took a seat opposite Catherine in a large wicker chair.

"I know I can trust you," said Maggie, inclining her head toward Midnight, "so I'm going to tell you a secret." She took a sip from her cup. "The other day I saw something in this." Maggie pointed to a crystal ball sitting on the table in front of her. "I saw you crying, and I had a feeling of sadness. I want you to know that if ever the day comes when you're in that much pain, you can come to me for assistance."

"Assistance? What do you mean?"

Maggie winked. "I am a witch."

Catherine smiled down at Midnight. "Thanks. I'll be sure to remember that."

"Uh-oh, look at the time. Hurry up and drink your tea. Your class is about to begin and I'm supposed to be on duty."

Catherine gulped down the remaining tea in her cup, set Midnight down on the couch and stood up to leave.

Maggie rose, the crystals she wore around her neck jingling like tiny bells. Catherine noticed for the first time what an elegant air she had as she walked. She tapped the mirror once and it slid open.

"Out you go, and by the way, that's a beautiful necklace you have on. Make sure you take care not to lose it."

Feeling renewed and healthy, Catherine walked briskly to the back of the library to meet her friends. She smiled when she noticed that every single student was wearing something that concealed his or her wrists. Alex was fiddling with a pair of lacy gloves. Morgan waved Catherine over and she took a seat beside him and Amber.

When River arrived, he told the class to stand and join him on the carpeted area to the left of the tables. All the students filed over and stood facing River, hands at their sides.

"I want everyone to lie down with your head pointing north and your feet to the south," River said. When the class had followed this instruction and stopped fidgeting, he continued. "Close your eyes, breathe in through your nose, and out through your mouth. Imagine yellow sun energy entering the top of your head and travelling through your body and out through your feet as you breathe in. When you breathe out, imagine blue moon energy entering your feet and travelling through your body and exiting your head. Your intake of air should fill you with positive energy. It should charge you. Your exhalation should release negative energy."

The class practiced breathing for a while. River then led them through a relaxation exercise, in which they released the tension from each part of their bodies, from feet to faces. When they were fully relaxed, River took them on a meditative journey, describing a beach where the sand was hot and the breeze was balmy as they visualized his descriptions. Catherine enjoyed every minute of her meditative state and felt her body and mind become calm and concentrated.

"Now you know how to relax," said River. "This skill can help you control energy and focus your powers."

For the rest of the class time, River taught them stretching techniques. He named all the poses he formed with his body as the class tried their best to imitate him.

After class, Morgan asked Catherine if she wanted to head to town for a bite to eat. Catherine agreed and told Morgan that she would meet him in the entranceway in an hour.

Hot and sweaty from the surprisingly intense stretching workout, Catherine stripped in her bathroom, carefully peeled off her bandage, and hopped into the shower. Hot water pounded at her back, soothing her muscle aches. She closed her eyes and let drops pelt her face.

Her thoughts kept leading her back to Morgan. It felt so right being in his arms, just being with him. She giggled remembering how excited she became every time Morgan took her hand. She loved the feelings that came with a new crush: the butterflies in the stomach, the dizziness in the head, and the yearning in the gut. Her exhilaration pushed her everyday worries aside.

She went to the cupboard for a fresh bandage for her thigh. Feeling clean and charged, she dressed, dried her hair, and grabbed her bag to go.

When she arrived in the front hall, Morgan wrapped his arms around her and breathed her in, then let out a long and happy sigh. He smiled nervously, but Catherine put him at ease by taking his hand and squeezing it tightly. "Let's go."

In town, they stopped for a slice of pizza and sat down to talk. Catherine couldn't stop smiling. She felt so happy that someone *wanted* her.

Morgan burst into laughter when he saw Zach and Amber stroll through the pizza shop door.

"Stop following us!" Catherine was laughing, as well.

"Whoa, this town *is* small," said Zach.

He and Amber ordered and joined Morgan and Catherine.

"I was thinking of throwing a Halloween party on Friday," said Amber.

"That sounds fun!" Catherine said. "It should be a costume party."

"Definitely," said Amber. "We can invite all Animal Kingdom members and anyone else who happens to be in the castle."

"We can decorate, and have candy and contests and prizes!" Catherine was excited at the prospect.

"We should also pull some tricks," said Zach. "Harmless ones, of course."

"Okay, we'll plan everything in my room tonight since we don't have any homework," said Amber.

Zach rolled his eyes at Morgan. "Let's leave the planning to the girls."

"Fine, you two. Then Amber and I get all the credit for the party."

When she went to bed that night, Catherine read from a book of horror stories she'd checked out of the library after she left Amber's room. She fell asleep with Halloween plans and the stories mingling in her head.

She dreamed that she was running through a field of sweet-scented wild flowers, frolicking and laughing. The light around her was bright. She spotted a boy wearing black in the distance. She ran up to him, wrapped her arms around his neck, and kissed him passionately. The boy held her tight and Catherine felt loved. Off in the distance, a yellow, horned demon laughed maliciously.

When Catherine awoke the next day, the dream was still fresh in her mind. All the way down to the ballroom, she thought about the boy in her dream. It hadn't been Morgan, of that she was sure, but who had it been? Catherine remembered the laughing yellow demon and shivered. To distract herself from obsessing about the dream, she focused her attention on choosing a perfect slice of toast. With her plate of toast and fruit and her cup of coffee, she wandered over to an empty table to eat alone in peace, and sat enjoying her breakfast over the book she had checked out the night before.

Morgan greeted Catherine with a hug. She sighed at the blissful sensation of Morgan's lean body enfolding her. Amber joined them for breakfast shortly afterwards, holding a stack of hand-made invitations she and Catherine had completed the previous night.

"Some of them have names on them and some of them don't," Amber told Morgan, handing him one. Catherine had drawn the image of a witch stirring a cauldron on the front of the card.

Morgan opened the card and read aloud. "You are invited to Amber's and Catherine's Halloween Party! Come in costume to Amber's suite at seven o' clock on Halloween night for a night of fun and fright."

"Doesn't it sound great?" Catherine was admiring how well her drawing had turned out.

"Yeah, especially the rhyming part," said Morgan, grinning. "So what are you girls going to dress up as?"

"Well, we can't exactly go out and buy fantastic costumes, so I'll probably make a nurse costume out of my old white dress," said Amber.

"I've always been scary things in the past, so this year I think I'm going to be an angel. Amber and I will both be in white, so people can spot us if they need our assistance, since we're the hostesses."

"I'm handing out the invitations today, and I'm asking River if there are any other kids in the castle."

Zach joined them at the table, and Catherine put her library book back into her bag. "Do you have any more smokes?"

"Yep. Let me get some coffee and then let's go out back."

The back door was to the left of the staircase and blended so well with the wall that Catherine had never noticed it before. She followed Zach to the outside courtyard with Amber and Morgan trailing behind. Dry leaves rustled over the paving and the air smelled of apples and fall flowers. Everyone took a seat on a bench by the pond to smoke. Amber handed Zach his invitation.

"I think I'm going to need some paint for my costume."

"Me, too," said Morgan.

"I have some fabric paints up in my room," said Amber. "You guys can pick them up after class if you want."

In class that afternoon, River lectured on the proper techniques of blood letting and drinking. Catherine took notes and replied when spoken to, but mostly she was wrapped up in her own daydreams and thoughts.

After the boys got their fabric paint, Amber and Catherine headed to town to pick up costume-making supplies, candy, snacks, candles, and streamers. Catherine bought her own pack of cigarettes. When they returned to the castle, the girls left their bags in Amber's room and raced to Zach's room to see what the boys had come up with.

Zach answered their knock and welcomed the girls into his suite. Posters of bands were taped to the dark purple walls. Paint bottles were strewn all over the place along with brushes, toilet paper, glue, books and scissors. Morgan, looking very concentrated, was busy painting in a corner.

"Like what I've done so far?" he asked when Catherine went to peer over his shoulder. He held up a black T-shirt with a white ribcage painted on the front.

"That's cool." Catherine reached out to touch the shirt, but Morgan hastily put it back down on the floor.

"It's not dry yet. So what did you and Amber buy in town?"

Catherine sat down next to Morgan. "Lots of the wildest candy you ever saw. Try this." She reached into her pocket and placed a tiny green packet on Morgan's palm. "It's sour, so beware."

Morgan tore the wrapper open and plopped the small, circular candy into his mouth. He slid it over his tongue a few times before his face contorted into what looked like delighted pain. "That *is* sour!"

"Told you so."

"Wanna taste?" He stuck out his tongue.

Catherine leaned in to kiss Morgan. Her lips quivered as sour juices gradually filled her mouth. Morgan slid the candy onto Catherine's tongue and continued to suck at her lips. Catherine had just taken Morgan's hand when a loud and annoying groaning arose in the room. Morgan and Catherine turned to find Zach, wrapped up in toilet paper, moaning like a mummy.

"Must kill humans," Zach groaned slowly.

"Mummies don't kill humans," said Catherine, laughing.

"But I have a curse on me!" Zach leaned down to pick up a can of Silly String.

"You wouldn't dare."

"I think I would." Zach shot a line of foam at Catherine, very accurately.

Catherine screamed and curled into Morgan for protection. Morgan helped Catherine up and they both ran to fetch a can of string to fight back.

"Me and Amber against you and Catherine."

"Oh, it's on," said Morgan, shaking his can.

"Give me the can," Catherine said to Morgan. "Zach needs to be punished."

"Sounds good to me." Zach was standing behind a kitchen chair with Amber, who rolled her eyes. Catherine ran up to the table and fired at Zach, but he jumped out of the way and hit his head on a pan that hung from the ceiling.

"Zach!" Morgan said. "Are you okay?"

Zach began to moan again, this time in real pain. He was on his back with his hands to his head, toilet paper scattered all around him.

"I'm sorry," said Catherine.

"It's not your fault," said Zach. "The toilet paper massacre was bound to happen."

Amber couldn't help giggling at the spectacle Zach made. "Come on, let's go decorate and work on our own costumes, Catherine. Besides, we have some girl stuff to talk about."

"We do?"

Amber nodded with a pleading look in her eyes.

"Okay, then." Catherine blew a kiss goodbye to Morgan, who was busy collecting a bag of ice for Zach's head.

When the girls got back to Amber's suite, Catherine said, "What did you mean *girl stuff?*"

Amber sighed and flopped down into a chair. "I have a problem. I can't stop thinking about Zach. We've been friends since the first day we met here at Blacklune, but ever since he kissed me, things have changed. I look at him differently now, but I don't know if he looks at me the same way. Do you understand?"

"Yeah." Catherine flopped down into another chair. "You want to know if Zach likes you back. You should hint that you have feelings for him. He might be scared to take the next step for fear of breaking the friendship you have. So make it clear that you're interested at the Halloween party."

"What should I do?"

"Flirt with him. Treat him like a guy, not just a friend. If it's meant to be, it'll happen naturally."

"That makes sense. Thanks. So what's with you and Morgan?"

"I can't stop thinking about him, either." Catherine sighed blissfully. "Ever since that night in your room, we've just become closer. We're more comfortable with each other now. I really like him. He's so handsome and sweet."

The girls worked past midnight on their costumes and decorating and finally got to sleep at around two o' clock.

Catherine woke up at eleven thirty, rolled out of bed, and got dressed. Morgan knocked on her door, kissed her on the cheek, and walked her to class. Still sleepy, Catherine rested her head on Morgan's shoulder while they waited for River to arrive.

River entered the library carrying a small pad of blank paper and eight pens. He handed a pen and one sheet of paper to each student. "I'd like you to decide on your favourite activity, and write it down on the paper. When you're finished, turn your sheet over so no one else can see it."

Catherine allowed her mind to wander back to her hometown. She saw the grassy fields and smelled the autumn air. She grinned when her imagination took her to The Cove. She closed her eyes and could almost taste the freshly brewed coffee. Jake, Rose, and the rest of her friends were there with her, smiling, enjoying life. But then her daydreaming changed directions and she saw herself dancing in the dark with her friends, lights flashing all around them, the music pumping loudly. She opened her eyes and wrote *dancing* on the paper, and began folding her paper into a swan while she waited for the rest of the class to finish.

River collected all the papers and picked up one of them to read. "All right, the first activity we have here is doing crafts. Whose activity is this?" Amber raised her hand and wriggled her fingers.

"What do you mean exactly by *doing crafts?*"

"You know, making things. Knitting, designing clothes, crafting."

"Thank you, Amber." River opened the next piece of paper. "Writing." He scanned the room and stopped at Morgan, who had a wry grin on his face.

"That's mine."

"What kind of writing?"

"Poetry, stories, anything."

River nodded and patiently unfolded the swan. "Dancing. Catherine, this is yours, correct?"

"Correct."

"What type of dancing do you prefer?"

"Something in the dark, like when you go clubbing."

"Very well." River sighed as he looked at the next sheet. "Camping."

"That's mine!" said Tyler. "What I mean by camping is sleeping in tents and making s'mores and swimming in lakes."

River smiled and went on, "Painting."

Emily raised her hand.

"Spas," River read.

Alex piped up, "What I mean by spas is well, getting pampered and shopping all day and eating in nice restaurants and having fun!"

Catherine smiled at Amber who was pretending to vomit her breakfast.

"Next we have video games."

"That's mine," said Zach. "I like first person shooter games, racing games, pretty much anything with violence—"

"Very intriguing," said River. "And finally, watching movies."

Kevin flashed a wide toothy smile. "I'm a big fan of old-style movies with classic actresses like Marilyn Monroe. I love acting, too."

River nodded. He collected all the papers into a stack and put them away in a folder. "You might be wondering why I'm asking you these things. The reason is simple. You are all here to make life easier for yourselves and to learn how to live happily. Now we are going to be sharing ways of achieving happiness. Each day the class will partake in one person's favourite activity."

"Sweet!" Tyler said. "Does that mean we actually get to go camping?"

"Yes," said River, as the class, wide-eyed and excited, began to chatter quietly.

"Today you will be writing, so get out your notebooks. Morgan, what type of writing would you like us to do today?"

Morgan ran his fingers along his jaw as he looked up at the ceiling, thinking for a few moments. "I want to write some creative prose. Let everyone else do whatever they want."

"Fine," said River. "Write whatever you would like. A short story, a poem, anything. Get your thoughts out on paper and don't be timid. You won't have to read us your work at the end of class, unless you want to. You may move around and find a private spot to work, but don't leave the library."

Some students sat thinking, tapping their pens against their teeth, annoyed and frustrated, while others scribbled away. Catherine and Morgan went to sit on a ledge beneath a window where natural light streamed in, providing the perfect writing atmosphere: calm, yet inspiring.

"Why don't we write about each other?" Catherine said.

"Okay."

Catherine's pen moved quickly as she wrote.

Through clouds of smoke we swam, our eyes glazed over in admiration of the world and one another. We drank in the sun and never paused for air. The stars were our blanket. We warmed ourselves with liquid intoxication and let our lips meet, thanking one another for the days spent together. Delirious and delinquent, we held each other tightly, felt content skin on skin, taking in each other's light.

Catherine read her work aloud to Morgan. Mesmerized, he smiled and leaned toward Catherine until his lips brushed hers.

"That was really nice." He gently bit Catherine's lower lip. Catherine smiled and bit back, and Morgan pulled away and grinned. "Now let me finish before I get too caught up in you."

Catherine nodded and touched her fingers to her lips, which were still tingling. She bided her time by doodling until Morgan finished.

"Viciously sweet," Morgan read aloud, "she pulls me into a place I cannot escape. Here, I am wrapped in seductive warmth, engrossed in melodic whisper, listening to never-ending laughter, on a bed of clover." He paused and shrugged. "It's not very good, but I couldn't focus all that well."

"I love it," said Catherine, sliding her hand along Morgan's jaw, and she slowly guided his lips to hers.

They sat there with lips locked, blood rushing and minds spinning with elation. They didn't need words—their hands did the talking for them. When River announced that class was ending soon, they rose to stand face-to-face, breathing heavily. Morgan pulled Catherine into a hug and squeezed her tight, as if she might slip away. He ran his hands down her shoulders and back. When they reached her waist, a dizzy current of elation swept through her, and she almost lost her balance. Catherine closed her eyes to fully absorb the moment and reminded herself that she wasn't dreaming. Somewhere deep down, she knew that this was right, that this was something good.

The students gathered at the back tables to finish up.

"Would anyone like to read their work?" asked River.

Alex proudly raised her hand, adjusted her paper, and cleared her throat. "I did a journal entry. Well, it's more like my thoughts on paper. Dear diary, I'm in the library right now writing for a class assignment. It's nice and calm here. The windows are letting in just the right amount of sun. I feel good. I'm in the fiction section and I'm staring at a book called *An Appetite for Love*. Kind of hilarious, I know. I guess my appetite for love is pretty big. I just broke up with Steve, my boyfriend. I feel upset I guess, but he wasn't the right one for me. We were just different people. I don't know when I'll find Mr. Right, but I really hope it'll be soon. I just want someone to hold and kiss."

Alex looked up from her paper and smiled at Morgan. Catherine pursed her lips.

"That was an entertaining insight into the personal life of Alex," said River. "Anyone else?"

Tyler, smirking, raised his hand. "In darkness it creeps, waiting in silence for prey. It longs for your blood," he read.

"A haiku," said River. "Nicely done."

After class was over, Catherine and Morgan went for a walk in the woods. They stopped at a pond and had stone-skipping contests. It had been getting colder with each passing day, and dark foreboding clouds had hidden the sun. But with Morgan at her side and the crisp fall air nipping at her cheeks, Catherine felt perfectly content.

They each took a pocketful of flat stones back to the castle for future contests. Inside Morgan's dark green suite, where it was comfortable and warm, Catherine sat down in front of the fire. Morgan sat next to her and they both were silent, gazing at the flickering flames.

It was a bit strange, Catherine thought, that she could be so comfortable just sitting and being around Morgan. She decided it was definitely a good thing.

5

On Halloween morning, Catherine awoke and dressed quickly. She raced down to the ballroom to grab breakfast, which today consisted of ice cream and candy. Since it was Halloween, River had made sure to set out copious amounts of sweets.

Morgan spotted Catherine from the entrance hall and laughed. He made himself a sundae and poured two mugs of coffee for himself and Catherine, who had been so excited by the candy and ice cream fixings, she had forgotten about her morning coffee entirely.

"Thank you!" Catherine said when she saw Morgan carrying two mugs. "Nice sundae, by the way. I see you've added some chocolate chips. Good choice."

"Nice work yourself. Those candy coated chocolates really add some colour."

Catherine smiled at him, scooped up some ice cream, and dipped it into her coffee. She put the melting spoonful into her mouth and began to laugh. Morgan laughed along with her.

"You guys are *seriously* too happy in the morning," said Amber, taking a seat next to Morgan. "So, Cat, we can't socialize after class today. It's work time. We have four hours to set everything up and get dressed. Okay?"

Catherine swallowed her coffee and ice cream and nodded enthusiastically.

The three of them walked to the library together. They broke into grins when they reached the back tables. River and Maggie had hung streamers from the ceiling and spider webs from the windows. They had strung lights along bookshelves and lanterns over the tables. One of the tables was covered in a bright orange plastic tablecloth, and pumpkins stood waiting on it.

"Goody!" Catherine gave Morgan an excited squeeze. "Let's sit down."

When everyone was settled in front of their own pumpkin, River began his little speech.

"Today we will be doing Amber's suggestion of crafts, and since it is Halloween, I thought some festive crafts would be fun. First off, we are going to have a pumpkin carving contest." He handed a sharp knife to each student. "At one o'clock we'll begin making our Halloween pals and at two, we'll finish off with making Halloween treats."

When River left the library, Amber whispered, "Let's do our A.K. names!"

Everyone took up their knives and began preparing their pumpkins, cutting off the tops and scooping mounds of pumpkin guts onto the plastic tablecloth. When Catherine was sure her pumpkin was empty enough, she took out her notebook and began sketching out possible tiger designs to carve.

Morgan was already carving away. He looked so determined he seemed angry. Catherine grinned at him and set to work on her own pumpkin. She carefully carved out stripes and ears and claws and fangs.

When the hour was up, everyone helped to heave the plastic tablecloth and pumpkin guts into the garbage bin in the back. When the class space was clean and tidy, the students took their pumpkins out to the front entrance hall. They placed their creations all along the stairs and put the candles River had given them inside their pumpkins.

"Everyone huddle together," River told the class. He went

around lighting the candles, turning the pumpkins into glowing jack-o-lanterns, then took a large camera from his bag. "On the count of three I'm snapping. One, two...three!"

Amber called out, "Happy Halloween!" and everyone joined her in a chorus of excited shouts.

River put his camera away after a few more shots and began handing out pieces of blank paper from his trusty pad.

"Take a good hard look at each pumpkin and decide which you think is best. You may not vote for your own pumpkin. Write down the animal on your paper and hand it to me when you're finished."

Catherine gazed at the luminescent creatures and sighed. Deciding was going to be harder than she thought it would be. *Everyone knows who everyone is so they might think I'm favouring.*

Catherine studied each pumpkin, trying her best not to think about whose it was. Amber's lion design was all right, but definitely not the best. Zach's wolf design looked like it was done by a four-year-old. Morgan's shark looked like a goldfish. Tyler's hyena looked like an ancient caveman painting. Emily's mouse was cute, but not amazing. Alex's poodle was good, but Kevin's bird was best by far. The robin's wings were carved spread out. Flames seem to soar out from the pumpkin, and in fact, the design didn't look like a robin at all, but rather, a glowing phoenix. Catherine wrote down *bird* on her paper and handed it to River.

When everyone had voted, River read the results aloud: "Wolf, robin, lion, mouse, mouse, fish, bird, bird."

"I won!" screamed Kevin.

Everyone clapped and cheered. River pulled an enormous chocolate bar from his bag and handed it to Kevin.

"Lucky," said Catherine.

As the class headed back to the library, Morgan nudged Catherine with his shoulder and shifted his eyes from side to side.

"So, who'd you vote for?" he whispered, as if he were breaking the rules.

Catherine giggled and she told him.

"Me, too! Cool."

River went to fetch supplies while everyone sat down at the tables.

"Who did you vote for?" Zach asked Amber.

"You," Amber said quietly.

"No way. I voted for you, too."

Amber smiled, her eyes sparkling.

River returned with a bucket of different coloured sheets of felt, a box of sewing supplies, and a bag filled with cotton balls and pens.

"Decide on a Halloween character you would like to make and sew away," River said, setting out the supplies. He held up a stuffed pumpkin and then let each student take a look at it. "Fold your felt in half, draw out your design, pin it, cut it, sew it, turn it inside out, and stuff it. Have fun."

Catherine picked out a sheet of black felt and folded it in half. She drew out a cat and pinned the two sides so they wouldn't move. She carefully cut out her kitty and began to sew.

Morgan was having trouble sewing his ghost. He kept pricking his finger and getting blood all over the white felt. Catherine took his finger and kissed it softly. Morgan smiled, but though his mood brightened, his sewing continued just as horribly.

Catherine hugged her cute little kitty and squealed with joy. She looked over at Morgan's bloody ghost, half stuffed, and burst out laughing. She ran her cat up Morgan's side and purred.

Morgan held out his ghost in front of him and sighed loudly. "I'm definitely looking forward to the sweet-making portion of today's class."

While everyone cleaned up their sewing scraps, River finished setting up the sweet-making table. He set out a large bowl of hot caramel and a tray of green apples with sticks already in them. Bowls with gummy candies, chocolate candies, cookie crumbs, and fruit were beside the caramel along with a tray for drying.

Each student took turns making their candy apple. Catherine took one look at the table and her eyes widened with eager delight. She coated her apple with as much caramel as possible and used every candy presented.

Amber and Catherine shot out of the library as soon as class ended, shouting out reminders about the party. They finished off their last bits of apple, shared a smoke, and set to work. They spread cotton spider webs over practically everything in Amber's suite. Catherine changed all the light bulbs to black light bulbs and filled up bowls and bowls with candy. Amber adjusted the ghosts she and Catherine had made the night before and strung more streamers along the walls.

Two hours later, Amber's place was dark and eerie, and yet mysteriously enticing all the same. Candles were set in high places where they couldn't be knocked over. A large cauldron filled with green punch was chilling in the fridge along with a bottle of vodka Amber had managed to score in town.

The girls changed into their costumes and let out screams of anticipation. By the time Catherine had made up her face in sparkles and shadow, it was six o'clock. She walked around lighting all the candles, her feathery angel wings fluttering slightly, then sat down in a chair and adjusted her white stockings. Amber began munching on candy while she waited for guests to arrive.

When they heard a knock, Amber spat her candy into the garbage, and nearly choking on her own excitement, answered the door. Morgan the skeleton and Zach the mummy wandered into the suite slowly, taking in the scene with awe.

"Damn, you girls did a good job, and you look hot!" Zach said.

"Thanks," said Amber, and remembering Catherine's advice, she slipped her arm around Zach's. "If you come help me set out cups, I'll give you a shot."

Zach grinned and followed Amber to the kitchen.

"Wow," Morgan said, staring at Catherine. "My very own angel."

Catherine giggled and wrapped Morgan in a hug. She kissed him on the cheek lightly so as to not smudge his makeup, then took his hand and led him into the kitchen.

"We need shots," Catherine told Amber.

"Whoa, whoa girly," said Zach, a plastic cup already in hand. "Eager, aren't we?"

Amber mixed two vodka and punch drinks and handed one to Morgan and one to Catherine. "Now, drink your medicine so you can feel better." Amber swayed her hips to show off her nurse costume. "And Morgan, I really suggest that you eat some candy. You are skin and bones, my dear!"

Morgan rolled his eyes and took a swig of his drink. Catherine took a few gulps of her own and ran to greet more guests when she heard them knocking.

Kevin, wearing a hot pink dress, stood at the door with a huge smile on his face. He adjusted his pink wig and shouted, "Happy Halloween!"

Catherine screamed and pulled Kevin into a hug. "Nice shoes! And your makeup! It's gorgeous! Damn, you look hotter than me."

Kevin laughed and went to join the others. Catherine waited by the door for more visitors and heard everyone in the kitchen start to shout and clap when Kevin arrived.

"Someone turn on the music!" shouted Kevin.

"I'll get it," Amber shouted back.

Emily, dressed as a cowgirl complete with straw hat and leather boots came next, with Tyler the caped magician. Alex arrived last in a devil outfit. She smiled at Catherine and stared at the suite, impressed. "You guys did a really good job."

Half an hour later, everyone was pleasantly drunk and watching Tyler perform magic tricks.

"Watch this," he said, taking off his tall black paper hat. He held it out in front of him, tapped it once with his magic wand and cried, "Abracadabra!" A small white toy rabbit popped out of the hat, and everyone shouted in amazement.

Cat the Vamp

Another knock came at the door. While Tyler continued on with his drunken magic show, Amber and Catherine got up to greet the visitor. "Did you invite anyone else?" Catherine asked Amber.

"River said Maggie's son might be in town today. I hope you don't mind." Amber opened the door to reveal a tall, masked phantom clad in black.

"Hi, I'm Amber, and the angel is Catherine. I take it you're Maggie's son?"

The phantom nodded. "Xavier. Pleasure to meet you both."

"Well, come on in!"

Xavier followed Catherine into the living room.

"Alakazam!" Tyler shouted at the crowd, waving his wand around in circles.

"Drunko needs a rest," Kevin called out.

Emily helped Tyler into a chair and whispered to him that he had done wonderfully.

"I know a few tricks," Xavier said, stepping into the centre of the room. He politely introduced himself and then picked up Tyler's hat from the floor. He twirled it around in his hands, concentrating on nothing else, and then tossed it into the air. He caught the hat in one swift motion, then held it completely still in front of him, and smiled. "I need a volunteer. Catherine, would you?"

Catherine smiled and walked up to the front.

"Reach inside." Xavier inched the hat closer to Catherine.

A little hesitant, Catherine slowly reached inside the top hat, fingers crawling across something hard and prickly. She pulled out the object and showed it to the audience.

"Aww!" said Alex. "A rose!"

Catherine smiled at Xavier, feeling her heart race just a little faster. "Thank you," she said, still amazed.

The group broke up and drifted in different directions after that, but the party was far from over. Catherine turned the music up louder and ran over to Amber in the kitchen. Before they even spoke, they each knew what the other was thinking.

"He's so..." said Amber.

"Charming," said Catherine, smelling her rose.

"Mysterious," Amber said dreamily.

The girls giggled and poured themselves another drink. Zach stumbled over, toilet paper dangling from every limb.

"Need more medicine," he said, holding out his cup.

Amber filled up his drink and they went off to talk in her bedroom. Catherine couldn't find Morgan anywhere. She gulped down her drink and poured herself another one. All that liquid had made her bladder ache, so she headed to the washroom, batting spider webs out of her face. One of the black light bulbs had burnt out, so Catherine had to rely on candlelight to find her way through Amber's suite. Finally, after nearly tripping twice, she reached the bathroom door. She flung it open and found Morgan and Alex there, kissing against the wall.

Catherine dropped her rose and drink and ran from the suite. This was too much to handle. She ignored Morgan's voice calling after her. All she could hear was the sound of her own heart breaking. In her own suite, she flung herself onto her bed and screamed into her pillow as tears flooded her face. She couldn't breathe or see, thinking of everything Morgan had said to her. Her mind wandered to the first time they had kissed and her chest went tight. All she felt was pain.

Maybe this is just a dream. Maybe when I wake up none of this will have happened.

"Hello?" Xavier said from Catherine's bedroom doorway.

Catherine wiped her eyes and sat up.

"Come in," she whispered.

Xavier entered and sat down on the edge of the bed.

"How did you get in?" asked Catherine.

"You left the door open."

Xavier took off his mask, and Catherine smiled slightly at his intensely green eyes. "You didn't have to come after me."

"I saw you run off and I wanted to make sure you were okay.

What happened?"

Xavier's dark hair reminded Catherine of Morgan, and she erupted into another fit of tears. "I'm sorry," she choked out.

"It's all right." He grazed her chin with his fingers and raised her head so she was facing him. "Beautiful girls like you don't need to cry over foolish boys."

Catherine nodded, her eyes still wet with tears. Xavier softly wiped the tears from Catherine's cheeks and kissed her lightly on the forehead.

The pressure in Catherine's chest lessened. She stared at Xavier, her vision wavering slightly, and attempted to smile.

"I have to go," Xavier said.

Catherine nodded silently and crawled under her blanket. Xavier slipped his mask on and left.

When Catherine awoke, she took a long, hot bath. She cried in the shower as images of the night before came flooding back to her. She dried herself and dressed, and turned on the fire. Just as she was about to curl up in a chair with her journal, a knock came at the door. Catherine didn't answer, but quietly crept over to the door and waited.

"Catherine, it's me," Amber said, knocking once more.

Catherine opened her door and let Amber in. They walked over to the green chairs in front of the fire and sat.

Amber, in a pink bathrobe and slippers, yawned audibly and rubbed her eyes. "Morgan was crying to me last night. He told me a pretty messed up story."

Catherine sighed and stared into the fire.

"Tell me what happened," said Amber.

"I opened the bathroom door and found Morgan and Alex together, and I ran off crying."

"Morgan told me he thought he was kissing *you*."

Catherine whipped her head around to face Amber. "So he's a cheater *and* a liar!"

"Well, technically, you weren't together," said Amber. "I mean, you haven't known each other for that long."

"That doesn't matter. We had something special. From the first day we met, it was like magic. We knew each other. I felt so complete with him." Catherine slid off her chair onto the floor. She crawled over in front of the fire and let the warmth soothe her. She closed her eyes and let her tears fall to the floor.

"Maybe you should talk to him," said Amber.

"No. I'm too upset. If he wants me, he can come and get me. I don't care if I ever get up off this floor. Let me rot here." She stretched out on her back and sighed.

"Come on, Cat. It's not good to dwell. I'll take you out for coffee and we can talk. Sound good?"

Catherine nodded. Amber changed out of her pajamas and met Catherine out front.

"I took some cigs from Zach," said Amber. "Want one?"

Catherine accepted the offer and put the cigarette to her lips. She inhaled as she lit her smoke and immediately her head spun with a comforting lightness. "So what happened between you and Zach?" she asked, breathing in cool air.

"We kissed," said Amber.

"I told you! My plan worked!" Catherine shouted, laughing almost hysterically. "So let me hear the details."

"We were both pretty drunk, but we knew what we were doing. We were talking in my room on my bed, lying down, and he just leaned over and kissed me."

"For how long?"

"We made out for a while. Nothing really major happened. We heard Morgan shouting and stopped to investigate."

"Sorry."

"That's okay, silly."

In town, they got coffees to go and walked over to the beach to stare out at the sea. "Xavier kissed me last night," Catherine said, watching waves crash against the shore.

"What?"

"Well, it was only on the forehead. I was crying in my bed last night, drunk and distraught, and he came into my room to console me." Catherine gulped down her coffee like water and continued to stare out at the ocean.

Amber sipped her coffee and grinned. "Lucky," she said, and Catherine grinned back at her.

The girls hugged goodbye. Amber assured Catherine that everything was going to work out. She walked back to Blacklune while Catherine stayed at the beach to think. Catherine needed some alone time.

The ocean was quiet today. The continuous ebb and flow of the waves soothed Catherine's nerves. She stared out at the horizon for quite some time, trying to forget yesterday for just one moment. A harsh wind caught her off guard and whipped at her back. Golden strands of her hair came flying forward, blocking her vision partially. She brushed them aside and shook her head to free it of torment. She turned to leave the beach and saw Xavier standing on the dock above her. Catherine's heart almost leapt from her chest. She laughed nervously. "Have you been watching me all this time?"

Xavier smiled and nodded. He beckoned Catherine to him with his finger. "Why don't you come up here? I have something to show you."

Catherine grinned and started to make her way up to the dock. Her thoughts took her to the previous night in her bedroom. Xavier had been so kind to her. He had been such a gentleman.

When Catherine reached the dock, she looked Xavier up and down, studying him soberly. He was taller than Morgan, with longer hair. He looked even more charming than he had last night. He continued to smile at her, confident and composed, yet there was something different about him that Catherine couldn't pinpoint. He was strangely enticing, and definitely handsome.

"So, what do you have to show me?" Catherine asked quietly.

Xavier stepped to the side to reveal a small orange kitten.

"Oh!" cried Catherine. "He's so cute!"

"He's yours to keep," said Xavier, picking up the kitten and handing it to Catherine, "that is, if you'll have him."

Catherine hugged the kitten to her chest. She scratched it behind the ears, making it purr. The kitten yawned and Catherine giggled at how tiny its teeth were. "He's adorable. Of course I'll keep him. Where ever did you find him?"

"On the beach. I really can't take care of him. I won't be here for that long."

"Are you staying with Maggie?"

"For now," Xavier said quickly.

"Thank you for this wonderful and unexpected gift." Catherine was smiling now.

"He's such a charmer," Xavier said, reaching to stroke the kitten's belly.

"Yes," said Catherine, staring at Xavier. "I'll call him Charmer."

They huddled with the kitten between them and continued talking until Catherine realized how much time had flown by. "I can't go back to the castle right now," she said, letting out a frustrated sigh. Her sorrow was transforming into rage. "I can't *believe* Morgan."

"You can talk to me about it. Let's have lunch, my treat."

"I couldn't eat anything right now, but I am thirsty."

"There's a hotel about fifteen minutes away from here, at the end of town, just before the other side of the forest. There's a fantastic restaurant there. How about we go sit down for a glass of wine and you can tell me the whole story. I'm a good listener."

Catherine took a deep breath and agreed.

The restaurant had a high ceiling. Quiet classical music played in the background. Beautiful wooden sculptures made by local artists stood all about the room, adding to the classy and calming atmosphere. Catherine sat across from Xavier in a tall comfortable chair. Next to her was a window that stretched from floor to ceiling.

Xavier had kindly offered to conceal the kitten in his leather jacket on the way in. Now, the kitten was fast asleep, curled up like a little orange ball of wool, on Xavier's lap. Catherine found it odd that the waiter hadn't noticed the kitten at all when Xavier ordered the bottle of wine. She was glad, but puzzled, that she hadn't been asked her age, as well. She brushed her questions aside and tried her best to focus on the moment. She tasted her wine and began to explain to Xavier why she was so upset and disconcerted. Xavier listened intently, his focus never once wavering from Catherine.

"I don't know what to do." Catherine took a large sip of her wine. "I feel terrible. *He's* the one who should feel terrible."

"For now you should just forget about him," said Xavier, taking Catherine's hands into his own.

Catherine suddenly felt content. All her worries disappeared and there was only Xavier. She was riveted by his stare—his eyes were pulling her in. She leaned forward and smiled, feeling dazed and light headed. She liked the way she felt and continued to grasp Xavier's hands.

"You're so pretty," said Xavier. "You're so feminine and delicate, and yet, I sense you have strength."

Catherine's lips parted, revealing her sharp fangs. Xavier caught a glimpse of them and raised his eyebrows, intrigued.

Catherine still felt as if she were sitting on a cloud. Her insides were warm, as if she was by a fire wrapped up in a blanket on a rainy day. "Thank you," she whispered, inching closer to Xavier's face.

For a moment, there was no other sound in the room aside from her own beating heart. Was this not the perfect moment? She tried to speak, but was cut off by Xavier's lips descending to hers. Catherine's heart began to palpitate quickly. Her warm insides started to boil. She gripped Xavier's hands tightly as he moved over her lips with his own in a kiss that was soft and smooth, long and slow.

Catherine was speechless when they parted. She felt completely calm and quiet, and time seemed to be stilled.

"I'm sorry," said Xavier. "I shouldn't have. I know you're going through a tough time with Morgan."

"Don't be. That was an amazing kiss." She let go of Xavier's hands and smoothed her hair, trying to collect herself. She took a sip of wine and touched her flushed cheeks.

"Another glass?"

"Sure, why not."

Something started to ache deep down in her gut, but she ignored the pain and kept her eyes on Xavier. When she stared at Xavier, everything seemed okay. She could forget for now...

After three glasses of wine each, Xavier and Catherine left the restaurant to go shopping. At a pet shop, Xavier purchased a litter box, kitty litter, kitten food, and two plastic bowls for Charmer. Catherine told him he didn't have to, but Xavier insisted. After all, he had sprung the kitten on Catherine, it was the least he could do. Catherine shrugged it off and thanked him.

On the way back to Blacklune, Catherine confessed that she was pretty drunk. Xavier laughed and took her arm. "I'll make sure you get back to the castle safely."

By the time they had reached Blacklune, Catherine was exhausted, not only physically, but emotionally. She felt drained and needed to rest. Panting slightly from their long walk, she thanked Xavier for the wonderful afternoon.

"It was no problem at all," Xavier said in a sing song voice, admiring the garden around him. They had stopped to catch their breath in the courtyard before parting.

"I'll make sure to take good care of Charmer," Catherine said, smiling.

Xavier slid his arm along Catherine's back and drew her to his chest. Their faces only inches apart, Xavier quietly said, "You take care of yourself too."

Catherine could feel her response to Xavier's strong arm holding her body against his. She felt that same comforting dizziness wash over her. It was not a normal reaction, she knew that, but before she could question any further, the dizzy spell grew stronger. She was floating on air again. Her body tingled with warmth. Her mind was at ease and there was only Xavier once again.

Xavier smiled his alluring smile and brought his lips closer to Catherine's. Catherine closed her eyes and succumbed to his invitation immediately, raising her lips to meet his. Xavier held Catherine tight, both arms sliding up her body. His hands came to rest on her neck where they massaged and stroked passionately.

From the balcony above them, Morgan watched frowning, then looked away, blinking back tears.

6

As soon as Catherine got back to her suite, she set down the litter box in her bathroom and filled it with kitty litter. She set out two bowls on her kitchen floor, one with water and one with kitten food.

When everything seemed just right, she went to sit in one of her big green chairs to relax and write in her journal. Charmer slept in her lap, purring softly. Catherine's mind raced. Her thoughts took her from Morgan to Xavier and back to Morgan again. Something wasn't right, she could feel it. The aching deep down inside of her was returning.

November 1

Dear journal,

I really thought Morgan and I were meant to be together. I guess not. Maybe he likes Alex more than me. She is beautiful. But Amber did say that's stupid. He kissed Alex. Obviously he doesn't care for me at all.

Maybe Xavier's the one I'm supposed to be with. He is handsome and seems intelligent. He's so...cool and confident all the time. Everything seems to go by so smoothly when I'm around him...almost too smoothly. He's seems too good to be true. He's so sophisticated and charming. Debonair. Ha! When he kissed me today, I felt strange, and maybe it was because I'm attracted to him, but oh, I don't know. It was as if I was in a dream...Come to think of it, the day is a little blurry to me. I am a little drunk on wine right now. Xavier took me out for drinks. But I can't help feeling like things aren't...right. He said he'd be in touch when he left me today. That was all. He just ran off after he kissed me. I don't even know much about him. Maybe I'm over thinking this whole situation.

I miss Morgan.

Boys are so frustrating. I can't think straight. I'm tired. But I don't think I'll sleep right now. I need to talk to someone who will listen...someone wise. I really hope I don't run into Morgan any time soon. I get really emotional when I'm tipsy...I might start crying in front of him.

Catherine closed the journal and decided to go and talk to Maggie. She was thankful that she saw no one on the way to the library. When she reached the counter, she took in a deep breath, trying to collect her thoughts. She suddenly felt embarrassed—after all, she had kissed Maggie's son. She prayed that the discussion wouldn't be too awkward.

"Catherine dear, come inside," said Maggie, poking her head out from behind the mirror.

Catherine did as she was told. She stayed quiet at first, afraid to speak.

"Please sit down and tell me what happened. Would you like anything to eat or drink?" asked Maggie.

"No, I'm fine, thank you. I wanted to come to you because, well, I know you saw me crying before. Your vision came true. I caught Morgan kissing Alex yesterday."

"Oh, sweetheart," Maggie said.

"I keep feeling these pains in my chest and in my stomach," Catherine said, verging on tears. "My head keeps pounding."

Maggie gave Catherine a hug. "It's all right, Catherine, things are going to be just fine. I can sense that Morgan is a good guy. When you're ready, talk to him."

"That's what everyone keeps telling me. I guess I really should. I just don't know how he could possibly redeem himself."

"Where's that beautiful necklace you always wear?" Maggie asked suddenly.

Catherine looked down at her neck and saw that she didn't have her crescent moon necklace on. "It must have fallen off," she said, sighing.

"Make sure you find it. I'm sure a lot of people would like to get their hands on such a precious piece of jewelry."

Catherine nodded and wiped her eyes. She thought twice about telling Maggie that she had gone out with her son, but she couldn't find the nerve. She thanked Maggie and got up to leave.

"Take some biscuits with you," said Maggie, fetching a tin filled with chocolate covered cookies for Catherine.

"Thank you," said Catherine, smiling.

She left, feeling more at ease after her short visit with Maggie, though her heart still ached. She returned to her room and munched on a few cookies. Then she searched her entire suite for her necklace, but found nothing.

She knew she would feel better after everything got sorted out, and after an hour of contemplating, Catherine finally decided to go talk to Morgan. She knocked on his door three times and waited, her chest still tight and painful. Morgan opened the door, and as soon as he recognized Catherine, his eyes started to water. He pulled Catherine into a hug, and began to laugh hysterically while tears streamed down his cheeks. Catherine, shocked, patted his back.

"People think I'm either lying or crazy," Morgan sobbed into Catherine's shoulder. "It was *you*, but I don't understand—"

"Shh. Let's go inside and you can tell me everything."

Morgan poured himself a cup of water and then took a seat at the kitchen table. Catherine sat across from him, unsure what to say or do. She knew, however, that she still felt more for Morgan than anyone else in the world.

"I remember I was in front of the bathroom and I saw you and smiled. I took your hand and led you into the bathroom and kissed you, well, at least, I thought it was you until you came into the doorway and dropped your drink. I saw you run off and I shouted at you to come back. Then I realized I had been kissing Alex." Morgan paused with a frustrated sigh. "It doesn't make sense! You have to believe me, Catherine." He dropped his head into his hands.

Catherine took his hands in her own and whispered, "I know your story sounds messed up...*really* messed up, but somehow, I know you're telling the truth."

"You do?" Morgan's head jerked up to look at her.

"Yes. I can't explain it. I really do hope I'm right, because I was so...hurt." Her face creased as she began to cry. "I know we aren't... together, but I really like you."

Morgan smiled, squeezing Catherine's fingers, and now he was crying tears of happiness. Catherine leaned forward and kissed Morgan's upper lip. Morgan flung his arms around her. "I like you too. I don't want to lose you," he said, breathing in Catherine's scent. "I want to *be* with you. Be my girlfriend?"

Catherine nodded and slid her hands up Morgan's neck. She drew his face to her own and kissed him passionately. Her heart no longer hurt. Her mind felt clear.

They went to Morgan's bedroom together. Side by side on the bed, they talked.

"Maybe Maggie can help us," Catherine told Morgan. "She's a witch."

"A real witch, with powers?"

Catherine leaned into Morgan and nodded.

"What were you doing with Xavier today?" he asked quietly.

"How did you know I went out with Xavier today?"

"I was out on the balcony and I saw you two together," said Morgan. "I saw you kissing him."

Catherine sighed. She tried to think up a good excuse, but there wasn't one. "I saw him on the beach. We went out and he kissed me. But, just listen before you say anything. Every time he touched me I felt...strange."

"What do you mean?"

"I felt dizzy and confused, light-headed," said Catherine. "Everything around me sort of vanished when he had his hands on me and I could only focus on him. I honestly cannot recall the entire day clearly. It was like a dream. Xavier's really...smooth all the time. There's something different about him. I can feel it."

"Maybe he's a witch," Morgan said simply.

"What?" said Catherine, grinning slightly.

"Maggie's a witch. It's possible that he's magic too. He probably has powers. That's probably why he was so good at that trick he pulled at the party."

Catherine gasped and sat up. "Now that I think back, it makes sense. He had such a powerful aura about him. I felt so drawn to him."

"That's it!" cried Morgan, sitting up to join Catherine. "He cast some sort of spell on me!"

"Maybe you're right," said Catherine, a cryptic expression on her face. "It's possible...I mean, anything's possible after finding out we're *fucking vampires!*"

"Xavier probably made me think Alex was you somehow. Think about it. If he could make you feel dizzy and drawn to him, if he could shut out everything around you two, if he's that powerful, maybe he could fool me into thinking someone else was you."

"But why would he do that? That's the part I don't get."

"Where did he go afterwards?" asked Morgan.

Catherine looked away and thought for a moment. "He went after me. He said he came to comfort me. Then he left. Didn't he go back to the party?"

"No. Weird. He must have known that you would get upset and run off. He must have wanted to get you alone."

"I don't know what he wants with me," said Catherine, letting out a deep breath. "I can't believe I fell for him. Amber and I thought he was a nice guy. I'm sorry for running off. I just didn't know what to do. That image really hurt me."

Morgan slid himself and Catherine back on the bed and then pulled the sheet over their heads. "It's okay. We're here now and that's all that matters. This is our own world." He reached up and skimmed the sheet with his fingers. A little light could be seen though the fibres. "We can do whatever we want in it."

"You say everything I've been waiting to hear for so long. No one has ever understood me like you do," said Catherine, filled to the brim with elation.

They kissed and filled themselves with love. Like a current, they travelled over each other's bodies, stripping away layers. Catherine was amazed that Morgan knew her body so well. He knew exactly where she liked to be touched.

At dinnertime, Catherine and Morgan decided to skip the ballroom and make their own creations in Morgan's kitchenette.

"We can eat dinner in pyjamas," said Morgan, grinning.

"I'll have to borrow some," said Catherine, tugging at Morgan's boxers.

Morgan slowly rolled out of the bed and went over to his dresser. He pulled out a large black T-shirt with a yellow happy face on the front and handed it to Catherine. "I hope this will suffice."

"It'll do just fine," said Catherine, pulling the shirt over her head.

They walked back into the kitchen and poured themselves a cup of water. Catherine sat in a chair admiring Morgan's behind as he bent over, studying the contents of his refrigerator.

"There's jam, peanut butter, bread, cheese, grape soda, and some candy from yesterday. My parents gave me some snacks before they left. I think I have some chips somewhere, too."

"Well, we can make sandwiches," said Catherine, walking over to join Morgan.

"Good idea," he said, taking out the bread. "Peanut butter and jam sound good?"

"Sounds great."

They each made a sandwich and sat down at the table to eat. They traded a half each so they could test whose tasted better.

Satisfied and finally happy, Catherine and Morgan went back to Morgan's room and lay entwined together on the bed, listening to the rain outside. Catherine sighed and hugged Morgan, happy to be indoors and warm, once again completely enamoured of him.

"You look good in my shirt," said Morgan.

"Thanks. Can I keep it?"

"Sure." Morgan ran his hand up Catherine's bare legs.

Catherine giggled and kissed Morgan's nose. He smiled and kissed her neck. Then he sighed heavily, pulling Catherine close, but turning his head away.

"What's wrong?" asked Catherine.

"Kissing your neck took me back to our first night here, the ceremony," said Morgan. "Then I remembered the time we were in Amber's bed. I don't ever want to be that out of control."

Catherine smiled at him. "Now you know when to stop, though. You can feel it, can't you?"

Morgan nodded. "It's so powerful, though. I could just keep drinking until death."

"Wow," Catherine said. "Well, you can drink from me again, but this time, I want to do it differently. Do you have any razors?"

Morgan's eyes widened and consternation spread across his face. But gradually, his alarm turned to intrigue.

"In the bathroom. Follow me."

Morgan took Catherine by the hand and led her to his bathroom sink. Just below it was a drawer with shaving supplies. Catherine took out a plastic razor and smiled.

"This will do," she said, beginning to pry off the plastic that surrounded the blade. She carefully bent back all the plastic and wrenched it off until only a clean metal blade was left. "Sorry about that." She threw the plastic parts into the garbage.

"No problem." Morgan was watching with fervent interest.

"Why don't you carve something into me," said Catherine.

"Are you sure?"

Catherine nodded and bit her lips with anticipation. "Carve your name into me." She sat down on the tile floor.

"Okay, but only if you do the same to me," said Morgan, razor in hand.

Catherine nodded and turned out her left foot so that the inner part of her leg was showing. "Right here." She pointed to the skin just above her ankle bone.

Morgan took a seat between Catherine's legs and steadied his hands. Catherine didn't flinch as he made the first incision—she gasped with delight.

After the entire name was cut into Catherine's flesh, Morgan set the razor on the counter and raised Catherine's leg to his mouth. He pushed his lips against her skin so his teeth wouldn't puncture her and drank. Catherine suddenly pulled him back by the shoulders. He came up with blood dripping from his lips, his pupils dilated.

"I can feel the energy pulsing though me. I can see everything clearer," he said, licking the blood from his lips. "You do me now."

"Gladly," said Catherine, giggling.

She took the blade, rinsed and dried it off, and settled down between Morgan's legs to cut. Morgan didn't stir as Catherine worked. She decided that *Cat* would work fine and didn't carve the entire name.

"That felt great!" Morgan shouted when she finished. "No pain."

Catherine smiled, put the razor on the counter, and began to suck on the letters she'd cut. Her head went light and her heart rate quickened. Her body was flooded with energy.

"Wow," said Catherine, panting, when she came up for air. "I feel fantastic. Squeeze me!"

Smiling broadly, Morgan squeezed her hard.

"No pain!" she shouted, pinching Morgan back. "Kiss me!"

Morgan kissed Catherine ferociously. Catherine tightly wrapped her legs around Morgan and pulled him toward her. Morgan peeled off Catherine's shirt and bra and dove into her chest with his lips. Catherine pulled Morgan into a hug, pressing his chest to her own and her cheek to his. Even the slightest brush of their skin was almost overwhelming.

Over Morgan's shoulder, Catherine could see the window. It was dark, but the moon shone brightly and the sky was flushed with light. There was something outside the glass, something human. Catherine gasped and pushed Morgan's face in the direction of the glass. They both sat up. Morgan held Catherine close as they searched the window for the figure, but it was gone.

"What was that?" Catherine asked Morgan.

He shrugged, but Catherine could sense fear in him. "Let's go to my room," he said, helping Catherine up.

Catherine slipped on her shirt, picked up her bra, and took Morgan's hand. Together they left the washroom, the tile and counter stained with their blood.

With energy still bubbling inside of them, Catherine and Morgan couldn't sleep. They sat up in bed telling stories and talking about their pasts. Morgan told Catherine how he had moved around a lot with his family. He had lived in Australia as a child, moved to the United States as a teenager, and finally moved back to Canada. They both continued to glance at the window for the rest of the night.

7

Catherine and Morgan got dressed and headed down to the ballroom for breakfast in the morning. They hadn't slept much and felt terribly exhausted. After two cups of coffee, some soup, and a cigarette, they were more relaxed.

"Let's go talk to Maggie," said Catherine. "I don't feel so good."

Morgan nodded and they stood up to leave. Dolores, a friendly old lady whom Catherine and Morgan had never met before, came over and collected their cups and dishes. She was a short, rather plump woman with a hairnet on her greying hair. She smiled at Catherine and returned to the kitchen through a door that was hidden along the wall.

"She must be the cook," said Morgan.

"She seems nice. Did you know there was a door there?"

"No. This castle has a lot of secrets."

When they reached the library desk, they found that Maggie was not there. Catherine spotted a bell on the counter and tapped it once. Soon after, the mirror slid open and Maggie popped her head out. "Come inside. I've been expecting you."

Catherine led Morgan through the opening into Maggie's comfortable home.

"I'm glad you two worked everything out," she said. "Take a

seat. I know you have something to say to me."

Morgan sat down next to Catherine and slid his hand over hers. Catherine smiled and gave Morgan's fingers a squeeze.

"Your son, Xavier, was at the Halloween party Amber and Catherine threw on Friday," said Morgan. "We wanted to know if he has powers, too, because we think he was up to something."

Maggie sighed and put her hands to her forehead. "Not again," she said sadly. "Yes, Xavier is a witch, and he's been known to do rather...naughty things. He likes dark magic, revenge spells and whatnot. He has such a thirst for power. It has gotten him in trouble on more than one occasion."

"We think he cast a spell on me, to make me believe Alex was Catherine."

"We just don't know why," added Catherine.

Maggie gave a little cry and said, "Then it's just as I feared. He took your necklace, Catherine."

"Why would he want it?" Catherine asked, confused.

"That necklace you had was a powerful magical item. When worn outside, under the light of the moon, when the sun has set, it will allow a person to fly. All the wearer has to do is say or think to themselves that they want to fly and they will. It can only be used ten nights in each year."

Catherine and Morgan glanced at each other quickly. Catherine knew Morgan was thinking the exact same thing as she was. "I wonder how my mother came across it."

"There are many magical items sold, all over the place," said Maggie. "The only difficulty is knowing where to go to find them."

"So what should we do?" asked Morgan.

"How am I supposed to get my necklace back?"

"Xavier will return," said Maggie, "and when he does, I will retrieve your necklace. Xavier may be a witch, but I am one too, and a much stronger one at that."

"What if he tries to trick us again?" asked Morgan. "I had a breakdown after that stunt he pulled. I thought I was going crazy.

Catherine hated me. I don't want that to happen again."

"Don't worry. You two have a stronger bond than any two people I've ever encountered. It's rare for such similar souls to meet, but not impossible. Stick together. Trust each other, and you'll be fine." She got up and walked over to a dresser and opened the top drawer. From inside, she took out two long, thin, black ribbons and handed one each to Morgan and Catherine. "Tie these around your necks just in case. They're blessed and will repel negative energy."

Catherine and Morgan thanked Maggie and immediately put on their ribbons. Catherine tied hers tightly around her neck and secured it with a bow at the back. Morgan let his hang a bit looser and secured it with a knot.

They left, thanking Maggie once again, and headed out back to the garden pathways. They took a seat on the bench beside the pond and skipped stones. The sky grew dark and the air became cold. Something was not right.

That night, Morgan slept beside Catherine in her room. Charmer also joined them. Morgan loved the kitten instantly, and because Catherine didn't want the look of happiness to leave Morgan's face, she hadn't told him who had given the kitten to her. She simply said she had found him on the beach, which was partly true.

A great wind had picked up and it rattled the windows every so often. At four in the morning, Catherine awoke to screams coming from outside the window. She woke Morgan up and together they peered outside to see what all the commotion was about.

Down below, Maggie was somehow pinning Xavier to the ground with magic. She had her wand out in front of her and in her other hand was Catherine's necklace. Xavier bellowed again.

"It's not fair! She doesn't even use it. I want it! I must have it!"

"I thought you already learned that stealing is wrong," said Maggie. "You're an adult now. There's no excuse for what you did. Scaring an innocent boy and girl. You should be ashamed of yourself. I wonder what the council would say if I reported this incident?"

"No!" screamed Xavier. "Please don't do that. I don't want to go back. I'll do anything!"

"All right," Maggie said, allowing her son to stand. "Return to your school and stay put. You're there to learn. How long have you been away?"

"A week," Xavier said, dusting off his black coat. "It doesn't matter, though. I'm better than all of them. I'll show them."

He ran off into the woods and left Maggie standing alone with the necklace. She looked up and smiled at Catherine and Morgan.

"Thank you," called Catherine, but not too loudly so as to not wake the other students.

"I'll give this back to you in the morning," said Maggie, as she went inside. Catherine and Morgan crawled back into bed and fell asleep.

They woke up and dressed for school the next day, deciding to keep their protective chokers on.

"Just until we're sure we're safe," said Morgan.

Catherine nodded and admired her ribbon in the mirror. "I actually like it. It's very Marie Antoinette." She grinned at Morgan and they walked downstairs to get breakfast.

Once they had their trays, they searched for a table and saw that Alex, looking miserable, was alone at one.

"Let's go talk to her," said Catherine, and Morgan agreed.

"Hey Alex," said Morgan, taking a seat with Catherine at Alex's table.

Alex looked up, her eyes sunken and dull. "I'm sorry, Catherine. I didn't know what was happening."

"It's fine," said Catherine. "We've worked everything out. Xavier is scum and well, he cast a spell over Morgan to make him think you were me. Don't worry about anything."

Alex's jaw dropped and she laughed in relief. They all ate breakfast, happy that they were not quarrelling anymore.

In the library, Maggie called Catherine over and handed her the necklace. "Keep it safe, and if you decide to use it, be careful."

"You don't have to be a witch to use it?"

"Everyone has power inside them. This necklace allows the user to bring out that power easily."

Catherine walked to class hand in hand with Morgan. They stopped at the carpeted area and took a seat. In front of them, a television was set up, along with a game system, ready to use.

"That's right!" shouted Zach. "It's game time!"

Catherine and Morgan chuckled and leaned against each another. Morgan brushed his right leg against the spot where he had carved his name into Catherine. Catherine smiled and brushed her leg against the spot where she had carved her name into him.

Amber beamed when she saw that Catherine and Morgan had made up. Everyone seemed happy and normal. Things were going smoothly. It was time to stir things up again.

"Tonight, I'm calling another Animal Kingdom meeting in my room," she whispered to everyone. "Be there at seven o'clock."

River arrived with a handful of videogames. Zach ran over to choose his favourite to play first.

"You're going to have a competition," River said. "Two people will play against each other. Whoever loses is out of the game and has to watch. The one who wins stays in the play and faces the next challenger. Zach has chosen *Ultimate Murder Zone*. Would you care to explain the rules, Zach?"

Zach got up and starting spitting out rules about the game and how to work the controller. A few people seemed lost, but Catherine kept up well enough.

Everyone laughed and had fun when they played. Zach ended up beating everyone except Tyler, who tied with Zach in the final match. Zach chose two more games and everyone watched and waited their turn to play. The class went by easily. Video games always seemed to allow hours to go by without anyone noticing.

Catherine and Amber talked outside after lunch. Catherine told Amber about the spell Xavier had cast on Morgan, but she kept the secret about her powerful necklace to herself.

"I can't believe it!" shouted Amber. "Good thing you didn't fall for him."

Catherine shrugged and stared up at the sky. She could hardly wait for nightfall to come. "I have a kitten now. Xavier gave him to me. He's so weird. I actually thought he could have been the one for me. It's totally fucked. He's fucked in the head."

"Yep. Fucked right up," said Amber, laughing. "I wanna see your kitty. What's his name?"

"Charmer."

Amber smirked, and Catherine punched her arm.

"I didn't see Zach all Saturday," Amber said. "I think he was sleeping off his hangover. But on Sunday we hung out."

"What did you do?"

"We just stayed in his room and played cards and talked and kissed...a few times. Things are good."

"That's great! I'm happy for you, really."

"Thanks. Oh! I just remembered! We get blood today at dinner. I can't wait. It's weird. Now that I know how good I feel with blood, I crave it almost. Don't you?"

"I drank some on Saturday."

"From who?"

"Morgan," said Catherine, pausing to roll up her left pant leg. "We carved our names into each other and drank each other's blood."

Amber's eyebrows rose slightly. "That's cool with me. I actually think it's hot, but don't go showing it off to everyone."

"Oh, I know," said Catherine. "It was so intense though. I felt so alive, so connected to Morgan. We have this bond. It's like I can feel him all the time. When he was sad, I felt it. We're boyfriend and girlfriend now. He asked me and I said yes."

Amber smiled, her eyes misted over.

"It's starting to rain," said Catherine, squinting at the clouds. "Let's go inside and find our boys."

"*Our* boys," repeated Amber. "I love it!"

With a little over an hour until dinner, Amber, Zach, Morgan, and Catherine all gathered in Catherine's room to hear scary stories. Amber and Zach flipped when they saw Charmer, and for the entire story, they took turns holding him like a baby.

Catherine turned off all the lights and lit a few candles. She wrapped a blanket around her guests and took up the horror book she had borrowed from the library a while back. Slowly, she began to read: "This is a true story. It was the late nineteenth century, at Blacklune on—"

"Wait a second," said Amber. "Are you talking about *this* Blacklune?"

"Is there any other?" Catherine asked calmly, trying to sound mysterious. "As I was saying, it was the late nineteenth century at Blacklune on a cold and stormy night when an old, grey-haired witch arrived at the castle doors. She had no place to go so she knocked on the doors, hoping that someone would allow her to stay the night. The owner of the castle welcomed the old woman in and told her she could spend the night. The woman thanked the man and settled into the last room on the left in the upper hall. The woman made no complaints during the night. She made not one sound. The next afternoon, the owner went to check on her. He knocked on her door three times, but there was no answer. He tried again and again, but still, no answer. He tried calling out her name, but she did not respond. He finally got out his master key and opened the door. His eyes fell upon a terrible sight." Catherine paused and eyed her listeners carefully. They were all huddled together, watching her eagerly. "The woman was sprawled out on the floor, motionless. The woman was...dead!"

Amber screamed, mostly at how loud Catherine had shouted the last word in her face. Zach pulled her close. Morgan kept his focus on Catherine.

"The owner walked over to the corpse, already beginning to stink of rotting flesh, and inspected it. The eyes were wide open. The woman's expression seemed to say something...but what? The man studied the woman's face and only came to an answer when he saw her lips were slightly upturned. She was happy to have passed so peacefully. The body was removed and life went on just as normally as before. A few weeks later, however, things changed. While the owner was cleaning up the bathroom in the last suite on the left side of the upper hall, he noticed something peculiar about his reflection. He stared at his face in the mirror and saw that his skin appeared wrinkled and old. His hair, usually full and brown, was thin and greying. His eyes were sunken and his skin was sagging. Immediately, the owner blew out the candles, set down his cleaning supplies and ran out of the suite, too frightened to continue with his work. The next day, he sent a maid to take a look at the mirror, but she saw no grey hair and no baggy skin. The owner, confused and frightened, re-examined his experience and came to the conclusion that only at midnight with the light of a candle and nothing else, could one see their future selves, old and grey. The memory of the old woman is kept alive through the mirror to this day. Her magic still exists. Do you dare enter the last room on the left side of the upper hall of Blacklune?"

"No way," said Amber, gripping Zach tightly.

"Yes way!" shouted Zach. "I say we do it tonight at the meeting. It'll be fun."

"Me, too," said Morgan.

"Well, I guess all the candles and stuff just got me a little freaked out," said Amber. "I'll do it if we all stick together."

"Fine," said Catherine. "I'll tell the story for the others and then we'll go on a mission. But what if the door is locked?"

"Why would it be locked?" asked Amber. "No one is in there."

"We'll see tonight," said Catherine. "If it's locked then we'll forget about it, but if it's open, then we're going in. Agreed?"

Everyone nodded and then stood up to head downstairs for dinner.

Catherine chose a pasta dish and a tall glass of blood. She took a seat at a table with Morgan, Amber, and Zach and began to eat. The four of them decided to save the blood for last. Catherine could hardly wait to drink hers.

"Just resist," Amber told everyone. "If we drink it last, we'll have more energy for A.K."

Catherine agreed and ate her pasta quickly, but her attention was on the glass and the thick, dark liquid inside of it.

When everyone had finished eating, they each took up their glass and brought it to the centre to clink with the others. Then they drank. Catherine felt energy pump into her system. Her eyes widened and she continued to drink, watching Morgan drink his blood down in one.

When all the glasses were empty and in the middle of the table, Amber smiled blissfully. Her smile caught the attention of the others and they joined in. Soon, everyone was smiling and squealing quietly.

"This is good," said Amber.

"Yeah," agreed Zach. "Let's go back to your room."

Catherine and Morgan followed them up the stairs. On the way, Catherine turned to Morgan and said, "I liked your blood better. I like it fresh and warm and alive."

Morgan smiled at her in agreement and kissed her on the cheek.

Amber turned on her fireplace and lit a few candles. Then she went to fetch her big red book. Zach cozied up next to her and kissed her ear. Morgan and Catherine sat in front of the fire, cross-legged, staring at each other. Catherine's heart was racing; she wanted Morgan all alone so she could kiss him over and over again. Morgan pulled Catherine close and kissed her softly on the lips.

"Well, evidently, you want the same thing," Catherine whispered.

"What?"

"Oh nothing. I just really want to kiss you."

"Me, too," said Morgan, moistening his lips. "Let's wait until the meeting's over."

Alex, Kevin, Tyler, and Emily arrived at the door all together and took a seat in front of the fire beside Catherine and Morgan.

"Welcome to the second meeting of Animal Kingdom," Amber said, writing something down in the red book. "Can you all say your nickname aloud to signify your presence, please?"

Everyone shouted out their nickname. Amber scribbled another note in her book and grinned. "We're all here to have fun, so tonight Catherine is going to tell you a spooky story."

Catherine un-cozied herself from Morgan, took out her horror book, and read. When she had finished the entire story, Amber pointed a flashlight at her guests. "Now it's time to find out if the mirror really is cursed."

Emily squinted and held a hand up to her eyes. "Are we all going to go, then?"

"Yes," said Amber, "unless you're too scared, that is."

No one said a word.

"Let's go then," said Zach, helping Amber up.

Everyone stood, still very much awake and enthused as they exited Amber's room. The outside hall was dark—only candles lined the walls. Zach led the way, a candle ready to light in his hand, proudly strutting down the corridor. Amber was right behind him.

"Try the door," Catherine whispered.

Zach turned the handle and everyone heard a clicking sound. The door had opened. Zach turned around and mouthed, "Holy shit," to everyone behind him. Catherine held onto Morgan's hand tightly and followed Amber into the suite. It was dark inside. The light switch didn't work.

"No surprise," Amber whispered loudly. "Ghosts like the dark."

They could only see the outlines of furniture.

"Watch where you're going!" Alex said. "These are brand new pumps."

"Sorry," whispered Tyler, gripping Emily like a lost puppy.

"Over here." Zach was pointing to the bathroom.

Everyone crammed into the washroom and stared at the mirror.

ଓଃ Cat the Vamp ଃଠ

Zach handed the candle to Amber and struck a match. Carefully he lit the wick and light filled the room. Everyone watched their reflection in anticipation.

"What time is it?" asked Kevin, sandwiched in between Tyler and Alex.

"One more minute until midnight," Morgan said, checking his watch.

They waited and stared at themselves in the mirror.

"Okay, it's midnight...now!" said Morgan.

Everyone studied their faces, but nothing much seemed to change.

"Oh, I think I see a hint of grey," said Amber.

"That's because we've been standing here for an eternity," said Alex.

Then, a strange moaning sound arose from outside the bathroom. Zach coughed and the candle went out. Alex screamed and soon everyone was shouting and pushing to get out the door.

"Run!" screamed Amber, grabbing onto Zach's shirt.

Zach and Amber fled back to Amber's room with Catherine and Morgan. Tyler and Emily came back next, huffing and puffing. Alex and Kevin came back a minute later. Kevin was crying and Alex was complaining.

"He sprained his bloody ankle," said Alex, pointing to Kevin.

"She stepped on me!"

"Look, it doesn't matter," said Amber. "What matters is that we're all here, safe and alive. The mirror might have not been haunted, but that room sure as hell is!"

"What was that?" asked Emily.

"Who knows," said Amber. "A ghost, a monster, an experiment perhaps. I'll have to record our expedition."

Amber began scribbling down everything that had happened in her red book. Catherine and Morgan went to the kitchen to talk.

"What do you think happened?" asked Catherine.

"I have no idea," said Morgan, "but whatever it was, it sure scared the shit out of me."

Catherine laughed and pulled him close. She kissed him long and hard and turned to look out the window at the moon. "It's night time. The moon is out," she whispered into Morgan's ear. "We should go out and play."

"What about Amber?"

"Take a look at her," said Catherine. "She's immersed in that book of hers. I'm sure she won't mind. I'll go tell her we have to go do something."

Catherine walked over to Amber and they talked while Morgan waited patiently in the kitchen. When Catherine returned, they both slipped out the door. Morgan gripped Catherine's hand. "What did you tell Amber?"

"I told her we needed to talk about what happened at the party. It's not like she would say no."

Together they raced down the stairs into the entranceway. Morgan took out his castle key and quietly unlocked the front doors. They crept out and Morgan locked the doors behind them. The night greeted them with cool kisses and brisk hugs. The sky was alive with shimmering stars. The moon was almost full.

"Wouldn't it be weird if the moon was just a light bulb and we were just some experiment?" asked Catherine.

"Yeah," said Morgan, "that would be cool. But we've been to the moon."

"I know, but it's fun to imagine things sometimes." She gripped her moon necklace, staring down at it. Then she focused on the moon. "I wish to fly," she said, still clutching the necklace, and before she could figure out what was happening, she was off the ground.

"Wow!" shouted Morgan. "You're flying! For real!"

Catherine looked down at the ground and laughed. She let go of the necklace and let her arms fall to her side. She was only a few feet above the earth, hovering. "I feel like I'm floating, but not totally. It's almost as if the air has turned to liquid. I feel like I can swim through it. It's very relaxing."

She raised her arms high above her head and thought hard about travelling up. She rose higher and felt her stomach swirl with excitement. "I can't believe it! I'm flying!"

She shot through the sky and landed on a tree branch. Morgan ran over and called up to her. "Let me fly with you!"

Catherine lowered herself to the ground. She took Morgan's hands and together they flew to the sky, past the trees, into the clouds. Catherine's heart was bursting with euphoria. She felt that same perfect feeling she did when Morgan kissed her. She was alive and there was nothing that could stop her from feeling happy.

"This is amazing," said Morgan. "You can control it just by thinking about it."

They hovered, surrounded by mist, hands still firmly clasped.

"We can sit too," said Catherine, crossing her legs. "If we imagine we're on the ground, we can sit in the air."

Morgan crossed his legs and let out an ecstatic shout.

"I wonder what would happen if I let go of you." Catherine released one of Morgan's hands. He wobbled slightly and they both sank closer to the ground.

"Please don't let go of me." Breathing rapidly, Morgan snatched Catherine's hand back.

"I won't," said Catherine, kissing both of Morgan's palms.

"What are you going to do with all this power?"

Catherine didn't answer. Vibrant with energy, she noticed sounds she normally wouldn't have heard. Her ears were attuned to the night and she could hear leaves rustling in the wind, pebbles rolling along the ground, and someone walking away from the castle.

"Look." Catherine pointed down at a woman with long dark brown hair.

"Who is she?"

They watched the woman walk below them. She carried no purse or bags, but wore a thick black coat and a bright red scarf.

"I wonder where she's going," said Catherine. "Come on, let's find out."

She pulled Morgan through the air to land on the castle's roof, from where they continued to watch the woman walk.

"Whooo areee youuu?" Catherine called out, trying to be ghost-like.

The woman froze on the spot and looked around. She raised her head to the sky, shrugged, and then continued on her way toward the main path.

"Tell us who you are or we'll come get you!" shouted Morgan.

The woman stopped again and looked back at the castle. She frowned and stuffed her hands into her pockets.

"Hey!" Catherine said quietly to Morgan. "That was mean."

"Well, it's rude of her not to introduce herself after we asked her so nicely."

"Please, whatever, whoever you are," said the woman, her voice shaky, "please don't harm me. I'm only visiting Blacklune."

"Why?" shouted Catherine, excited by her power to frighten the woman.

"I'm a donor." Although the woman spoke quietly, both Catherine and Morgan heard her.

"She gives blood," said Catherine, "to us. She must be a normal, clean human or River wouldn't accept her. She looks so helpless. Let's scare her."

Catherine took Morgan's hand and they drifted down off the roof to float just above where the woman stood trembling. The woman looked up and screamed.

"Demon!" She began to run back toward the castle.

"Catch her!" shouted Morgan.

Catherine shot toward the fleeing woman and they caught her and pinned her to the ground. Together, they muffled her screams.

"What should we do?" asked Morgan.

Catherine's mind was spinning wildly. "Drink." She plunged

her fangs into the woman's neck.

Warm, intoxicating blood filled her mouth. When she rose, Morgan bent down to feed, as well. Catherine roared with victory and flung her arms around Morgan, who was laughing uncontrollably. Feeling ready for anything, she took Morgan's hands and they flew to the rooftop once more and gazed down at the earth below, King and Queen of the night. They fell into each other and kissed under the moonlight.

Catherine closed her eyes as Morgan's hands travelled down her body. Things were moving quickly once again and before she could even speak, her pants were at her ankles. Morgan groaned, like an animal in heat, and tugged at Catherine's underwear. Catherine opened her eyes and stared at Morgan. She knew what he wanted. She knew she wanted it too. She nodded and went to work on unzipping Morgan's jeans. He moaned again and slid Catherine's underwear off along with his own. Catherine hugged Morgan to her chest and waited, legs spread. She felt him enter her like a knife, twisting inside her, but she embraced the pain. She wrapped her legs around Morgan and pulled him into her. They were one with each other, with the night, with life itself. They were invincible. Their bodies slid in rhythm with the branches of the trees that gracefully arched and bowed in the wind, whispering dark secrets to the moon.

Overwhelmed and exhausted, Catherine and Morgan collapsed on the roof and slept until sunrise, their bodies tingling almost unbearably.

Catherine awoke and immediately knew that something was wrong. She felt...empty. She no longer was energized. She saw Morgan asleep beside her. She smiled and shook him gently. When he woke, she kissed him softly on the lips.

"How are you?" she asked.

"My body feels different," he said, stretching. "I don't feel good at all."

"Me either," said Catherine. "It's so bright. I can't stand it."

They helped each other up, legs weak and wobbly, and brushed themselves off.

"What time is it?" asked Morgan, taking Catherine's hand.

Catherine's heart rate quickened as she stared at the sun. "The sun is out. We can't fly anymore. How are we going to get down?"

They walked over to the edge of the roof and peered down. The stone path leading to the castle was glistening from a light rain that had fallen during the night. Neither Catherine nor Morgan had even noticed that they were getting damp as they slept.

"What are we going to do?" asked Morgan, giving Catherine a little shake.

"Calm down. Let's sit for a moment and talk about this. I feel strange."

Morgan kept staring down at the ground, as if he was searching for something. When he did finally face Catherine, there was a frightened look in his eyes.

"What's wrong?" asked Catherine. "Come over here and sit down. We need to talk."

But Morgan didn't move. He pointed to the ground, looking terrified. "What happened to the woman?"

Catherine gasped and stood up. "I forgot about her!" she cried out, amazed at herself. "I was too caught up—"

"Do you remember what we did to her?"

Catherine looked down at the ground. No one was there. She sat down beside Morgan and tried to clear her mind. "We bit her," Catherine said, her voice shaking.

Morgan nodded and sighed loudly. "We just left her there bleeding. Who knows what might have happened to her. She could have been dragged off by some rabid wolf pack for all we know!"

"Don't be stupid," said Catherine, taking Morgan's hands. "Look, we drank too much blood. We were excited. We weren't thinking of the consequences. It's not our fault—"

"Yes, Catherine," said Morgan, "it is."

Catherine fought back tears and pulled her hands from Morgan's grasp. She dug her fingernails into her palms and breathed in deeply, trying to calm herself. At the moment, she could think of nothing to assuage the situation. "She's not dead."

"Where is she?"

"I don't know!" shouted Catherine. "Let's get down from here and go find River."

"Do you know how much trouble we'll get into? I don't want to see River."

"We have to talk to him. We'll explain everything. Don't worry. Things will be fine. I promise."

8

They found a trellis covered in vines leading to the balcony. They climbed down silently. Catherine felt like crying. "I hate it when you're angry at me. I was so happy the first time you brought me here," she said as she stood on the porch, waiting for Morgan to climb down.

He smiled and pulled Catherine into a hug. "I'm sorry I yelled at you. We have to stick together, like Maggie said. We're stronger together."

Catherine closed her eyes, letting Morgan's warm embrace calm her. "Let's go inside," she said quietly, taking Morgan's hand.

They went in through the balcony door and walked down the upper hall. There was no sound and no curious doors opened.

"There they are!" River said from the bottom of the stairs.

Catherine's heart skipped a beat when she heard River's voice. He was standing alone, waiting for them, a very contemptuous look on his face.

"Follow me to my office," he said and walked off toward the library.

Catherine and Morgan didn't utter a word. They followed him all the way past the back tables, where students were busily painting, to the one wooden bookshelf on the wall. River pulled an orange book from the shelf and inserted a key into the space where the book had been. The bookshelf slowly began to rotate. When it had rotated ninety degrees, River stepped through the space into his office, Catherine and Morgan following right behind him. Once all three were inside, the bookshelf returned to its original position.

More bookshelves lined the walls in River's office. He took a seat in a large red chair behind his massive desk of dark wood. Morgan and Catherine tried to make themselves comfortable in the seats opposite him. Black and white photos sat all around the room, some of them old with a sepia tint. A few newspaper clippings were pinned to a bulletin board on the wall.

"Last night, I heard something peculiar outside," River began, "so I went out to check what it was. I found my friend, Lilly, lying on the ground covered in blood." He stopped to stare at the students before him, penetrating their souls with his wise eyes. "She was taken in and tended to, of course. She was badly injured, but conscious, luckily. After a few hours rest, she awoke refreshed and told me a rather frightening story involving you two. Before I go on, would either of you care to explain yourselves?"

"We were playing around at first, calling out to her and all, but then she started screaming and I panicked. I bit her," said Catherine.

"Then I did," said Morgan, squeezing Catherine's hand.

"We were really excited. We got out of control. We're sorry."

River nodded. "I can understand these things," he said calmly, "but what you did could have seriously harmed Lilly. I'm going to let you off this time, but if I ever catch you doing anything like that again, you might not be able to stay here. I expect you to apologize to Lilly and from now on, there will be a curfew for not only you, but your classmates as well. You must be in your own room by eleven o' clock on weeknights, excluding Fridays. Checks will be made."

Catherine nodded and Morgan thanked River for his leniency. They were getting up to leave when River said, "Lilly is in the last room on the left side of the upper hall." He was grinning very slightly.

Catherine rolled her eyes and dragged Morgan from the room.

"See, it wasn't so bad," she said when they were out of earshot. "We just can't do anything like that again."

"It was fun though, wasn't it?" said Morgan.

Catherine nodded in agreement. She heaved her tired body up the stairs to the upper hall.

"So the ghost last night was Lilly all along," said Morgan. "Let's not tell Amber."

Catherine agreed. They knocked on Lilly's door and heard a quiet voice call them in.

"Hello?" said Catherine, stepping hesitantly into the suite.

"In here."

Morgan followed Catherine to the bedroom. Lilly was resting in the bed, her neck wrapped in bandages, her eyes droopy. The room was cheerful and light. A glass vase filled with purple flowers stood on a side table covered in lacy cloth.

"We're really sorry," said Catherine.

"We didn't really know what we were doing. We just were so happy and we liked it and we wanted to get even more happy and then you came along and things just got out of hand," Morgan spat out in one breath.

Lilly nodded and sighed. For a moment, she was silent, thinking. "It's all right. This is a school for vampires after all. Sometimes these things happen with newcomers. What I really want to know is what you kids were doing in my room last night. I got up to use the bathroom and my light wouldn't turn on. I started to complain about it, out loud, and all of a sudden, a pack of kids came running out of my bathroom."

"We were checking to see if your mirror was haunted," said Catherine, smiling a little.

Lilly grinned. She told Morgan and Catherine she needed to rest. They apologized once again and left. With only a few more minutes before class was over, they decided to go back to Catherine's room to wait for Zach and Amber.

ଓଃ *Cat the Vamp* ଃଠ

Catherine lay on her bed with Morgan, and rubbed her eyes. "I miss the darkness. I miss how beautiful everything was last night," she said, staring out the window. "I miss flying."

"That was awesome," said Morgan. "The whole night was just... fantastic." He slid his hands on top of Catherine's and sighed. "I want more blood. I feel so empty and drained now."

"We drank too much last night. Now normal life isn't as fun. I feel so exhausted compared to last night. I feel...sad. I don't know why. I mean, you're here with me. I should feel totally happy, but I don't."

Morgan pulled Catherine onto his chest and wrapped his arms around her. "I know, but it was worth it."

"Yeah."

"I think I love you," Morgan said suddenly, staring into Catherine's eyes.

Catherine smiled as her heart melted. "I love you too."

"I wanted to say that before," said Morgan, giving Catherine a quick kiss. "I love you."

Catherine returned the kiss, feeling at peace. Her heart had found its home. For a moment, her body tingled with a contentment that went beyond satisfaction. She felt perfectly and utterly whole. *I'm in trouble. I nearly killed a woman. I don't know what the hell is going on with my family or friends back home. I don't even know what time I woke up today... but Morgan loves me.*

Amber and Zach burst into the bedroom and hopped onto the bed, their eyes alight with excitement and alarm. "What the hell?" shouted Amber, although she was smiling. "We have a curfew now because of you two!"

"River told us what happened," said Zach. "That's pretty serious."

"Seriously awesome!" shrieked Amber, putting her hand out for Zach to slap. "I can't believe you like...attacked her."

Charmer came strolling into the room meowing. Amber and Zach ran over to greet him with kisses.

Catherine spent a few minutes telling her friends what had happened, although she left out the flying part. She felt better, surrounded by people who cared for her.

"So what are we going to do with the rest of the day?" asked Amber.

"It's raining outside now," said Morgan, pointing to the window. Spears of water shot past the glass pane, which was speckled with tiny drops.

"We could go outside and run around in the rain and have a water fight," said Catherine. "We'd just have to make sure to get inside and warm up right after."

"That sounds fun, actually," said Morgan. "A little mental, but fun."

Amber and Zach agreed, so they all went to get changed into rain gear. They met in the entranceway and started laughing at one another. Amber and Zach had taped garbage bags over their clothes. On their heads were colourful shower caps. Morgan wore an old T-shirt and sweater and some cut-offs and Catherine had donned a baggy sweatshirt and shorts.

"Why are you guys wearing shorts?" asked Amber. "It's freezing out there."

"And wet," said Morgan.

"Your pants legs are going to stick to you like jam on toast," said Catherine, giggling at herself.

"Very funny," said Zach, hitching up his garbage bag pants. "These babies will keep me nice and toasty."

"Nice garbage bags," said Morgan.

"Don't hate me 'cause you ain't me," said Zach, grinning.

"Stick to you like jam on toast isn't even a real saying," said Amber.

"It will be when you go crying home to your mama in your wet pants!" said Catherine. "Oh, by the way, I have four towels. I'll just leave them here so we can dry off before we go upstairs."

"Let's go!" said Zach, opening the castle doors.

෴ Cat the Vamp ෴

They all shivered as a gust of cold air hit their faces. They stepped out into the rain and began squealing.

"It's so cold!" shrieked Amber, running onto the grass, her head to the sky. Zach chased after her.

Catherine stood still, letting raindrops soak through her clothes, into her skin. Her body went icy. Morgan took her hand and told her they had to hide. He led her behind a tall willow tree by the entrance to the forest.

"They're filling up their shower caps with water," Morgan whispered to Catherine.

"Oh damn," said Catherine, clinging onto Morgan's wet sweatshirt. Her head was freezing and water kept running into her eyes, but she loved it.

"Let's find something to get them with," she said, searching the forest floor.

How about this?" asked Morgan, digging his fingers into the sludgy mud of the path.

"You're so bad! Good idea!"

Together they scooped up handfuls of mud and crept out of the forest. They huddled by a rock to watch Zach and Amber, who were drenched and clutching water-filled shower caps.

"Where did they go?"

"They'll be back," said Zach.

"On the count of three," whispered Morgan. "One, two, three!"

Catherine jumped up and ran full speed with Morgan to where Amber and Zach stood unsuspecting. Catherine took the first fire. She threw her ball of mud at Amber's stomach and laughed victoriously as it splattered on the plastic garbage bag.

"You are going down, bitch!" Amber shouted at Catherine, beginning to run.

Morgan fired a mud shot at Zach and hit him just below the waist. Zach burst out laughing and raised his cap, taking aim.

"Oh crap," said Morgan, running after Catherine.

"Help!" screamed Catherine, laughing until her lungs hurt. Amber caught up with her and poured her entire cap over Catherine's head.

"How does that feel?"

Catherine continued to laugh. She rubbed the water from her eyes and opened them just in time to see Morgan get splashed all over the front part of his pants by Zach.

"Victory is mine!" shouted Zach, holding his shower cap high.

Shivering and smirking, Morgan walked over to Catherine. He wrapped his wet arms around her and they stood hugging, tiny needles of rainwater bouncing off their heads. A cool breeze sprang up, and Zach and Amber joined Catherine and Morgan's huddle for warmth. They made a tight circle facing each other, freezing, yet blissful, happy to be outside and alive in the rain.

"Let's drink the sky," said Catherine.

She tilted her head back and let drops tickle her tongue and trickle down the back of her throat. The others joined her and soon everyone's face was numb.

"I want to go inside now," said Amber. "These garbage bags aren't holding up too well."

Catherine snickered and they all headed back for the castle. Catherine's clothes were soaked and the towels she had set out didn't go far toward drying herself off.

"I have to go upstairs," she said, taking Morgan by the hand.

Amber and Zach went off to sit in front of Zach's fire. Catherine took Morgan to her suite to get warm. "I need a shower," she said, peeling off her sweatshirt.

"Can I join you?" asked Morgan.

Catherine stared at Morgan and smiled. "Okay."

They stripped down and left their sopping clothes in a heap on the tile. Carefully, they stepped into the tub, still shivering. They faced each other, taking turns standing with their backs against the rush of warm soothing water. Catherine took Morgan's hands and pressed her body against his. She closed her eyes as the warm waterfall stroked her back and ran all the way down to her heels. Morgan picked up a bottle of shampoo and squeezed out a dollop of it into his palm. He ran his hands through Catherine's hair, massaging her scalp. Catherine took in deep breaths of citrus scent and steam. She shampooed Morgan's hair, and ran soapy hands up Morgan's back and all over his body. Morgan moaned and raised Catherine's face to his own. They stared at each other silently for a moment before they kissed. Wet and soapy and fruity, they continued to kiss as the bathroom mirror steamed over and lines of water began to run down the window. The entire bathroom was in a fog. Catherine imagined that she was under a waterfall in a tropical paradise, surrounded by exotic fruit and trees.

"I don't want to leave," she said, sucking on Morgan's wet cheeks.

Morgan laughed and squeezed Catherine. "We don't have to. But I'm getting really hot, so let's continue our tropical adventure outside."

Catherine stroked Morgan's chest and kissed him once more before turning off the water. They stepped out of the tub and wrapped themselves up in towels. Catherine breathed in the steam before opening the door to go to her bedroom for dry clothes.

"What am I going to wear?" asked Morgan.

Catherine stared at Morgan for a moment. All she could do was admire his beauty. His hair was slicked down in waves across his face, ends dripping. His chest was covered in glistening drops of water. A pink towel was seductively wrapped around his hips. Catherine had to force herself to stop staring so she could answer his question. "Why don't you just quickly run back to your room and get some clothes? We can do our laundry together if you want."

"Good idea. I'll meet you back here in a bit." Morgan stepped into the hall and hurried to his suite to unlock it.

"Nice towel."

Morgan turned around and grinned sheepishly. Zach was wrapped up in Amber's pink robe.

"You're one to talk," said Morgan, opening his door.

"I think this looks good on me, thank you very much," said Zach, returning to Amber's suite.

Morgan quickly pulled on some underwear and shorts. He picked up his bag of dirty clothes and returned to Catherine's bathroom to add his wet clothes to the load.

"Looking good, hot stuff," said Catherine, standing with her bag of clothes just outside the bathroom. She had put on a flowery top and dark jeans. "The laundry room is at the end of the hall, by the staircase." They hefted their bags and headed down the hall. "Here we are," she said, pointing to a door that had *Laundry Room* printed on it.

Morgan turned the handle and opened the door to a very white and bright room. No one was inside. There were two washing machines, so Catherine emptied her clothes in one and Morgan took the other. They added some soap from a box on a nearby table and turned on the machines. The large, white squares groaned and grumbled, much like Catherine's heart was starting to do.

"What should we do while we wait?" asked Morgan, eyeing Catherine earnestly.

Catherine smiled at Morgan, but her heart sped up, this time out of fear and confusion. Her eyes told Morgan something wasn't right.

"What's wrong?" he asked, suddenly feeling a pang of guilt.

Catherine walked over to him and sat down on the table. Morgan sat next to her and wrapped his arms around her.

"Last night was like heaven. I felt like nothing could bring me down. I never got bored, not even once. I was just eternally happy. The world was mine and I felt like I could do anything. I thought I was invincible, but later, I realized, I'm not. When we were on the roof, I was so in love, just overloaded with energy and happiness. I was just living for the moment. I felt like I was in a dream. I felt... perfect, like nothing could ever go wrong. I didn't realize until later how serious everything was. I don't want to get..."

Morgan pulled her head into his chest and sighed. "I know," he said, anxious and relieved at the same time. "We won't let that happen again. We'll be more careful. I'm sorry."

Catherine snuggled into Morgan and felt a tear roll out of the corner of her eye. She wiped it away and lifted her face to Morgan's. She kissed him on the chin, touched that he understood completely.

When their washing was done, they transferred their clothes into the driers. While they waited, they talked. Morgan mentioned seeing Zach in Amber's pink robe and Catherine laughed long and hard.

They piled their clean clothes into their bags and left the laundry room feeling accomplished and at ease. Morgan slipped on a clean shirt, threw his clothes into his room, and went back with Catherine to her suite.

"It's almost six o' clock," said Catherine. "Let's get dinner. We haven't eaten all day."

Morgan agreed and they left the suite and went to knock on Amber's door. Zach greeted them, still in his pink robe.

"Hello again," he said, smiling broadly. "Are you guys heading down to eat soon?"

"Yeah, are you?" asked Catherine.

"Yep. I guess I need to put some clothes on. Damn, I'm so comfortable in this."

"You can wear it over some shorts," Amber called from her room.

"Good idea!" said Zach, pushing past Morgan and Catherine to get to his own suite. He came back out a minute later in black boxers, the open robe revealing his chest.

"Oh, goodness," said Amber, rolling her eyes at Zach, but she took his arm and started to walk with him down the hall.

Catherine and Morgan followed them down to the ballroom. The four of them each took a tray of food back to a table and began to eat.

"I wish I had blood," said Amber, forking some broccoli.

Everyone nodded. Catherine glanced at Morgan. He smiled at her. They both raised their brows and grinned, knowing that Amber and Zach felt almost the same way about blood as they did. It scared Catherine just a little.

After dinner, Catherine and Amber said they wanted their alone time, so Zach and Morgan went off to talk in Zach's place. Amber collapsed on the floor in front of the fire when she and Catherine got to her suite. Catherine plopped down beside her and took in a deep breath. She turned her head to face Amber and smiled. "So tell me about you and Zach."

"Everything is just really good," said Amber, hugging her knees. "We just joke around a lot. He's so funny and cute. How are things with you and Morgan?"

"He told me he loved me."

"When!"

"Just before you and Zach came into my bedroom today."

"Did you say it back?"

"Yeah," said Catherine. "I really do too. I know it seems fast, but I feel like I've known him for longer than some of my closest friends. He's always in my mind." Catherine paused, but Amber didn't speak. She sat listening, expecting more. "We had sex."

Amber practically jumped out of her skin and threw her head back. "You naughty girl! How was he?"

"Good," Catherine said, grinning. "Really good, but I was out of my mind. It was after we drank from Lilly. We were both so ecstatic that we weren't really thinking of the consequences. We just did it."

"Did you use protection?"

"No."

"Are you on birth control?"

"No," said Catherine, cringing slightly.

"Dude, that's really dangerous."

"I know," said Catherine, almost tearing up. "It's retarded! I

Cat the Vamp

think back now and feel stupid, but at the time, it felt like I was doing nothing wrong. I was surrounded in this sparkling darkness. I could only hear pleasant sounds and smell Morgan against me. It was so surreal that I wouldn't have been surprised to have woken up in the middle of it all."

"Be careful. I don't want to have to worry about you," said Amber, sliding next to Catherine to hug her.

Catherine nodded and felt tears welling in her eyes. "Thanks for listening."

"No problem, sweetie."

Amber made hot chocolate for both of them and they talked at the kitchen table until ten o' clock. "I'd better get back to my room," Catherine said.

"Have a good night."

In the hall, Morgan pounced on Catherine and smothered her in kisses. "I had to catch you before you went off to bed," he breathed into her ear. "Stay with me until eleven. Please."

Catherine nodded and went with Morgan to his suite. They listened to music, sprawled on the floor, trying to enjoy their last moments together before the morning.

At eleven o' clock, Catherine ran back to her room. River knocked on her door a minute later. Catherine answered the door with an innocent smile.

"Goodnight, Catherine," said River, walking off to check the other suites.

Catherine slept comfortably that night. She had settled her inner turmoil and felt at peace with herself.

In class the next day, Catherine curled up with Morgan to watch a horror movie about Dracula that Kevin had chosen. Catherine enjoyed herself immensely, although the blood on screen made her cravings more intense. By the look on the other students' faces, they felt the same way.

Catherine and Morgan spent the rest of the afternoon together. After dinner, they returned to Morgan's room. They took a seat on

Morgan's bed and were silent for a moment.

"I really want to," said Catherine.

"Me, too."

"We can just drink a little. It'll be fine."

"You first."

Catherine smiled and took Morgan's wrist into her hands. She sank her fangs into his skin and sucked hard at the pungent red liquid that filled and excited her.

When she finished, she sighed and put her arm out for Morgan to drink. Morgan bit into her wrist. Catherine's pain turned to pleasure at the sight of her blood staining Morgan's lips and fangs.

They bandaged their wounds with cloth and safety pins and went to lie on Morgan's bed. Catherine felt like she was floating. She stared out the window at the moon. She couldn't look away. It was calling her. Suddenly she had the strong urge to jump out of the window. She stood and began to slide up against the glass. She rested her hands on the sill and pushed her head and torso outside the window. Her feet left the floor. Morgan noticed Catherine's flailing legs out of the corner of his eye and snapped out of his reverie. He ran over to her, took her by the arms, and pulled her back inside. When she was firmly back on the bed, he shut the window, locked it, and stared at Catherine in disbelief.

"What were you doing? Don't waste the necklace."

"I wanted to see the moon. I was just looking."

She rested her head on a pillow and closed her eyes, feeling slightly guilty for having lied.

Morgan kissed Catherine on the forehead and wrapped his arms around her. They lay on the bed gazing into each other's eyes.

"I feel good," said Catherine, tracing the lines on Morgan's shirt with her finger.

"Me, too," said Morgan, running his hands along Catherine's sides. "Close your eyes and imagine this. You're on a beach. You're relaxing on the sand. It's warm and radiant. You can feel the warmth sinking into your skin. The air is soft and balmy. Just above you is a tall palm tree providing you with just the right amount of shade. You dig your hands and toes into the sand and feel every grain tickle you. The air smells like coconut and you can hear birds cawing overhead as they circle the sky. You hear waves crash against the shore and the smell of salt begins to waft through the air. You look up and notice a red band of colour in the light blue sky. Then you see an orange band appear just beneath it. Then yellow. Then green. Then blue. Then indigo. And finally, violet. Now you can see the entire rainbow shining brightly in the sky."

"Wow," said Catherine, opening her eyes. "It seems so real."

"You can get into some really enjoyable meditative states that way, through visualization, but it just looks really cool to imagine when you're high on blood."

"I thought we needed blood to make our energy levels normal," said Catherine. "Shouldn't blood just make us feel normal? Why do we feel so awesome when we drink it?"

"Well, we've been drinking more than we're supposed to, I guess. We've been over-drinking, but I like the feeling I get when I have an excess amount of energy. I feel so alive, like I'm above everyone else, you know?"

"Yeah, it's amazing." She smiled and pulled Morgan against her. They kissed until Catherine had to leave, colours still swirling in her mind's eye.

She slipped back to her room and waited until River came to check on her. She made sure not to let him see her wrist and said goodnight politely. Then she hurried to fetch her journal. She sat up in bed writing about the last few days.

She collapsed on her bed at three in the morning and dreamt of a tropical island. She was there with Morgan, bathing in a hot pool of rainbow water.

9

Catherine tumbled into class the next morning, tired, but she looked good. She wore the outfit she had chosen the night before: a tight black top and a denim skirt. Her body ached a little, but when she saw Morgan, all the pain was forgotten.

"Tonight at eight there will be a dance," announced River. "Maggie has kindly volunteered to supervise, but for class today, we have to start setting up. Everyone follow me to the ballroom."

All the students got up and walked over to the ballroom. Boxes of equipment and decorating supplies were scattered all over the floor.

"Choose a box and start setting up for the dance," said River.

Catherine and Amber ran over to the same box and opened it.

"Decorations!" Amber said. "Sweet!"

"I've got the sound system," said Zach. "Nice turn tables."

"Lighting equipment," said Emily.

"Bubble machine," said Tyler.

"Glow sticks!" Kevin hugged his box to his chest.

"Fog machine," said Morgan.

"Bottled water," said Alex. "Phew. This shouldn't be too bad, and if I get thirsty on the job, well, I have water."

Everyone helped each other set up. River walked over to Zach, who was carefully adjusting some very large speakers. "I've been informed that you DJ."

"Yeah, for a little while now."

"Would you like to DJ at this dance? I'm prepared to offer you cash in return."

"How much are we talking here?" asked Zach, highly interested.

"Three hundred for the night."

"Done," said Zach, grinning. "I'll have to take a look at the music selection beforehand."

"Of course. Thank you for agreeing to do this."

"Thank you for asking. What would have happened if I had said no?"

"Maggie would have taken care of it," said River, winking.

Three hours later, the ballroom was cleared of all the tables and covered in balloons and streamers. Lights were set up along the ceiling rafters. A bubble machine stood next to the entrance along with buckets filled with glow sticks and bottled water. The sound system was where the food tables usually stood. Beside it, the fog machine was set up and ready to use.

"Nicely done. You kids deserve a dance," said Maggie. "River told me to inform you that your curfew has been extended until midnight today." She paused to let the students cheer. "Also, lunch will be served in the library today. Enjoy!"

Everyone's spirits were up. They all sat in the library eating lunch, laughing, excited about the dance. The cheerful mood continued at dinner. Everyone seemed overjoyed. Catherine loved it.

At six thirty, Amber leaned over to Catherine and whispered, "Get dressed for the dance and come to my room with Morgan. We're going to have a little pre-party get together."

Catherine nodded and scarfed down the rest of the food on her plate. She pulled Morgan up from his chair and nudged him in the direction of the stairs. They left quickly. In the upper hall, Morgan turned to Catherine and whispered, "What?"

"We're having a pre-party," said Catherine. "Go get hot for the dance and come to Amber's as soon as you can."

Catherine ran to her bedroom and began searching for something to wear. She decided on the black dress she had worn for her ceremony, but to spice it up a little, she cinched up the skirt so it was half its original length, with the hem well above her knees. She quickly applied eyeliner and added extra mascara to her lashes. She pinched her cheeks and smiled at her reflection before racing to Amber's suite.

Amber was wearing something short and sparkly when she answered the door. "Come on in."

"You look so sexy!"

"I just wrapped this fabric around me," said Amber, shrugging. "Thanks. Now let's drink!"

Catherine felt her heart jump with anticipation. Amber went to the fridge and pulled out the bottle of vodka from the Halloween party. "There's so much left," she said, taking off the cap.

Catherine sighed. She'd been hoping for blood, but alcohol would suffice.

"Bottoms up," said Amber, and together the girls downed a shot each in one.

Zach and Morgan walked into the kitchen. When Zach saw the bottle, he burst out laughing. "I told you, dude," he said to Morgan, as he wrapped an arm around Amber. "I know this girl."

The boys downed a shot each. Zach abstained from more drinking and headed down to his DJ booth. Morgan, Amber, and Catherine drank another shot together after Zach left. Catherine and Amber each took two last shots, finishing off the bottle.

"You look amazing," Catherine told Morgan, staring at his simple white shirt and blue jeans.

"You look better," he said, sliding his arm over Catherine's back.

They sat at the kitchen table and talked excitedly until eight o' clock. When Morgan heard loud music coming from the ballroom, he stood up and announced that it was time to leave. He led the girls downstairs and into the entranceway. The ballroom was dark aside from the flashing rainbow lights darting about the room.

Catherine, surrounded in bubbles, grabbed two glow sticks, cracked them, and then ran into the centre of the room and spun around, her hands waving in the air. Amber, after nearly tripping, joined Catherine. Zach waved to them from above and the girls waved back. Morgan walked up to Catherine and blew in her ear. Catherine screamed, spun around, and pointed her glow sticks at Morgan, ready to attack.

Tyler and Emily came in all dressed in white. Their attire glowed under the lights. Amber waved them over and they all chatted and laughed. Tyler and Emily nearly fell over from being hugged and pulled so enthusiastically by Amber and Catherine.

Alex came in next, wearing slim black jeans and a hot pink top. She giggled as she ran over to the group of people. Kevin, in a tight black top and pants, went up to Alex and gave her an exaggerated once over.

"Nice outfit, slut," he said.

"Thanks, manwhore," Alex said, imitating his tone of voice.

Maggie sat in a chair in the corner, smiling and waving when she was acknowledged. She watched the kids for the first hour and stuffed ear plugs in her ears for the second.

By ten o'clock, everyone was hot and sweaty from dancing and laughing, surrounded in sound. Catherine's heart was pounding.

"I'm so tired," Emily said.

"Let's go take a rest," said Tyler. He escorted Emily back upstairs.

Everyone else continued to dance. Catherine gave up trying to look good and simply began to jump up and down in place with her hands in the air, still a little dizzy from the vodka.

"Who wants a slow song?" asked Zach.

"Me!" Alex practically sighed, exhausted. She wrapped her arms around Kevin, happy to stop moving.

"You have to swerve a little bit," said Kevin.

"I can't do it. My feet are so sore."

"That's what you get for wearing designer stilettos."

Kevin agreed to walk Alex back to her room, where they collapsed on Alex's couch to eat chips and watch a movie on Alex's portable video player.

Catherine, Morgan, and Amber threw their arms around one another's shoulders, their bodies wet and sticky. They all began swaying and belting out lyrics until the song ended. Zach hopped down from his booth, raced over to Amber, and gave her a kiss on the lips.

"You looked so good out there, I couldn't resist." Amber laughed and pulled Zach into a hug.

Catherine, out of breath and her heart racing, stumbled up the stairs with Morgan all the way to his room, where they tumbled laughing down onto the kitchen floor from sheer fatigue and passed out. They were still there when River came knocking at eleven. Catherine woke up, her head pounding, and realized that she had to leave. She answered the door, told River she knew, and stumbled off to her own bed.

The next day, only slightly hung over, Catherine went to class excited to find out what activity they would be participating in.

"Today, we're going camping," said River.

Tyler made a little cry of joy and gave Emily an excited shake.

"Get changed into some outside gear," said River. "Some jeans, runners, a sweater, and a coat are some good things to keep in mind. I'll be supplying you with tents, food, first aid equipment, and sleeping bags. Bring whatever else you think you'll need. We'll be leaving in half an hour. Everyone be in the entranceway by then."

"Where are we going and for how long?" asked Alex, looking quite worried indeed.

"We're just going to take a little trip to the forest, set up camp, and sleep over for one night," said River. "We'll be back in time for lunch tomorrow." Alex smiled wryly.

Catherine went up to her room, grabbed her coat and cigarettes, and nothing else. Then she went to check on Amber, who was busy stuffing a bag full of magazines and electronic toys. "It's going to get really boring at night," Amber said.

The girls headed to the entranceway together and met up with Zach and Morgan, who were both empty handed.

"We're roughing it," said Zach, patting Morgan on the back.

"Not even cigarettes?" asked Catherine.

Zach looked away and shrugged with a smirk on his face.

"I knew it," said Catherine. "So much for roughing it."

"Good luck," said Amber, showing the boys her bag. "I'll have plenty to do at camp."

When everyone was assembled, River handed out sleeping bags. On his own back, he carried a large backpack filled with camping supplies. The group left the castle grounds and ventured into the forest. Tall trees loomed above them, their branches still. There was no breeze. They passed a pond and came to a clearing, circled by a ring of tall willows.

"It's beautiful here," said Catherine, admiring the orange, red and yellow leaves around her.

"Girls, take one tent and set up. Boys, take the other," said River. "No boys in the girls' tent and vice versa."

Catherine frowned at Morgan and then went to help set up the girls' tent.

"This sucks," said Alex, shoving a support pole into the tent.

"Careful!" shouted Tyler, running over to help. The girls watched in awe as Tyler pitched their tent in a matter of minutes. Then he did the same for the guys.

"Get settled and be outside for lunch in an hour," said River, setting up his own tent.

Alex unrolled her sleeping bag and started digging through her bag. She pulled out a magazine and sat silently reading. Amber spread out her sleeping bag, pulled the same magazine from her own bag, and began reading. Catherine and Emily started to giggle.

"What?" Amber and Alex said in unison. Then Amber realized

what the other two were laughing at. "Oh lord."

"You read *Femme Fashion!*" said Alex, delighted. "Who's your favourite fashionista?"

"Well, I wasn't impressed with most of them, but Mandy stood out to me for some reason," said Amber.

"No way! That's exactly who I'd vote for," said Alex, smiling. "Wow. Camping isn't that bad after all."

"Yeah, I guess not," said Amber.

Catherine had no idea what Amber and Alex were talking about. While they continued to chat, she unrolled her sleeping bag and lay down next to Emily.

"So are you and Tyler a thing?" asked Catherine, staring at the roof of the tent.

"Sort of," said Emily. "We kissed at your Halloween party and then again after the dance."

"Aww," said Catherine, her heart melting at how sweet and innocent Emily sounded.

"He's a really nice guy, but I've never had a boyfriend and I'm afraid I'll screw up. I don't even know if I kiss well."

"Don't worry about things like that," Catherine said, turning to look into Emily's eyes. "He likes you. He wouldn't kiss you a second time if he didn't think you were a good kisser."

"I guess you're right. Thanks, Catherine. I knew you were nice when I first met you."

Catherine laughed quietly. "I wonder what the guys are doing."

In the boys' tent, Zach was giving Tyler some useful advice. "If you want her in the pants, play it cool. Make her feel safe. Also, girls want what they can't have, so don't get too close, but don't get too far away or she'll forget about you. You have to balance things out. Compliment her and just be yourself. If it's meant to be, then in no time you will be surfing the waves of love." Zach rolled onto his stomach and began humping his sleeping bag in demonstration.

"Stop it," said Tyler, throwing a sleeping bag at Zach, although there was a small grin forming at the corners of his mouth.

"Lunchtime," River called.

Catherine crawled out of the tent and saw that River was handing out sandwiches. She chose a cheese sandwich and then took a seat on a log with Morgan to eat.

"So what have you girls been up to?" asked Morgan.

"We just talked," said Catherine, "about school."

"Same," said Morgan.

The class went on a hike through the woods, stopping to pick edible berries every once in a while. River pointed out the wildlife and named a few of his favourite birds. The air was still and stagnant. When the wind did finally pick up, it howled eerily as it swept through the leaves.

Back at camp, River announced that the students would be doing a scavenger hunt.

"Get in pairs," said River, handing out a list of items to everyone. "Be back in one hour. Don't stray too far from the tents."

"One rock as large as your head, five dry sticks, one extra long and dry branch, one feather, and a box of graham crackers," Catherine read aloud from her paper.

"Same, except I don't have the graham crackers," said Morgan. "I have a bag of marshmallows."

"It says that for the final object, I'm supposed to look up," said Catherine.

"It says I'm supposed to look in."

"Let's get a move on," said Catherine, taking Morgan's arm.

They came across a tree with dry brittle branches. Some had already broken off and fallen to the ground. "Let's pick them up," said Catherine. "Five each, and we can take a big one from the tree." She took hold of a branch and snapped it off the tree.

"Catherine!" said Morgan, laughing. "You're supposed to find them on the ground."

Catherine, kneeling down to collect her sticks, looked up, and rolled her eyes. "The tree is dying anyway. I'm sure it didn't mind...

lending a hand." She took her long branch and waved it in front of Morgan's face, laughing at her own joke.

"Fine," said Morgan, breaking off his own branch.

They continued to walk on through the forest with their sticks, Catherine's eyes focused skyward and Morgan's scanning every nook and cranny he came across. They each found a nice white feather and a big, heavy grey rock. "Let's go drop these off at camp," Morgan said.

They left their finds by River's feet and went in search of their last items. Morgan brought his large branch along to poke things with. They ran into Zach and Amber.

"I challenge you to a duel!" shouted Zach, holding out his branch.

When Zach finally "stabbed" Morgan, Morgan and Catherine walked off in search of their final item once again.

"Oh look!" said Morgan, spotting something poking out of a hole in a tree.

They both ran over to an ancient maple tree and found the marshmallows tucked nicely into a hollow in the trunk. Morgan seized the bag and checked it a few times. "Looks good. Now let's find your crackers."

They went off with their heads pointed upward, through the forest, their eyes scanning treetops for the box.

"I found it!" cried Morgan, pointing to a blue box nestled between two low-lying branches.

"I might be able to jump and reach it."

"No need," said Morgan, tapping his stick against Catherine's head. He carefully tipped the box out of its resting place so that it fell into Catherine's hands.

"I have a feeling we're making s'mores tonight," she said.

By the time everyone had returned to camp, there were piles of sticks everywhere. "Put your long branches in your tents and then come help put all the smaller sticks into one pile," said River.

Everyone started chucking their sticks into a little pit River had dug. Inside, there were already a few, short dry logs. The students were then instructed to place their big, heavy rocks around the hole for protection.

"We're making a fire," said Kevin.

"Correct," said River, adjusting the rocks. He went to his own tent and took out a long, thick stick. "This will be the speaking stick for tonight. You may use your feathers to decorate it if you wish."

"How are we supposed to get the feathers to stay on?" asked Alex.

"Use the forest," said River. "Be creative."

"I have to go use the washroom," said Emily.

"Take a partner and take this," said River, returning to his tent. He leaned out with a roll of toilet paper and tossed it to Emily.

"Can you go with me?" Emily asked Catherine.

Catherine nodded and the girls walked off into the woods. It was getting colder as night time neared. Emily stopped at a large tree and walked behind its broad trunk. "Make sure no one comes near."

"Don't worry, I will."

Once Emily was done, the girls hiked back to camp. Everyone was wrapping vines around the speaking stick and sticking their feathers in where they would fit. Catherine took her feather and tucked it behind some vine. Zach found a large pinecone and bound it to the top of the stick. Soon the speaking stick was a speaking sceptre.

"Let's light this baby on fire," Zach said, holding the sceptre above his head.

"Can we start the fire?" asked Tyler.

"Sure. I'll supply you with the matches. The rest is up to you," said River.

Tyler lit the wood. Immediately, a crackling sound rose as the fire spread slowly through the small sticks.

"It worked," said Alex, amazed.

After dinner, it grew dark and everyone sat around the fire

roasting marshmallows on their long branches and making s'mores. When Catherine sniffed the air, it smelled of firewood, chocolate, dry leaves and Morgan. She nudged Morgan with her leg and grinned at him. Morgan smiled at her, his mouth sticky with white goo. Catherine laughed at him and wiped his lips with her finger, yearning to kiss him.

Tyler led the group in some camping songs. Everyone joined in, no matter how childish they thought they were being, and in the end, they all had fun. They played improvisation games for a bit and told scary stories. Catherine and Morgan whispered to each other, huddled close for warmth.

When the embers started to die out, River told the students to go to their tents. Catherine kissed Morgan quickly before heading off to her tent. She glanced back at him once more before entering girl world to collapse with a longing heart on her sleeping bag.

"What's wrong?" asked Emily.

"I want to be with Morgan," said Catherine.

"Oh, forget about him for one night," said Alex. "Besides, we have magazines, a radio, snacks, and gossip to entertain us."

"And nail polish," Amber reminded Alex.

"Oh yeah," said Alex. "I totally forgot about makeup. Who wants their nails done?"

"I wouldn't mind," said Catherine, sitting up.

Amber turned on her radio and made sure that the volume was not too loud.

"What colour do you want?" asked Alex.

"Black," said Catherine.

"Yikes. Well maybe I have a bottle of dark purple, but...oh, I have black polish from two Halloweens ago when I was a witch."

Catherine spread her fingers on Alex's knees, and Alex set to work. Amber worked on Emily, who had chosen red polish in hopes of attracting love.

Catherine sat blowing her nails dry while Amber read everyone's monthly horoscope. "Catherine, this month brings a whirlwind of excitement, adventure, and romance. Your spirits are high. Don't get too caught up in the wave of bliss for there are consequences for every action."

Catherine smirked and snatched the magazine from Amber's hands. "This month, you've noticed that you've fallen in love with someone new, someone exciting, someone with a large package, but is he who you really think he is or does he secretly want Kevin in the pants?"

Amber ripped the magazine back from Catherine's hands, rolled it up, and swatted Catherine's arm with it. "That's for lying, you naughty wench."

The girls sang along with the radio and flipped through magazines, picking out their favourite products and models.

Tyler and Zach were listening to a hockey game on the radio while Morgan and Kevin were talking.

"Is it sick of me to miss her?" asked Morgan. "I just really want to be with her for some reason."

"Not at all," said Kevin. "She's your girl. Why would it be sick?"

"I just feel more attached to her than any other girl I've been with."

"Do you love her?"

"Yeah," said Morgan. "I've never loved anyone before, but I love her."

Kevin sighed, his voice tremulous. "You should be with the person you love. Go to her. I'll cover for you."

"Thanks," said Morgan, giving Kevin a hug. Morgan pulled on his coat and shoes. "Hey guys," he whispered to Zach and Tyler, "I'm going out for a bit. Kevin will explain. Try not to miss me too much."

Morgan eased out of the tent and carefully crept across the ground, making sure not to step on any twigs, to the girls' tent. He heard music coming from inside and smiled, relieved that they were still awake. He whispered Catherine's name and tapped on the tent once.

Catherine's heart fluttered as she unzipped the door flap.

"Come out with me," said Morgan.

Catherine slipped on her coat and boots and waved goodbye to the girls. She took Morgan's hand and crawled out of the tent. They quickly, but cautiously, skipped off into the forest feeling marvellously devious.

They slowed down when the tents where no longer in view. Catherine pushed Morgan up against a tree and kissed him. A harsh wind swept past them. They shivered and clung to each other for warmth. Morgan swam over Catherine's face with his lips.

The black sky above them was filled with stars. Catherine looked around and realized she had no clue where she was. She told herself she was okay, that Morgan would make sure she was safe. He would take care of her.

"I want you so bad," said Morgan, taking Catherine's sleeve. He looked into Catherine's eyes. She nodded and he bit. Her blood rose like a red river into Morgan's mouth. The sight of it caused Catherine's stomach to lurch in excitement.

"I need blood, too," said Catherine, lifting Morgan's sleeve.

She bit him hard, making him yelp. She didn't care. He had her first. He could take it. She was filled with satisfaction as the warm liquid rolled down her throat. She stared up at Morgan and sucked harder and harder until Morgan looked uncomfortable.

"Thirsty tonight," he said, squeezing Catherine's sides.

Catherine kissed him on his neck, his chin, and finally, his lips. Her mind spun wildly. Morgan began laughing and placed his hands on Catherine's cheeks. He pointed her face at the trees around them and Catherine began laughing too.

"I can see all the leaves perfectly," she cried. "I can see the ridges on the bark. I can see an owl. Look!"

"Wow. Come on, let's run."

He took Catherine by the hand and they ran through the woods, ducking under low-lying branches, jumping over fallen logs, and cutting through the bushes as if they were air. The night was theirs to claim.

They stopped in an open space clear of the trees. "The King and Queen of the night have returned!" shouted Morgan.

"What a beautiful meadow. Oh, look at the stars. What a perfect place to look at the sky. Not one tree in sight! Come here daydreamer."

"Nightdreamer," Morgan corrected. He took Catherine's outstretched hands. They spun in a circle, their heads back to watch the stars turn into white lines of cosmic dust. Catherine broke away and ran through the meadow, enjoying the sound of the tall grass swishing against her boots. Morgan chased her and pinned her to the ground. They lay there kissing until they were too tired to move. Their minds calmed as they gazed up at the stars. They stopped talking and fell asleep.

Catherine awoke shivering, yet the sun was burning hot on her face. She opened her eyes and saw green all around her. Morgan was asleep beside her. She blew on his face and he awoke groggily. They sat up and listened. Birds chirped softly in the distance. The grass swayed in the wind.

"The light seems blue," said Morgan. "It's like we're in a fantasy."

"It does seem sort of ethereal."

"I don't exactly remember falling asleep. I remember the meadow, but my concept of time is all off."

"Mine too," said Catherine. "Let's get up."

They stood and tried their best to dust off the dirt and leaves they were covered in, but they didn't have time to get picky.

"We should get back," said Catherine. "Maybe everyone's still asleep at camp."

"I hope so," said Morgan, taking Catherine's arm.

They trudged through the brush, finding it a lot harder to navigate than the night before. All the trees looked similar. There was no path and some bushes were filled with prickly leaves.

"How are we ever going to get back through this?" asked Catherine. "I'm so tired."

"We can't drink. Our eyes won't be able to stand how bright the world will seem. Remember how easy it is to see in the dark? Besides, if we drink now, we'll just want it even more later."

"You're right," said Catherine, pushing a branch out of her face.

Half an hour later, they found the campsite, but no one was there. All the tents were gone.

"I guess we should head back to the castle," said Morgan.

"Oh, no! River said that if we did anything bad again, we might get kicked out!"

"Yeah, but we don't really have a choice. Whatever happens, happens. I love you."

"I love you," said Catherine.

She squeezed Morgan's hand. Morgan kissed her gently and then turned his eyes in the direction of Blacklune. Catherine sighed and they began the trek back. "That was fun, last night, dancing around in the meadow."

"Yeah," said Morgan. "Hey, do you remember the owl?"

"Oh yeah! He was huge!"

"His eyes were amazing."

"Are you ready?" asked Catherine, pointing to the castle doors.

Morgan nodded. They walked up the steps and opened the doors. No one was in sight.

"Let's go upstairs," whispered Morgan.

They crept up the stairs quickly and as soon as they got to the upper hall, they heard River clear his throat. He stood with his arms crossed in the entranceway. "Get out of my sight. I'll deal with you two later."

Catherine and Morgan hurried to their own rooms, their hearts racing. They both had a shower and then collapsed asleep on their beds.

10

Three hours later, Zach and Amber knocked at Catherine's door. Catherine swung her legs over the side of her bed and slid off the edge onto the floor. She walked, a little dizzy, to answer the door.

"We brought you some cake." Amber handed Catherine a piece of pink-frosted cake on a plate. "We just made it. It's still warm."

Catherine smiled wanly at her and took a seat in the kitchen. She began to pick at the cake with her fingers.

"Here, use a fork," said Zach, passing her one.

Catherine took the fork and sliced into her cake. She picked up a small chunk and placed it on her tongue. "That's pretty good. What time is it?"

"About three o'clock," said Amber. "So, where did you guys go?"

"We ran off into the forest and we were just playing around. We decided to drink from each other, and then we went running through the woods and found this meadow. We danced around and played tag and then fell asleep."

"You can't keep doing this," said Amber. "You're going to get hurt. You woke up on the ground."

"With Morgan," said Catherine. "I'm fine. I appreciate your concern, but this is my life and I can live it however I choose."

"We're just worried about you, Cat," said Zach. "Be careful, seriously."

"You don't know because you haven't experienced it yet," snapped Catherine. "When you do, you'll realize."

"What are you talking about?" said Amber.

Catherine took in a deep breath. "Once you feel what I've felt, you'll understand why I don't care if I wake up in the dirt." She walked off to her bedroom and crawled underneath the covers to sleep.

Amber and Zach whispered to each other, but Catherine couldn't hear what they were saying.

If I had blood I would be able to hear their whispers. Just rest now, Catherine. Morgan will come. Morgan. Morgan, come to me.

A few minutes later, Morgan walked into her bedroom. She stretched out her arms and pulled him on top of her. "I knew you would come," she said, kissing Morgan over and over again. "I feel much better now. Are Zach and Amber gone?"

Morgan rolled off of Catherine and snuggled up beside her under the blankets. "Yes. I had to see you. I was sleeping, but I could feel you calling me."

"Amber and Zach came to see me," said Catherine. "They gave me cake."

"Someone knocked on my door, but I didn't answer."

"They're worried about me," said Catherine, smiling at Morgan. "They told me I'm going to get hurt and that I can't keep doing this. I kind of flipped out on them. Well, I didn't yell at them. I just told them that I could live my life the way I want to. I said that they didn't understand how I felt. They haven't felt like we have. They can't judge us."

"Exactly. I know they're concerned, but they can't talk."

They slept for the rest of the afternoon and didn't bother to get up for dinner. At seven o'clock, they got out of bed and wandered into the kitchen. The cake was still on the table. Morgan began picking at it with the fork. He tasted it and moaned with delight.

"Still good."

They finished off the cake and sat at the kitchen table thinking.

"Maybe we should invite Amber and Zach over," said Catherine. "I don't want them to be mad at us."

"Okay, we'll get them back on our side. We could get them to drink from each other and then from us. We could have a blood bash!"

"Yes! But we'll have to lure them in. They're not going to agree right away. We'll play a game of truth or dare. I'll dare one of them to drink from the other. Once they do, they'll realize how it feels and they'll want more."

"Good idea." Morgan leaned forward to kiss Catherine. She broke off the kiss quickly.

"Let's go invite them now."

No one answered when they knocked on Amber's door, so they tried Zach's. "Hey man," Zach said when he saw Morgan at the door. He raised his eyebrows at the smirk on Catherine's face. Amber was peering curiously from behind him.

"We were wondering if you and Amber wanted to come over to Catherine's," said Morgan.

"Yeah, okay," said Zach, turning his head to glance at Amber. "We'll be over in a few minutes."

Catherine and Morgan walked back to Catherine's place and high-fived. They waited at the kitchen table, silently. When the knock came, they both jumped up to answer the door.

"Welcome," said Catherine. "Do you want anything to eat or drink? Actually, I don't have much to eat. I have water."

"I'll have a glass," said Zach.

Catherine turned on the tap and ran the cold on full blast. She filled up a cup and handed it to Zach. "Let's go sit by the fire."

They all sat on the floor in a circle while the fire hissed.

"Let's play truth or dare," said Morgan.

Catherine stayed quiet so she wouldn't seem too eager. She

smiled so she wouldn't appear totally uninterested.

Amber recalled how wonderfully her last game of truth or dare had gone. "Okay!"

"Fine," said Zach, thinking of the same thing.

"Good idea," Catherine said. "Who wants to go first?"

"I do." Amber turned to Zach. "Zach, truth or dare?"

"Truth."

"Who was your first love?"

Zach laughed as he searched the crevasses of his mind. "In grade three, I remember I was in love with Sally. She had long blonde hair and big blue eyes and she shared her snack with me every day. She moved to Australia in grade four."

"A tragic tale," said Amber. "Okay, now you go."

"Catherine, truth or dare?" asked Zach.

"Truth."

"Would you kiss River for one hundred bucks?"

"Ew!" Catherine paused to think. "He's old, but he's not bad looking. Maybe."

"Dude!" said Amber. "Nasty!"

Catherine just shrugged. "Amber, truth or dare?"

"Dare."

"I dare you to bite Zach," she said, knowing full well that Amber was not one to back down from a dare.

Amber looked at Catherine strangely. Catherine couldn't tell if she was angry or intrigued. Then Amber turned to stare at Zach. Hesitantly, she asked, "Do you want to?"

Zach glanced at Morgan and Catherine, and then turned back to Amber. "Fine." He held his arm outstretched.

Amber took his arm in her hands and sunk her teeth into his flesh. She began to suck. Zach watched her with wide eyes. She came up and took a deep breath, her pupils dilated. "Zach, I dare you to drink from me," she said thrusting her arm onto Zach's lap.

Zach took her arm and bit into it slowly. He let the warm liquid fill his mouth. When he swallowed, his entire body shook with satisfaction. Zach and Amber took each other's hands and started laughing.

"I've forgotten how fantastic it is to feed off someone," said Zach, gazing around at the room. "I feel so alive!"

"Oh my God," said Amber, still grinning broadly. "I can feel the carpet moving underneath me. I feel so energized!"

They stood up and stared at each other.

"We're still playing the game," said Catherine.

"Oh right, it's my turn. Morgan, I dare you to drink from Catherine and then Catherine, you do the same to Morgan. I can't play anymore. I have to run around, or something," said Zach. He took Amber by the arm and they raced to Catherine's bedroom to bounce on her bed together. They laughed raucously, their heads spinning and their hearts racing in their chests.

Morgan gave Catherine his wrist and Catherine gave him hers. They bit, drank and stopped in perfect unison. For a minute they sat still as their bodies began to change. When they felt as if they were floating on a rapid current, they rose and went to join Amber and Zach.

"I feel so good," squealed Amber.

They all held hands and continued to jump in a circle on the bed. The world spun and danced in perfect clarity. Everything around them was beautiful and had meaning. The world was an amazing place to live in. They had no worries. They only lived.

They stopped jumping and rested on the bed. Catherine felt her heart reverberating in her throat. She took in a deep breath and tried to calm herself. She was hot and normally would have been tired, but she still felt like she could run a marathon, like she could do anything. No one was tired.

"Let's listen to music," said Amber.

She raced back to her room, picked up her radio, came back to Catherine's and turned it on, at high volume. Zach, Catherine, and Morgan got up and started to dance with Amber. They all held hands in a circle again, spun around and around and jumped as high as they could.

Amber broke the circle, ran to Catherine, and hugged her. "I'm sorry about what I said."

"No, I'm sorry," said Catherine, squeezing Amber close.

Morgan and Zach leaned against a wall, their bodies tingling all over. Morgan stared at Zach, mesmerized by how vibrant his hair was. Zach stared back, drawn to Morgan's eyes. "I never noticed how cool your eyes are. They look like they have little golden flakes in them."

"Your eyes look like water," said Morgan, in awe. "I can see them swimming."

Zach ran his fingers through Morgan's dark hair. Morgan brushed the spikes on Zach's head with his hand. Zach saw Morgan's wrist out of the corner of his eye and without thinking twice, he pulled it toward his mouth and drank. Morgan watched Zach's lips redden with his blood. Morgan's heart raced. He wanted, no, he needed blood. When Zach stopped, Morgan took Zach's hands and pinned them to the wall, dove into Zach's neck and drank. Zach's blood tasted different. It was stronger and more powerful than Catherine's. Morgan pushed himself up against Zach and squeezed him. Zach moaned and broke free from Morgan's grip. Carefully, he pulled Morgan's face away from his neck. They stared at each other, panting, their bodies warm and wanting. They didn't move until they heard Amber laughing loudly. Morgan pulled away from Zach without speaking. Zach went into Catherine's bathroom and shut the door.

Morgan walked over to Catherine and Amber and took a seat. His mind was racing. The world was turning too quickly. He felt amazingly energized and told himself to brush his uneasy feelings aside.

Zach came out of the bathroom, holding his neck, and sat down next to Amber. He too ignored the strange ache in his gut and told himself to enjoy the moment. He glanced at Morgan and felt his stomach flip.

"We want to go outside and make a fire," said Amber.

Morgan and Zach immediately agreed and the girls squealed with joy.

"We'll have to be extra quiet, though," said Catherine.

"Want me to grab my lighter?" said Zach.

"Yes, go," said Amber.

They snuck down the stairs into the main hall and quietly exited through the front doors.

"I feel like I'm a secret spy," whispered Catherine as they walked stealthily into the forest.

When they were far enough into the woods that they couldn't see the castle, they stopped and began to make a pile of wood.

Zach started the fire and Catherine poked at it with a stick, trying to spread the flames through the dry branches. Amber started dancing around, still laughing. She grabbed Catherine and they skipped around the fire, singing quietly.

Zach took out a pack of cigarettes and offered one to Morgan. They lit up and sat taking deep drags off their smokes, trying to clear their heads a bit.

Fire swirled in front of Catherine's eyes. The world was a painting and she was the painter, splashing orange flames over her canvas. She told Amber they were wood nymphs and Amber began to climb a tree, claiming it was her home.

Catherine applauded and joined Amber atop the small tree. Together, they stared down at the earth below, still pretending to be mythical woodland creatures.

"I have wings, glowing ones that are yellow," said Catherine. "What colour are your wings?"

"Mine are bright red because my element is fire."

"Okay, you're a fire fairy and I'm an air fairy. What are your powers?"

"I can shoot fire from my hands and I can control the temperature," said Amber, grinning with glee.

"I can control the winds, and I can disappear and fly."

"Wow!"

"I'm cold," said Catherine.

"Here, I'll warm you up," said Amber, placing her hands on Catherine. "Do you feel warmer?"

"Actually, I do. You're magic!"

"Maybe this tree is magic."

"It looks magic," said Catherine, stroking the branches fondly.

Down below, Morgan and Zach were finishing up their smokes, listening to Amber and Catherine. They started to laugh. Zach patted Morgan on the back and they stood up to join the girls in their magic tree.

Time flew by. At around eleven o'clock, they all jumped down to sit around the fire and watch the last flames die. They headed back to the castle and all high-fived when they reached Catherine's room.

"We pulled it off," said Amber.

"We don't have a curfew today," said Zach.

"But you're around *us*." Catherine pointed at herself and Morgan. "If we do one more thing wrong, River is going to send us home, I swear."

"We'll take it easy then," said Zach.

Everyone nodded. They sat by Catherine's fireplace, listening to music. Every once and a while, Amber would start singing along with the radio. At midnight, the girls began to feel drowsy.

"I'm still really happy," said Amber, "but my energy is wearing off."

"Mine, too," said Catherine.

They fell back onto the floor and curled up together like two little puppies.

"Are you awake?" Zach asked Morgan.

"Yeah, I'm not tired at all."

"Me, either. What do you want to do? We're going to stay like this for a few hours at least."

"We could go to town and get coffee or something," said

Morgan. "That place we went to get ice cream before is open twenty four hours."

"Okay," said Zach, looking over at the girls. "They're asleep."

"I'll write them a note," said Morgan, getting up to grab a piece of paper and a pen.

"What are you going to say?"

Morgan wrote his note and then read it aloud: "Dear girls, Zach and I have gone to town. Be back soon. From Morgan."

"I doubt they'll wake up before we get back."

Morgan nodded and they left the room quietly. They exited the castle with even more caution and practically tiptoed across the grass. Once they were on the main path, they sprinted toward town. Within five minutes, they had reached Café Crème.

"Hello, boys," the lady with the flowery apron said to them when they entered the coffee shop. Morgan could see the woman's nametag from where he was standing.

"Hi, Bonnie. Can we get two cups of coffee please?"

"Sure thing. I usually don't work this late at night, but the boy who does called in sick, poor thing. He always has the most rotten luck."

"Thank you," said Zach, taking the coffees and heading over to a table by the large glass windows.

Morgan paid Bonnie and went over to join Zach. He took his coffee and sipped it slowly.

"Do you think she noticed my neck?" Zach asked.

"No. She was too busy talking about that sick kid worker." They spoke so softly that no one else would be able to hear them. Their sense of hearing was still heightened.

"Is there anyone else here?" asked Zach.

Morgan glanced over Zach's shoulder and then back at Zach. Zach nodded. He continued to sip his coffee for a full minute before turning around to see who else was in the café. "Is that Xavier?" he asked, raising his voice slightly.

Xavier, reading the paper, looked up and smiled. Suddenly,

Morgan wished he had not taken off his black ribbon charm.

"How nice of you to join me," said Xavier, taking the seat between Zach and Morgan.

"What the hell are you doing here?" said Morgan. "I thought you were supposed to be at some school."

"They don't miss me," Xavier said bitterly. "I saw your fire in the forest. I saw Catherine and Amber dancing. I know what you've done. I can see it in your eyes. I can see it on your body."

Zach slapped a hand to his neck.

"Look, what do you want?" asked Morgan, glaring at Xavier contemptuously.

Xavier smiled and sat back. "I want you to make me one of you."

"You can't do that," said Zach. "You're born a vampire."

"Try again," whispered Xavier. "Vampires lack life energy. If you drain me and then let me feed on you, my body will crave blood."

"No," said Morgan. "Leave us alone. You've already done enough."

"I've read about you," Xavier said, his voice rising. He paused to collect himself. "I want to feel what you feel when you drink. It must be amazing. And there's hardly any comedown!"

"Xavier, you'll feel depressed if you don't get energy. You'll want more and more. It's fun for a while, but it's hard to live with," said Zach. "You're already balanced. Why would you want to become unstable?"

"If you haven't noticed already, I'm pretty damn unstable now," Xavier hissed through clenched teeth. "Look, what do you want from me in return?"

Zach and Morgan glanced at each other.

"I want you to leave Catherine alone," said Morgan. "I don't want you to come near her ever again. I don't want you playing tricks on any of us at the castle. I don't want you around."

"Done," said Xavier.

"I want something useful," said Zach. "You're a witch, right? I want magic."

Xavier nodded and slipped a chain off his head into his hands. He held it out, dangling it in front of Zach. On the end was a light blue crystal. "If you're in a tough situation, ask this crystal for help. It will give advice that only you will hear. It's very useful, and it saddens me to give it away, but it's for a good cause. Now will you agree?"

Zach slipped on the necklace and looked at Morgan.

"Tomorrow," Morgan told Xavier, "come to Blacklune at midnight. Wait out front. We'll come for you."

Xavier shook their hands and fled the café with his paper. Morgan and Zach continued to sip their coffee.

"Ask your necklace something," Morgan said.

"Should we tell the girls about Xavier?" He closed his eyes and heard a calm voice reply, *Only if you are prepared to fight.* "It said only if you want to fight."

"I don't want any more conflict. Let's not tell the girls, or anyone. Xavier will leave once he gets what he wants, hopefully forever."

Zach nodded. When they finished their drinks, they stood to leave.

"Bye, dears," Bonnie called to them.

Morgan and Zach ran back to the castle, crept up to Catherine's room, and joined Amber and Catherine on the floor to sleep.

They had a lazy Sunday morning. Morgan awoke first. He grabbed his note off the kitchen table, crumpled it into a ball, and threw it in the garbage. Exhausted from the night's adventures, they all stumbled into the ballroom for breakfast, still half-asleep.

Catherine, much to her relief, had gotten her period, and for the first time in her life, she was more than happy to have it. She munched on her toast, her eyes droopy. Her body ached slightly, yearning for blood.

Zach gulped back a cup of coffee. He had tied a red bandana around his neck to cover up Morgan's bite mark. He didn't want to have to think up an explanation when he had more important things to deal with.

"I'm going back to bed," said Catherine, pushing her plate away. "Anyone's welcome to come with me."

Morgan rose and smiled. He waved goodbye to Amber and snapped his fingers at Zach. Then he went back to Catherine's bedroom to sleep.

They cuddled up together in Catherine's bed with Charmer, their bodies intertwined. They held hands and kissed when their mouths met. They got up at noon to have lunch and go smoke. They went out to the top balcony and stared out at the sky. Catherine rested against Morgan's body and watched the end of her glowing cigarette.

The day went by fast and smoothly. Catherine and Morgan were both calm and still recovering. They slept and talked and smoked and were happy just to be with one another.

At ten minutes to midnight, Morgan told Catherine he had to go to his room to do something, and that he needed some alone time. Catherine nodded understandingly and kissed him goodbye.

Morgan stepped out into the hall and spotted Zach. He grinned, relieved. They didn't speak as they paced down the stairs and out the front doors. Xavier was already there waiting for them.

"Where should we go?" Zach whispered to Morgan.

"Follow me," said Xavier, leading Zach and Morgan into the forest.

The air was pleasant and smelled sweet, but the forest was dark and the trees looked twisted. Deep in the woods, Xavier stopped in front of a large stump and sat down on it.

"I'm ready," he told them, slapping his hands on his knees.

"Are you sure you want this?" asked Zach.

Xavier nodded. Zach and Morgan looked at each other hesitantly, then nodded silently. Zach breathed in deep and took Xavier's right arm in his hands. Morgan took his left and gripped it tight. In unison, they sank their teeth into Xavier's wrists and sucked hard.

After only a few seconds, Morgan stopped and gasped with amazement, his eyes already dilated. "His blood is so powerful."

Zach raised his head, blood running down onto his chin. "It's so good," he said, through clenched teeth.

Morgan and Zach dove in once again. Morgan could hear Xavier groaning slightly in pain, but he ignored it. With Zach's help, he pushed Xavier back forcefully until their victim's back was flat against the stump.

"Let's get his neck," Zach whispered to Morgan.

Morgan nodded and they gracefully moved up Xavier's body to feed on his neck. Xavier was crying softly, but Zach and Morgan took no notice. They were wholly focused on drinking and the rush it gave them. When they finally drew back, saturated with energy, they looked around, breathing heavily. They could see every detail of the forest as if it were daylight, but clearer. Morgan stared at Zach's skin, glowing under the moonlight.

"We should let him drink very soon," said Zach, motioning to Xavier. "He's lost a lot of blood. He might pass out."

"He can drink from me," Morgan said happily.

Zach took Morgan's wrist and bit into it but only drank a tiny amount of blood. Morgan felt no pain. Every move he made was enjoyable. A simple wave of his arm through the air made his body tingle with excitement. The wind was a warm current tickling his limbs. When he shifted closer to Xavier, he felt like he was flying. He had to let his head clear for a moment before he could speak. "Drink now."

Xavier continued to cry. His eyes were closed. He was fading fast. Zach slapped Xavier's cheek and told him again to drink. Morgan pressed his bleeding wrist to Xavier's lips and waited. Xavier tasted the blood, then he drank. He clung to Morgan's arm when his strength began to return.

"That's enough!" Zach shouted, prying Morgan's wrist from Xavier's jaws.

Xavier sat up, his lips stained red. He didn't speak. He only stared at Morgan and Zach, and then at the trees and the sky. He gazed down at his hands and chuckled.

"Are you all right?" asked Zach.

"I'm fantastic!" said Xavier, standing. He jumped up and plucked a leaf from a tree. He blew it off his palm and watched it drift to the ground. "I have to go explore. This magical moss-covered land is calling me. Wow. I can feel my mouth changing!"

Morgan licked his own fangs. They weren't all that long, but they did the job extremely well.

Xavier ran off, leaping over logs with ease. Zach and Morgan watched him until he was out of sight among the dense brush.

"It seems a little dangerous for him to have powers in that state," said Zach, watching the sky for any strange sparks.

"He'll be fine," said Morgan. "We've done what we promised, and I feel fantastic!"

"Me, too," whispered Zach.

They stood, their arms outstretched, letting the wind caress them. They walked through the forest, and each step felt like a leap, each breath, a gulp from a sweet, refreshing spring.

"What are we going to do with all this energy?" Zach said.

"Anything!" shouted Morgan, spinning on the spot. "We can't go to the girls though."

"Let's go swimming!" said Zach, as if it was the most brilliant idea he had ever come up with.

"Yes! We should! But we'll need towels."

"I'll go get them," said Zach. "Let's head back to the castle. You can wait out front. Keep quiet. Don't spin around."

"Okay," said Morgan, giggling like a child.

They raced back to the castle, laughing, not tired at all. Zach went inside and grabbed two towels and came back out flailing them in the air, a mad grin on his face.

"Let's book it," whispered Morgan.

They ran down the main path, the forest a smudge of green and brown. They stopped when they reached the town, amazed by how quickly they'd covered the distance.

They headed down to the sand, took off their shoes and socks, and began laughing. Zach looked at Morgan and smirked broadly.

"I know!" shouted Morgan. "The sand!"

They stripped down and ran toward the sea. As soon as Morgan's body hit the water, he felt like hundreds of ice cubes were sliding all over his body. It felt marvellous. He dunked his head underwater and let liquid swirl around him. He came up a minute later when he realized he still needed air to survive.

"There you are!" said Zach. "You were gone for so long. Doesn't the water feel great?"

Morgan nodded, sucked some water up into his mouth, and spat it out like a fountain. He parted the water with his hands and watched in awe at the magnificent patterns that formed on the surface.

"Look out there," said Zach, pointing to the distance.

Morgan turned his head and saw the stars reflected on the black sea. He felt like he was in a magical, dark sphere where nothing could go wrong. He lifted his head back and smiled, his body radiating with pleasure.

When the cold began to affect them slightly, they swam back to shore and dried off. They dressed quickly, still intensely alert.

"We can't go back now," said Zach. "I'm still alive."

"I know," said Morgan, shaking his head dry. "We could go get hot chocolate."

"Yeah!" shouted Zach, whipping Morgan with his towel.

Morgan chased Zach up to Café Crème, but they both stopped abruptly at the entrance.

"Bonnie's not there," said Morgan. "How do we know we can trust this guy?"

"Stop being paranoid. What could he do? We could easily take him down if we had to," said Zach, tapping his teeth as he winked.

"You're right," said Morgan, opening the door.

"Hey," the young man said, looking up from a book.

"Hi," said Morgan, forgetting about his wet hair and towel. "Can we get two hot chocolates?"

"With whipped cream?" the boy asked.

Zach and Morgan nodded. Zach paid this time. When they received their drinks, they sat down at a table underneath a window with a clear view of the sea.

"Mmm," said Morgan, sipping his cocoa slowly.

"This is about all I can stand. I don't think I'd be able to eat right now."

"Same. I'm so energized I don't feel the need to eat at all. It's weird."

They sipped their drinks silently, lost in their own thoughts. They both could feel the boy at the counter watching them suspiciously. Eventually, the feeling grew so strong, Morgan turned around and glared. The boy's eyes widened and then returned to his book.

"Nice," whispered Zach.

At three o'clock, Zach and Morgan stood to leave. They brought their empty mugs to the front counter. Zach read the boy's nametag. "Thank you, Peter."

Peter nodded and took the mugs with trembling hands.

Zach glanced at Morgan's dilated pupils and grinned. Then they turned to leave.

"Wait," said Peter.

Zach and Morgan spun around, eyeing the boy questioningly.

"Are you from the school by the woods?"

"We could be," said Morgan, feeling sly and important.

Peter's eyes bugged out a little. He glanced at Zach's neck, nodded, and waved goodbye.

Once Morgan and Zach were outside, they started cracking up. They joked and roughhoused back to the castle, ignoring the pain that started to rise in their heads.

11

It was bright in the morning, too bright. Catherine awoke and changed quickly. She smiled when she spotted Morgan in the library and skipped over to him. "Good morning," she said, kissing him on the lips.

Morgan smiled and pulled Catherine onto his lap. He kissed her neck and squeezed her tight. Catherine stared at him. He looked worn, but he seemed attentive.

All the students rose when River arrived with the news of an outing. "We're going to a spa in town."

"Finally!" shouted Alex, gripping Kevin's arm.

The spa was located on the outskirts of town, apart from all the other shops. It was surrounded by trees and silence. The inside was warm and smelled of candles and greenery. The calm sounds of flowing water, serene voices, and relaxing music surrounded the students.

Everyone got a massage and then chose one other activity offered. Catherine and Morgan decided on the mud bath. They each relaxed in their own tub of hot mud, silent, enjoying the warm liquid earth on their skin.

Catherine heard a faint dripping sound coming from another room. She closed her eyes and allowed herself to succumb to fantasy as all light vanished. She was somewhere she had never been before.

She was on a stony path and her feet were adorned in bright red shoes. There were shops all around her and sweet aromas of fresh bread and coffee floated on the air. She began to dance. She spotted Morgan. He was saying something to her. What was he saying?

"Catherine," Morgan said firmly.

Catherine opened her eyes. She had been dreaming. She sat up a little and lifted her muddy hands to her head. She gazed at Morgan and smiled. He smiled back and said no more.

When the students were showered and ready to leave, they gathered at the entranceway. Everyone seemed to glow, looking refreshed and happy. Alex sighed with contentment as she studied the rock gardens around her.

The students were treated to dinner at a nearby restaurant. Catherine, sitting next to Amber at the table, asked, "What did you do at the spa?"

"I went swimming. Zach said he was sick of swimming and had some seaweed wrap done."

Zach and Morgan started to crack up.

"Splish splash," Morgan whispered, causing Zach to crack up even more.

"What?" said Amber.

"Nothing," said Zach. "Seriously, it's a guy thing."

"Fine," said Amber. "Catherine, let's talk about girl things. It sure was a good thing I didn't have my period today. Do you have yours, Catherine?"

"Actually, I do."

Amber stopped joking around when she realized how important Catherine's last statement was. She immediately hugged her. "Thank God!"

"I know," said Catherine, placing a hand to her heart.

"I don't even *want* to know," said Zach.

Catherine giggled. Morgan stared at her and sighed in relief. He slid his hand onto her leg and squeezed it. Catherine did the same to him.

After a hot meal, the students walked back to the castle. In the main hall, River announced that it was time for their weekly energy drink. Catherine squeezed Morgan, her breath quickening. "You two will not be joining us tonight," River told Catherine and Morgan. "I expect you to be upstairs. I don't care where, but at eleven, you are to be in your own room."

Catherine felt her heart stop for a moment. Morgan yelped. Catherine looked down and realized she had dug her nails into Morgan's hand.

While everyone raced to the ballroom, Morgan and Catherine slowly made their way upstairs to Morgan's room.

"I can't believe it!" Catherine shouted as soon as they were inside. "It's not fair!"

Morgan sat on the floor, his hands to his head. He sighed loudly and punched the carpet with his fist. "We did attack Lilly, and we did ditch the camping trip."

"I know, but we can't be expected to be perfect. Sometimes I just can't control myself. He doesn't understand."

"It's only one night. We'll survive."

Catherine crossed her arms and sat down beside Morgan. She stared at the unlit logs in the fireplace and cursed to herself.

They turned to each other and kissed. Catherine felt her body go warm. If she couldn't have blood, then she would have Morgan, all of him. She sucked at his neck and caused him to cry out. She massaged his sides and slowly caressed his chest with her lips. She unbuttoned his pants and pulled down his underwear. Morgan moaned with anticipation. Catherine smiled and devoured him. She filled her mouth with Morgan and focused her energy on pleasing him, on warming him, on giving him absolute pleasure.

"Oh my God," said Morgan, his head tilted back in ecstasy.

Catherine smiled as he poured into her mouth. She swallowed and felt complete and satisfied with her work. She kissed Morgan on the lips. Morgan was still recovering, his eyes half open.

"I don't think I can move," he said, grinning.

"You don't have to."

She got up and went to the kitchen for a small knife. She grabbed a cup and set it on the table. Then she put the knife to her wrist and cut swiftly. Blood dripped from her incision into the cup. There was just enough for Morgan to feel something. She licked the knife clean, threw it in the sink, and picked up the cup. She walked back to where Morgan lay peacefully on the floor. Morgan's eyes shot open at the smell of blood, and he sat up, smiling.

"Drink, my darling," said Catherine, putting the cup to Morgan's lips.

Morgan drank it in one swallow, and groaned from the sensation it gave him. Revived, he pulled Catherine's wrist to his mouth and licked her wound. Catherine got up and went to the bathroom to get a bandage. Morgan stayed where he was, his eyes following her. "Why are you being so nice to me?"

"Because it makes me happy," said Catherine sincerely, as she returned to sit next to him on the floor.

Morgan pulled her close and they kissed. Catherine could taste her blood on his lips. She laughed as they collapsed back on the floor together.

At eleven, Catherine kissed Morgan goodbye. She squeezed his hands. She owned a part of him. She had him inside her. He was hers. She took a sharp intake of breath and told herself that yes, everyday was real. Love was real. Morgan was real. His love was real.

She spent the night writing in her journal. She had a lot to think about. She wrote to keep her mind on Morgan and off the fact that she didn't have blood. She wrote to keep herself from harming anyone.

At breakfast, Morgan showered Catherine with kisses. "Good morning, beautiful."

"Good morning, sexy." Catherine rested her legs on Morgan's lap and wrapped her arms around his neck. She pressed her body against his, kissed him lightly and blew softly on his ear. "I have an idea you're going to like," she whispered.

Morgan grinned at her, his eager eyes speaking more than words could.

"Tonight, after dinner, we should sneak out. We can go to town and feed."

Morgan's eyebrows twitched upward. He pulled back to stare at her. "Are you serious?"

Catherine nodded and took a casual sip of her coffee. From the look in Morgan's eyes, she knew he liked her idea.

The class lesson that day was on controlling urges. River told his students that they didn't want to become reliant on blood for happiness. "Fill yourselves only with the necessary amount of energy. Too much energy sometimes leads to devastating results."

Catherine and Morgan laughed. River ignored them.

The class was taught how to summon energy from nature and certain activities. Catherine and Morgan didn't pay attention. They closed their eyes and ears and held each other as they drowsed.

"That was an interesting lecture," Amber said at the lunch table. "I can't believe River talked about sex."

Catherine smiled at Morgan, thinking of the night before. She had fed off him and she had felt renewed.

At dinner, Catherine, Morgan, Zach, and Amber all sat talking about their home lives and friends. Catherine and Morgan participated, but they fidgeted and twitched the entire time, eager to leave.

At seven o'clock, Morgan and Catherine started to formulate a plan in Catherine's suite.

"We should wear all black," said Catherine, "to blend in with the night."

"Do you have a black shirt or something that you're willing to cut up for fabric?"

Catherine nodded and went to her bedroom. She came back holding a cotton knit black t-shirt and handed it to Morgan, slightly confused. Morgan took the shirt, inspected it, and nodded approval.

"Do you have any scissors?"

"Amber left some here," said Catherine, retrieving them from the kitchen.

Morgan cut out two black masks from the shirt. Each mask was simple: a piece of fabric with two eye holes and long ends to tie with. Morgan handed one to Catherine and raised his brows meaningfully.

"They look like raccoon masks," said Catherine, fiddling with hers.

"No, they look sweet."

Catherine fastened her mask at the back of her head and pulled her hair over the ties. She gazed at herself in the mirror and smiled. She looked different. She was recognizable, yes, but she would seem mysterious to strangers, almost dangerous. "I like it. Go get some black."

Catherine changed into tight stretchy black pants, a black shirt, and a coat. She pulled on her slouchy boots and studied herself in her mirror. She went to meet Morgan, now changed into black jeans and shirt, in the hall. They quietly walked down the stairs and out of the main doors, and headed unhurriedly down the main path. When they were completely out of sight of the castle, they giggled a little and hugged each other.

"What time is it?" asked Catherine, searching the dark sky for the moon.

"It's just after eight."

Catherine smiled and took Morgan's hand. She kissed him lightly on the cheek and watched his eyes light up as they both lifted off the ground.

"Your necklace! I almost forgot about it."

Catherine wrapped her leg around Morgan's knee to support him securely, and continued to fly upward until they were above the treetops, heading to town. "Let's have fun tonight. I don't want to be upset anymore. I just want to live and be happy."

It didn't take long for them to reach the outskirts of town. They recognized Café Crème below them. "Look," said Morgan. Peter, the young counter boy, was walking alone just outside the coffee shop.

"Where is he going, do you suppose?" asked Catherine, slowing down.

"Let's follow him."

They watched Peter stroll along, unaware of the hunters above him. "He doesn't seem to be going anywhere," said Catherine. "He's just taking a walk."

"Let's feed. No one is around. No one will see. Put on your mask."

Catherine did so, although she felt a pang of guilt as she lowered herself and Morgan closer to their prey. Peter suddenly shivered.

Morgan was silent and still. Catherine tapped him once. He nodded, and together they swooped down to attack.

It happened in one swift movement. They landed and pinned Peter to the ground, their bodies fuelled with adrenaline, excitement, and need. Peter was no match against two ravenous vampires. Helpless, he was fed on, drained and left lying on the sidewalk as Catherine and Morgan flew off.

"Where should we go?" Catherine said.

Morgan pointed to the beach. They drifted over to the sand and found a small cave in the cliff by the water. They flew into the darkness and landed on the soft sand.

"It's nice in here," said Catherine, admiring the wavy creases in the stone walls.

The cave was not dark for them. It was perfectly light and comfortable. The soft glistening sand made a wonderful bed. They took a seat and watched the sea with intense concentration. They couldn't be seen from the outside. Only a black hole in the cliff wall was visible on the beach. They, on the other hand, could see everything beyond the cave with perfect clarity.

After a little while, Morgan raised his head. "Listen."

Catherine huddled close and focused, feeling a chill. She pulled off her mask. "Is that screaming?"

Morgan slid off his mask and rolled onto his back. He stared at the roof of the cave, at the indents and swirls of rock, and sighed. Someone far away was shouting for help and Morgan and Catherine knew why.

"He's not hurt," said Catherine, choking on her words, "badly."

When the screams faded, they focused on the sea. Catherine told herself she was fine, that everything was fine and she was okay.

This isn't bad. I've fed. I feel fantastic. It's a new day and I'm with Morgan, the one I love. I'm warm and safe and happy. Nothing else matters.

She curled against Morgan and felt fulfilled and alive. Morgan ran his hands along Catherine's sides, under her shirt. Shivers shot through her body. She turned to Morgan and released her energy into him through her lips. He returned the energy along with more of his own, and they forgot about the screams outside.

Catherine awoke to the sound of Morgan coughing loudly. She rubbed her eyes. The back of the cave was still very dark, but sunlight was spilling in the entrance and it was bothering her. She felt tired and wanted to go back to sleep. She had spent the entire night loving Morgan and listening to the sea, only sleeping for a few hours. It was now ten o'clock in the morning and she was finally exhausted.

"We've got sand on us everywhere," said Morgan, brushing off his jeans.

"Come here, sugar," said Catherine, reaching her arms out to him.

He smiled and collapsed next to Catherine, but he didn't relax. His attention was drawn to someone speaking outside of the cave mouth.

"Did you hear about all the excitement?" a whiney woman's voice said. "Some couple found that Peter boy lying on the ground outside the café, covered in blood."

"What happened to him?" a screechy old woman's voice asked.

"They're not quite sure. Peter keeps saying he saw two, black creatures swoop down and attack him. Apparently, they can fly and they feed on blood."

"Oh my, that sounds a bit ridiculous, don't you think?" the old woman said. "Is the boy okay?"

"He's in the hospital to make sure he has no poison in him and such. I think the boy's suffering from a mental breakdown, personally."

When the voices faded, Catherine and Morgan shut their eyes and fell asleep.

When they awoke again at eleven o'clock that night, Catherine began to whimper slightly as she realized she could no longer see clearly in the dark. She clung to Morgan's arm. "Don't let me go!"

"I won't. Don't worry. It's pitch black in here, let's get outside."

They stood up together and carefully felt their way out of the cave. Catherine squeezed Morgan's hand and slowly, they flew up onto a ledge on the cliff face to get their bearings. Below them, on the beach, four teenagers were running around shouting and roughhousing, oblivious to Catherine and Morgan's presence.

"Isn't it great!" shouted a small brunette girl. "Our town is haunted now!"

"It's not haunted," said a blonde girl. "It has vampires."

"Vampires don't exist!" said a boy in a red shirt, waving an empty bottle at the blonde.

"My grandpa told me to watch out for the Blood Villains," said a tall boy in blue. "Peter almost died."

The brunette girl's eyes widened and she quickly took a swig from her bottle.

"He did *not* almost die," said the blonde girl. "They just took a little blood from him. I find the whole thing...romantic. Two young vampires on the search for blood. They don't kill people!"

"You're crazy!" the boy in red laughed.

"No, I'm not," said the blonde. "I know I'm right. Vampires exist. The Blood Villains are real. I wish they would come down and drink from me right now!"

"Don't say that," the brunette girl whispered. "They might be watching."

"As if!" said the boy in red contemptuously. "Come out, come out, wherever you are!"

Catherine and Morgan glanced at each other and smiled. They took hands and stepped off the ledge, hovering in the air. They seemed mere shadows against the night sky.

"Hey!" shouted Catherine.

The teenagers stopped talking all at once and looked up at the cliff face. The boy in red dropped his bottle and the brunette girl ran to the taller boy. The blonde stood completely still.

"It's them!" shouted the brunette girl's boyfriend. "It's really fucking them!"

"Holy shit," whispered the other boy. "They *can* fly."

"So blondie wants to play?" called Morgan. Catherine giggled at him.

The blonde nodded and stepped forward.

"Let's take her," Morgan whispered to Catherine. "She looks tasty."

They gracefully lowered themselves to hover just above where the blonde was standing awe struck.

"Tell us your name, girl," Catherine said.

"Cindy," the trembling girl said.

Catherine and Morgan nodded and then they each took hold of one of Cindy's arms. They rose with her a few meters above the sand. Cindy didn't flinch, even when her friends below started to shout.

"Put her down!" screamed the boy in blue.

Morgan put Cindy's wrist to his lips and breathed in her scent. Catherine did the same. Together, they punctured her soft flesh and began to drink. Cindy didn't cry out, even when she saw her own blood ooze from her veins, but she began to squirm slightly in fear.

When Catherine and Morgan were done feeding, they gently lowered Cindy to the sand. Catherine kissed Cindy once on the head. She took Morgan's arm and flew off toward the forest.

"Have fun, kids!" Morgan shouted, hugging Catherine tightly and laughing as he was pulled through the air.

Cindy's friends crowded around her and began asking her questions, bemused and frightened when they saw her bloody wrists.

"Are you all right?" the small girl asked.

Cindy, still lying on the sand, only nodded. She stared down at her wrists. She was too drunk to feel much pain. She was dizzy and excited. "They chose me. They know my name. Did you see them? They're gorgeous! I met them! I was in their arms."

"Dude, I don't know what the fuck just happened," said the boy in red.

"Cindy just got bitten by two vampires," said the tall boy. "My grandpa was right. The Blood Villains are real."

"They're young too, like us," said the brunette. "The guy looked handsome."

"The girl was pretty fine too," said the boy in red.

"Do you know what this means?" said Cindy. "There's more to the world. We keep searching for something, anything, to make life worth living. It's here. Magic exists. Anything is possible."

"Especially when you've got alcohol!" the boy in red added. The brunette slapped his arm.

In the forest, Catherine and Morgan stopped to skip rocks at a pond. They were close to the castle.

"We missed school today," said Morgan.

"I know," said Catherine, who was watching green light dancing around her. "I think those kids liked us. Maybe we won't get such a bad reputation, after all."

Morgan stared at the ripples in the water, concentrating. "What we did to Peter was crossing the line a little. It was exactly like Lilly, but we weren't even energized. We just wanted blood. We could have controlled ourselves. We chose not to."

"He's fine. Stop worrying about him. If it makes you feel any better, Cindy offered herself to us."

"True," said Morgan, focusing on the sound of silence. "Her blood was sweet. Did you notice?"

Catherine nodded, grinning. "Not as sweet as you."

Morgan chuckled.

"Do you think River knows?" Catherine said.

"News must have reached Blacklune by now. If we go back, we'll be sent home for sure."

"We can't stay in the forest forever. Let's go to our meadow."

"Where is it?"

"We'll find it," said Catherine. "We have all night."

They started walking through the woods, putting thoughts of River and Blacklune out of their minds. After two hours, they found the meadow and danced under the moon, fearing nothing. When they were exhausted, they sat in the grass and held each other.

They slept the day away again, in the open meadow, cringing in their sleep at the sun. At midnight they awoke, starving for blood.

"I haven't eaten in two days. I'm going to need even more blood than usual," said Catherine, jumping to her feet.

"We can't attack any more people," said Morgan, holding his head. "I need it too, but we can't."

"What are we supposed to do, just sit here and do nothing? There's a town of helpless people out there with plenty of blood to spare."

Morgan looked at her for a moment. "We'll stay here until tomorrow."

"No!" Catherine snarled, her fangs bared.

She flew at Morgan and pinned him to the earth with all her strength. Rage fuelling her, she tore into Morgan's neck and sucked harder than she had ever done before. Morgan screamed with pain and tried to push Catherine away, but with her necklace, and his blood inside her, she was stronger than he was. She drank until she was dizzy and finally came up for air, panting hard. She laughed in ecstasy and flew up to sit on a tree branch as her world grew brighter before her eyes.

Morgan coughed and clutched his wound, weeping helplessly because he was too weak to stop. He had no idea where Catherine had gone and decided that he was going to die. His world was white. He couldn't move. He couldn't hear Catherine anywhere.

Catherine sat swinging her legs and picking at some moss on the tree, until she realized that something wasn't right. Morgan wasn't with her. She looked down and her heart dropped. Her stomach flipped and she puked everything she'd drunk. Frantic, she wiped her mouth and flew down to where Morgan lay unmoving.

"Morgan!" she shouted. "Answer me!"

Morgan did nothing but stare up at the sky. He had given up on taking in enough air for words. Breathing was too big an effort to make.

Her mind spinning, Catherine bit savagely into her wrist and shoved it into Morgan's mouth. "Drink now!"

Morgan's mouth twitched when he tasted Catherine's blood on his tongue. He began to drink.

"Keep drinking, sweetheart," said Catherine, shrugging her other arm out of her coat.

She clutched the neck of her shirt and tore half of it off her body. She pressed the shredded shirt to Morgan's bleeding neck and prayed to the moon that he would survive.

Finally, Morgan pushed Catherine's wrist away and sat up. Neither of them spoke for a minute. Morgan continued to hold the black shirt to his neck.

"I'm sorry," whispered Catherine. "I don't know what came over me."

Morgan nodded, tears still brimming in his eyes.

They sat nursing their wounds for an hour, tired from fighting, tired from fleeing, tired from feeding off each other. Catherine took Morgan's hand. She pulled him close.

"I don't want to hurt you," said Catherine, tears welling in her eyes.

"Stay with me. We'll sleep here and return to the castle tomorrow in the day."

Catherine nodded and stroked Morgan's cheek. She knew this would probably be the last night she spent alone in the forest with him.

Morgan was up at nine o'clock. He woke Catherine and they stood to leave. They were silent as they started on their way back. Catherine felt awful inside. No matter how hard she tried to cheer herself up, she couldn't shake the feeling of melancholy. Sadness was being pumped through her heart and was flooding her veins. She felt worse than when her grandmother had died. She knew she needed blood and she began to hate herself for it. Half way to the castle, she stopped abruptly and began to cry. She crouched down and hugged her knees, her head buried in her chest. "I can't take it, Morgan."

Morgan crouched down beside her, and though he felt the same sadness, he knew he had to be strong. He didn't cry. He put a hand on Catherine's back and rubbed, trying his best to comfort her. He told her things were going to be all right, even though he didn't know anything for sure.

"Just leave me here," Catherine suddenly shouted, lifting her head and baring her fangs.

Morgan jumped back slightly. He stared at the dirt and dried blood all over Catherine's face and clothes, at the tears spilling out of her eyes. Suddenly everything was illuminated and he realized that he had been lying to himself. Something needed to change. For a moment, staring at Catherine, he was disgusted, because he knew he was looking at what he had become. "Get up," he said, his voice shaking.

Catherine continued to cry, her face streaked and filthy.

"Get up!" shouted Morgan, grabbing Catherine by the arms.

Catherine started to scream. Morgan jerked her up, forcing her to stand, to get up and face him and reality. His grip was hurting her. Catherine calmed herself, but she continued to cry. She looked desperately into Morgan's eyes, imploring him for help. Morgan wanted to stay strong, to protect his lover, to be a man, but he crumbled at the emotion in Catherine's eyes. He let out a cough and the tears came. He gripped Catherine tighter, feeling helpless.

"I'm sorry," Catherine whispered, her voice cracking.

Morgan let go of Catherine's arms and lifted his head to face her. He closed his eyes and wiped them with his hands. The sight of Morgan crying made Catherine's heart ache.

"We'll be okay," she said quietly.

Morgan nodded and wrapped his arms around her. They didn't speak again until they had both stopped crying.

"We need to change, Catherine," Morgan said solemnly. "I can't go on like this anymore. It was fun at first, but now, it's tearing us apart."

"I know," said Catherine, her head resting on Morgan's shoulder. "I'm sorry. I love you."

"I love you, too."

They took hands and walked back to the castle without another word. Catherine ignored the sick feeling rising in her gut. She pushed the sorrow from her heart. She had to be strong.

"You look all dusty," Catherine told Morgan as they reached Blacklune's doors.

"So do you," Morgan said, picking a leaf out of her hair.

They entered the castle and peered into the ballroom. "We should eat something," Morgan said.

They walked into the ballroom hand in hand and ignored the stares they received from the other students. Zach and Amber were nowhere in sight. Morgan and Catherine filled their trays with food and sat down to eat, weary and aching.

"Blood Villain," somebody whispered into Catherine's ear.

Catherine turned around and smiled at Amber. Morgan waved

at Zach.

"River knows everything," Amber told them, setting down her breakfast tray. "Peter's okay now, just so you know. So is Cindy. She's been telling everyone how wonderful you two are."

Catherine smirked and shovelled some cereal into her mouth. She didn't really care about anything Amber had to say. She was pissed off that she was awake in the daytime with no blood. She closed her eyes and focused on the crunching sound the cereal made as she chewed.

"You guys look haggard," said Zach, noticing Morgan's bloody neck. "You have dirt all over you. You look...sick."

"Because we didn't get to feed last night," said Catherine, eyes still closed. "Well, not properly anyway."

She sighed and began to cry. She dropped her spoon and let her head fall into her hands. Morgan wrapped his arms around her and whispered into her ear. "It'll be okay."

Catherine opened her eyes. She could sense something bad about to happen. She brushed herself off and straightened her back. She took Morgan's hand just as River walked through the entrance to the ballroom. He stopped there and glanced at her and Morgan. He waved them over and waited.

Catherine felt tears trying to escape her eyes once more, but she held them back, more afraid now than sad. She rose with Morgan and walked over to River. He led them once again to his office to talk.

Inside the small room filled with books and photos, Catherine suddenly was aware of just how awful she looked. She stared at River in his clean black attire and sighed once again. She began picking chunks of dirt and blood out of her hair.

"I know this seems like fun and games, but if you two continue on the way you've been going, someone will end up seriously injured or dead," said River, settling into his large leather chair. "Drinking blood from strangers is not only rude, but extremely dangerous."

Catherine and Morgan were silent.

"You are here to learn how to live as a vampire and, ultimately, to learn how to control your urges. Drinking blood in moderation to achieve the proper amount of life energy is fine, but in excess, it turns into an obsession. Blood can be resisted, but you two have chosen to abuse it, and now you crave it more than the others here do. That craving is dangerous. If you continue to consume large amounts of blood, your body will change. It will try to adjust and those large amounts of blood you are consuming will become the minimum amount you need in order to achieve perfect energy levels. It will become harder and harder for you to feel normal, to feel happy. I've let you off the hook in the past, but this time, I am afraid, I will not be able to. You will be staying at Blacklune, but there will be strict rules for you both from now on."

Catherine was surprised she was being allowed to stay at the castle. She stared at River unblinking for a moment, taking in every detail of his appearance. He was being so understanding. It was almost as if he had gone through a similar ordeal, as if he had lost control in the past. In fact, she *knew* River was only letting them off easy because he felt for them.

"You will only receive half a glass of blood on Mondays. Your energy levels are overloaded. You both need to take a break from feeding. You will no longer have free weekends. You will be in your own rooms by eleven o' clock every night. You have your own bedroom for a reason. Use it. You will also have to remain on castle grounds as long as you live here. No trips whatsoever to town."

Catherine frowned, but still didn't speak.

"Luckily, a new class is beginning on Monday that deals with controlling urges. You will both attend this class for the next two Monday evenings. Now, let me warn you that you will not be the only ones attending these classes. Vampires come from all over to seek help from our teachers. Some of them are not friendly."

Morgan swallowed hard. Catherine bit down on her lower lip.

"Your parents will be informed of your atrocious behaviour as well," River said, disappointment etched onto his face. "I'm afraid that if something like this ever does happen again, you will be sent home immediately. Three strikes and you're out. You may exit."

Catherine and Morgan stood up to leave when River added, "And by the way, you will not be allowed to sit with one another during class." He cleared his throat and looked directly into Catherine's eyes. "You two have committed serious crimes. Luckily Lilly is in our little secret so she felt no need to contact the authorities. I have a strong feeling Cindy won't either. Peter is in the hospital and to our advantage, no one believes that the Blood Villains exist." He turned his gaze on Morgan and shook his head. "Please think about what you've you done."

Catherine turned on her heel and fled from the office with Morgan. They stumbled back up to Morgan's suite and collapsed on the floor to think.

"Maybe we're just bad people," said Morgan.

"We're not bad people. We're good people who like doing bad things. We're good at being bad."

"We could have controlled ourselves."

"We could have, but we can't change the past. I guess I like experiencing things to the fullest."

"You're right," said Morgan, "but we went too far. We did hurt people."

"We didn't kill anyone and we learned our lesson. We'll fill ourselves with other things. We won't drink as much anymore, and if we do drink, we'll drink from willing donors. We'll get better. We won't feel like *this* anymore."

Morgan pulled Catherine into a hug and sighed. "We can't have sleepovers anymore. We can't sit together anymore. We can't even go to town again."

"We'll make it work. I promise you, we'll be okay." She rubbed Morgan's back. "It's not that bad. We'll still see each other every day. We'll get through this."

"You're right," said Morgan, and even though he felt awful inside, he made an effort to smile.

12

Catherine awoke groggily on Sunday. She felt miserable and she knew why. She wanted to go on sleeping, but the prospect of seeing Morgan pushed her to get up. She dragged herself to the bathroom to wash and brush her teeth. She stared at her reflection for a long time after she was clean. She looked...different. She felt her face—her skin felt tighter. Her complexion was pallid and she definitely looked exhausted, but there was something else. She looked...predatory somehow. She snarled at her image, flashing her fangs, then composed herself and smiled slightly. She felt beautiful and dangerous. She could feel power emanating from her.

What is this? I feel so strange. It's so different than normal. It's almost as if–

Catherine suddenly spun around. She had heard Morgan's voice. She went to her door, but no one was there. She sat in a chair, waiting. She knew, without understanding how, that Morgan would be arriving soon.

Just as Morgan was about to knock, Catherine rose, opened the door, and quickly welcomed him in. Oddly enough, Morgan seemed completely unsurprised. He smiled and kissed Catherine on the head before sitting down.

"I heard you this morning," he said, turning toward the fire.

"I heard you, too," said Catherine, "in my mind."

Morgan nodded. Staring at the fire he said, "I think we're changing. I feel...stronger."

Catherine shot Morgan a broad smile. "I think the blood has changed us. I think somehow our bodies and minds are more advanced."

"When did this happen? I only remember feeling powerful when I fed."

"Maybe while we took in some of our victims' energy, we attained some of their individual powers, their strengths."

"Could be." Morgan turned to face Catherine. "Remember when we were energized, how we didn't have to eat or sleep much? Remember how it felt like we weren't even human sometimes?"

Catherine nodded, listening intently.

"Maybe, since we didn't have to worry about necessities like food and digestion, we somehow evolved. Since our minds were freed from mundane everyday matters, they changed. We started thinking differently, using different parts of our brains."

"So you're telling me that by drinking blood, by getting in that state, we somehow opened up a new part of our brain, one we never used before?"

"Most people only use ten percent of their brains," said Morgan. "Maybe we're using more. It makes sense. We drank too much. We had too much energy. We were *above* normal humans. Why couldn't we somehow have gotten super human powers? Our bodies got used to that state. We changed, Catherine."

They sat silent for a while, staring at the fire. Catherine smiled to herself. "Yesterday, when we were talking to River, I had this feeling. I *knew* River was letting us off the hook because he sympathized with us. He had lost control before. It was like, for a moment or two, I had a glimpse into his mind."

"Really? Do you think he knows you could do that?"

"I'm not sure," said Catherine. "I don't know what's happening. We have to learn more about it. We have to practice. Remember when River showed us how to transfer and shield energy? We could do that, with our thoughts."

"What did you do when you got a glimpse yesterday?"

Catherine looked up, remembering. "I was thinking about River. I was thinking of only him. My mind was clear of everything else."

"Okay," said Morgan, becoming excited. "Try again with me. Focus on reading my thoughts."

Catherine turned to look directly at Morgan. She continued to concentrate only on him. She closed her eyes and saw black. Suddenly, the image of a long, white stick formed in her mind. Her eyes shot open. "A stick!"

Morgan laughed. "A cigarette," he corrected. "I'll try now, and then let's go have a smoke."

Catherine nodded and closed her eyes. Mentally, she drew a red heart. She thought of it over and over again and pictured it as clearly as she possibly could.

Morgan smiled and whispered, "A heart."

"Yes! Oh, my God! Do you know what this means? We have powers! We can read thoughts!"

"Not very well, and sometimes it comes randomly. I bet we can read each other's mind so well because we're so close."

"Aww," said Catherine, curling into herself.

"I meant because we're sitting only a foot apart, but that works, too," Morgan said, grinning. "Maybe there are more people who can do this. There have to be."

"More vampires, yeah," said Catherine. "But that means we have to practice shielding."

Morgan agreed and they left to smoke on the balcony.

It was a cold, windy day. Trees were swaying back and forth and leaves were dancing about in the air. Catherine shivered as she exhaled. "I only have a few smokes left."

"Me, too. We can't even go into town for more. We'll have to get Zach or Amber to go for us."

Catherine nodded. When she was done smoking, she put out

her cigarette and went back inside with Morgan.

"Let's go get some coffee," Morgan said. "Breakfast should still be going on."

They settled at a table by themselves in the ballroom.

"I'm starving," said Catherine, taking a large bite out of a croissant. She had filled her plate with fruit and bread and cheese.

"So am I," said Morgan, forking eggs onto a piece of toast.

They ate quickly. Immensely satisfied, Catherine leaned back in her chair and sighed. She looked around the room. She and Morgan were the only ones in the ballroom except for a rather mysterious looking brunette girl standing at the buffet table.

"Who is that?" Catherine asked Morgan.

Morgan swallowed a mouthful and turned to look at the girl. He shrugged and returned to his food. "Probably a new student."

"Maybe she's going to that class."

"What class?"

"The Monday night class. You know."

Struck by the thought, Morgan looked more closely at the girl. She appeared about the same age as he was, and looked normal enough. When she turned around, Morgan saw that she had a pretty face. Her eyebrows were thick and dark, like her hair, and they were raised curiously.

"Hello." Her voice was smooth and calm. "I'm Charlotte."

"Hi, I'm Morgan, and this is Catherine."

Catherine smiled and waved to the girl.

Charlotte smiled back and turned to leave with her mug of coffee.

"What are you here for?" asked Catherine suddenly.

Charlotte paused to look back at her. "A class taught by Saje."

"Monday night?"

Charlotte nodded.

"See you there," Catherine said.

Charlotte raised one eyebrow and took a sip from her mug. She smiled at Catherine and Morgan and left the ballroom without another word.

"I wonder who else will show up on Monday," said Morgan. "She didn't seem too bad."

"I bet we don't either."

The wind had become even stronger over the last hour. Some trees with thin trunks had snapped and fallen in the forest. The windows rattled, creating a constant reminder of the chaos outside.

"It's going to rain, I think," said Catherine. "Come on, let's go find Amber and Zach and do something fun inside."

Morgan stood up and took Catherine's hand. They walked up the stairs together and stopped in front of Zach's door. They knocked and waited anxiously.

Amber answered the door and instantly pulled Morgan and Catherine into a hug. "Come in. Sit down and make yourselves comfortable. Zach's in the shower."

Catherine and Morgan took a seat at the kitchen table while Amber busily began adding cups to a sink filled with dirty dishes. When she had finished pouring boiling water into a clean mug, she took a seat at the table and stared at her friends. "So, what exactly were you two thinking? You were gone for a while. You didn't even say goodbye. You didn't say anything."

"I know," said Catherine, taking Morgan's hand under the table and squeezing it.

"We wanted blood," Morgan said flatly. "We weren't thinking of anything else."

"You really pissed River off," said Amber. She took a slow sip of her tea and frowned slightly. "Peter's still in the hospital."

Morgan's head dropped. "I feel terrible, about everything."

"Me, too," said Catherine, "but it's not like we can change the past. What happened, happened. River punished us, anyway."

"What did he do?" asked Amber, setting down her mug.

"We have curfew every day," Catherine said. "We only get half a glass of blood on Mondays."

"We can't sit together in class anymore," added Morgan, his

head still bowed.

"Worst of all, we can't go to town. Oh, can you buy me a pack of smokes when you have time?" She reached into her pocket, pulled out a ten dollar bill, and handed it to Amber. Morgan handed her a twenty.

"Two packs for me, please."

"I'll go into town tonight with Zach," said Amber.

"Thanks," Morgan and Catherine said in unison.

"You know, Alex, Tyler, Kevin, and Emily think you two are dangerous."

Morgan looked up and laughed loudly. "What?"

"Yeah, they're scared of you. Probably because they don't know you as well as me and Zach do. You *did* hurt people. You *attacked* people. Everyone knows about Peter—everyone in the castle at least."

"We're not attacking people anymore," said Catherine, slightly annoyed. Her eyes almost watered. "We're asking before we take."

"We asked Cindy," said Morgan, hoping for sympathy.

"That's the other part, though. Some people think it's cool that you two drink blood. I heard someone in town talking about how there are mysterious, flying creatures in Meadowshell. I don't think River likes the attention at all."

Catherine and Morgan listened to her in silence.

"I'm just glad you guys are okay," said Amber. She stared into her cup, trying to find the right words. "You have to try harder."

"We're going to a class on controlling our urges every Monday night, here at the castle," said Morgan.

"That's great! I really want you guys to stay here, you know?"

Catherine nodded.

Zach emerged from the bathroom in shorts and a T-shirt, his hair slightly wet.

"Yo!" he shouted when he spotted Morgan and Catherine. He wrapped his arms around his friends and squeezed them tight. "You guys *fucked* up," he said, taking a seat.

"We know," said Morgan. He explained the new set of rules River had given him and Catherine.

"Blood Villains, eh?" said Zach. "Kind of cool."

"You're not helping, Zach," Amber said, slapping Zach on the arm.

Catherine smirked and got up to get herself a glass of water. She leaned against the kitchen counter for a moment. She stared at Morgan and knew he didn't feel right. A wave of nausea washed over her and immediately was gone.

"Are you okay?" she asked Morgan. "Here, drink some of my water."

"I have to go lay down for a while," said Morgan, standing up to leave. He took a sip of water and held onto Catherine for support. "Cat, help me."

Morgan and Catherine said goodbye to Amber and Zach and slowly made their way to Morgan's bedroom, where Morgan dropped onto his bed and pulled the blankets around himself. "I feel awful."

Catherine crawled into bed beside him and frowned.

"I feel sick to my stomach," said Morgan, curling up into a ball, his head at Catherine's chest.

"Maybe it's guilt."

"Ha!" shouted Morgan, his eyes closed. "Probably. Everything's different now. I'll never be a normal guy again. I'm a vampire. I have fangs. I could fucking kill someone if I wanted to. What are my friends back home going to say? What is anyone going to say? They'll say I'm a freak."

"No," said Catherine, rubbing Morgan's back. "You're not a freak. I'm not a freak. Yeah, it's going to be hard. It's going to be annoying at times, but I don't care in a way. Don't you understand that being different from everyone else is amazing? That it's a blessing? We get to experience what no one else does. People won't see us and run away. We look normal."

"No we don't," said Morgan. "Not anymore. We look different.

We look sick."

"Sorry for being born pale," said Catherine, rolling her eyes.

"We've changed. We see things differently now. We react quicker than others. Our senses are heightened. We're more...perceptive. I can see better at night even without drinking blood. My eyes have changed. We act differently. We're not even human."

"Yes we are!" shouted Catherine, sitting up in bed. "If you're not happy about having powers, *whatever*. I am. I *like* being different. I *like* being powerful. We're above normal people, Morgan, don't you see? We don't need them!"

"We're pushing people away, Cat. You don't see that."

Catherine turned away with a frustrated sigh. "Look, I know we did a lot of messed up shit. I feel bad. I feel terrible, okay. But I don't feel bad about changing."

Catherine lay back down, her back to Morgan. They didn't speak again, and soon they both fell asleep.

When Morgan awoke, he realized he was alone. He felt like crying, but he pushed his sadness aside. He rubbed his eyes and thought of Catherine. An image of her feeding Charmer arose in his mind. He got out of bed and ran his fingers through his hair, mildly amused at how useful his powers were becoming. He felt refreshed and well, and his mind was clear. He went to Catherine's room.

Catherine sat in her bedroom with Morgan practicing shielding and sending thoughts until dinner. They didn't speak about their little fight earlier—they didn't have to.

At dinner, they sat with Amber and Zach. Everyone was happier and more at ease now. Alex, Tyler, Emily, and Kevin sat at another table far away, eating quietly. Alex stared at Catherine. Catherine tried to focus in on Alex's mind, but found it much harder to read than Morgan's. She got the feeling of fear mixed with contempt, but no actual words or pictures entered her mind.

"It only works with you," Catherine whispered to Morgan.

"I know," said Morgan. "It sometimes works if I focus really hard. I can't control the receiving all that well either. Words will just pop into my head."

"Alex is angry and scared. That whole table is the same."

"I know. They haven't even said hello."

Catherine focused on her food. It had started to rain outside and the falling drops provided the perfect backdrop to the silence.

Alex and Kevin were the first ones to leave the ballroom. They shook their heads at Morgan and Catherine as they passed. Tyler and Emily left next. Emily stopped next to Catherine and timidly whispered, "I'm sorry, Catherine. I just can't risk it."

"They haven't been speaking much to us, either," said Zach.

Amber shrugged.

"Sorry," said Morgan, glancing from Amber to Zach.

They all went out for a cigarette on the balcony after dinner. Catherine watched the raindrops splattering as they hit the ground below. She was upset that even Emily, the sweetest girl ever, was mad at her.

Catherine and Morgan went to go play with Charmer and relax in Catherine's suite until curfew.

In bed, Catherine thought goodnight to Morgan and heard him say goodnight back to her in her mind. She tossed and turned all night, questioning.

Will Rose still want to be my friend when she sees me? Will she even accept me if I tell her what I've done?

Catherine pulled her hair into a ponytail the next morning. She changed into a pair of jeans and a loose teal sweater. As she was pulling on her sneakers, her body started to ache. It wasn't hunger pains, Catherine knew. She ran her tongue over her fangs and pushed the thought of blood from her mind. She needed to get some fresh air.

On the balcony, Amber, Zach, and Morgan were already smoking. Amber handed Catherine her new pack of cigarettes. Catherine lit up a smoke and joined them.

It was much warmer today and the wind had died down

completely. Catherine felt calm for a moment as she inhaled, but her anxiety returned when Amber told her that it was time for class.

Amber, Morgan, Catherine, and Zach took their seats at the same table in the library. Beside them, Alex, Tyler, Kevin, and Emily sat at another table, huddled together in conversation. This was the first time the students had chosen to sit apart. Remembering her new restrictions, Catherine sat at one end of her table while Morgan sat at the other. Amber had kindly taken a seat close to her to keep her company. Zach sat with Morgan.

River entered the room and noticed the two groups of four. He raised his eyebrows, though he was obviously not amused.

"Good afternoon, class," he said, clasping his hands together. "Today I'm going to be talking about how to deal with your… gifts."

"Perfect," Catherine whispered to herself.

"You have all changed," said River, pacing in front of the tables. "You have all grown fangs, you have all developed an appetite for blood, and you have all felt what it's like to be full of life energy. You're all experiencing the same changes, the same new feelings. However—you've all been secluded here at Blacklune. What will other people say about your gifts? To be honest, most won't notice or care unless you point out your fangs to them. You're all vampires yes, but you're all still human. You all have human emotions." He stopped and eyed his pupils. "Okay, feedback. Any questions? Does anyone want to share a moment when you felt excluded because of your new state of being?"

Kevin raised his hand slowly. "Sorry, this is a little off topic, but how come we didn't need blood when we were kids? Weren't we born vampires?"

"Yes, very good question, Kevin," said River, starting to pace again. "Your life energy levels were much more stable in childhood. When you hit puberty, your levels became less balanced and you felt the effects more than when you were younger. That's why most parents only allow their children to drink blood after they become adolescents. It's not necessary before then."

"I've been thinking," said Alex, "about being a vampire. It's weird. I know I can't change it, but I've noticed like...now people are scared of me if I show them my fangs or whatever. Why wouldn't they be right? I could be like Catherine."

Catherine glared at Alex and then turned to Morgan, pleading with her eyes for some support.

"If you're a good person, people will see that," River said.

Zach raised his hand and River nodded in his direction. Zach took in a deep breath before he spoke, seeming nervous. "Is it normal to be experiencing changes like umm...feeling...stronger?"

"Could you explain, please?"

"Well, I feel a lot stronger," said Zach, "physically."

"Hmm," said River. "Having the right amount of energy can definitely make you feel happier and even healthier, but it won't usually have a large effect on your overall strength. It's not a common change, but it isn't abnormal. Everyone should be feeling their best. Those who are feeling differently are either drinking too much or too little."

Zach glanced at Morgan. Morgan nodded at him. Zach looked away, slightly disturbed.

The class continued with students asking questions and River giving explanations. Near the end of class, River took Catherine and Morgan aside and told them to be in the library at seven o'clock for their urges class.

Catherine took Morgan by the hand. "Let's go eat. Class was interesting, don't you think?"

Morgan agreed and collected his things. He was about to start walking toward the ballroom with Catherine for lunch when Zach took him by the arm, and pulled him away from Catherine, into the entranceway.

"Sorry, Cat," called Zach, forcing Morgan along. "We need to talk."

"Well, the guys need their alone time, I guess," Amber said to

Catherine, shaking her head in confusion at Zach. "Come on, let's get lunch." The girls left for the ballroom while the guys headed out front.

"What's going on?" Morgan asked Zach once they were alone.

"Something's been happening to me," whispered Zach. "I feel stronger. My vision is better too."

"I've changed, too." Morgan took out a cigarette for himself and offered one to Zach. "Catherine and I have been reading each other's minds."

"What?" said Zach, lighting his smoke.

Morgan exhaled and nodded. "We both feel different. I think it's because of drinking too much blood, having too much energy. We evolved somehow."

"Like Pokemon?" asked Zach, grinning.

Morgan rolled his eyes.

"Fucker," said Zach suddenly, punching Morgan in the arm. "In class, I was thinking to *myself* that maybe Xavier gave me powers, and you nodded. You knew what I was thinking, didn't you?"

Morgan admitted it. They finished their cigarettes.

"I don't have telepathy," said Zach, "but I do feel stronger."

He walked over to a moss-covered rock the size of a basketball and lifted it off the ground as if it weighed nothing. He threw it up into the air once and caught it easily. Without warning, he threw the rock at Morgan. Morgan was surprised to find that he had no trouble catching the rock whatsoever. In fact, he found it extremely easy to handle.

"You bastard!" said Morgan, throwing the rock back to Zach. "I knew I felt stronger, but I didn't know I was *this* strong!"

Zach caught the rock, this time with one hand. He threw it back to Morgan, who also caught it with one hand.

Morgan started laughing. "Are we the only ones?"

"I think so. I think this is because of Xavier. I asked that necklace and it said Xavier's blood allowed me to become what I am. Come on, let's head back."

○³ Cat the Vamp ○○

After lunch, Morgan whisked Catherine up to his suite. Once they were alone, the door locked, Morgan told Catherine to stand still. "Don't get scared. I'm going to try something. Morgan lifted Catherine off the floor, threw her into the air, and caught her like a baby.

"What have you been eating?" Catherine said, laughing.

"I just found out about this today."

He adjusted his stance and threw Catherine into the air once more. She squealed with delight as she landed in Morgan's arms. Morgan set her down and threw his hands up in disbelief.

"How come you have this and I don't?" She went over to Morgan and tried to pick him up, failing miserably.

"I'm not sure," Morgan said quickly, trying his best to shield his thoughts.

Xavier suddenly popped into Catherine's mind. She looked over at Charmer and sighed, slightly embarrassed.

"I'm starting to change my mind about having powers," said Morgan. "I'm getting used to it. I like it."

"Good," said Catherine, taking Morgan's hands. She kissed him once on the lips and gazed up at him. "My strong, strong, sexy man!"

"My little girl," said Morgan, pulling Catherine into a hug.

"No one's ever called me little! Skinny, yeah, but little, never," said Catherine, smiling. "You make me feel like, well, a girl."

Morgan lifted Catherine and she wrapped her legs around his back. "This is amazing," she said, kissing Morgan again. "You're driving me crazy!"

"I know," said Morgan, leaning in for a kiss. "I got Zach to buy some, uh, protection."

Catherine raised her eyebrows, slightly shocked, but intrigued. She smiled and kissed Morgan once again, her hands around his neck. She nodded in the direction of the bedroom and giggled.

Morgan smiled, flashing his fangs, and walked to his bedroom with Catherine in his arms. He laid her on the bed, his heart pounding, though his head was completely clear. It was bright outside—not even closing the blinds would shut out the light in the room.

"Well, take off my shirt," said Catherine, her hands above her head.

Morgan smiled and began to remove Catherine's clothes, layer by layer. When she was completely naked, he pulled off his shirt and with Catherine's help, was quickly stripped of the rest of his attire.

It was different, being naked together in daylight. It was scarier, but more exciting in a way, Catherine thought. She could see every part of Morgan's naked body. She could feel his most private parts hard against her thigh. She laughed as Morgan kissed her neck, making his way down to her erect nipples. Watching Morgan caress her body and feeling his fingers slip between her thighs drove her wild with passion. His skin against hers, the novel excitement of the situation, was pushing her over the edge.

"Let's fuck," Catherine said suddenly, opening her eyes.

Morgan grinned, and rolled off of her to grab a condom. When he was ready, he once again climbed on top of Catherine. Catherine spread her legs wide and arched her back. She felt him enter her slowly. Morgan groaned and squeezed Catherine's sides as he pumped, sweat collecting on his chest. Their bodies rocked with the rhythm of their breath. Pleasure was spreading throughout Catherine's entire body and she let out short cries. She dug her nails into Morgan's back, perhaps a little too hard.

"Fuck!" Morgan winced, baring his fangs.

He hugged Catherine to his chest and rolled off the bed, still inside her. Catherine found herself up against the bedroom wall, her legs wrapped around Morgan's back. Catherine screamed as he thrust into her. She was on the brink of exploding. Then, Morgan gave a cry so loud and drawn out that Catherine knew he had come. She felt him releasing inside of her. His cries of pleasure gave her the final push and then she was flying higher and higher and she was free.

They collapsed on the floor, breathing hard and covered in sweat. They lay there naked and silent for a while, Catherine stroking Morgan's back lovingly.

"That was almost as good as blood," said Morgan, turning to face Catherine.

"Almost," said Catherine, sliding her tongue over her fangs. "We'll have to do it more often, you know, since we're trying to get off blood and all."

Morgan laughed and drew her into a hug. He smiled at how wonderful it was to be so comfortable naked in front of the person he loved.

At five minutes to six, Catherine and Morgan entered the ballroom holding hands and smiling. They were the only students there. River stood by the glasses of blood at the buffet table, monitoring them. He had never had to oversee dinner before. After picking out their dishes, Catherine and Morgan walked up to him silently. River handed them two half glasses and nodded. Morgan nodded back and led Catherine back to a table.

They ate in silence, saving their blood for last. When it was time to drink, they took each other's hands under the table and downed their drinks in one.

Catherine smiled at how everything suddenly seemed more enjoyable. She wasn't out of control. She felt confident and alive. She looked over at Morgan and grinned. She heard Morgan's thoughts clearly in her mind. *I like it. Me too*, she thought, and she saw Morgan nod.

"This is going to be fun," said Catherine aloud.

Do you think River knows? Catherine thought at Morgan. *He's watching us.*

Morgan looked over at River and then turned back to Catherine.

No. Catherine heard it perfectly in her head. They continued to speak without words for the next hour. They ignored the stares from the other students. Zach and Amber never showed up for dinner. Eventually, the clarity of their messages wore off, but they could still make out each other's feelings. At a quarter to seven, they left the ballroom and headed to the library.

"I can't believe we actually had a conversation," Catherine whispered to Morgan.

"I know." Morgan took Catherine's hand and kissed her. "At first, it was cool, but it was also annoying because the messages weren't always clear. But when we drank blood, it was like our powers were heightened even more. Your words were so clear in my head, and I know mine were clear in yours."

"Are you still upset about having powers?"

"No, I'm not. I'm sorry I had that breakdown. I was feeling really upset, probably from a lack of blood. I feel okay now, though." But he was starting to worry. *This isn't exactly a good thing. This makes me want to drink more blood.*

"Stop it," said Catherine. "I can feel your...neediness. It's making me want it too."

"Sorry," said Morgan, looking away.

When they reached the back tables, they spotted Charlotte sitting alone at a seat by the windows. Morgan and Catherine both said hello and took a seat beside one another at the same table.

"River doesn't teach this class," whispered Catherine. "We can sit—"

"Yeah, I know," said Morgan. "Don't talk about it."

A woman of about thirty entered carrying a binder full of notes and pamphlets. On top of the binder was a clipboard with a pen attached to it by a piece of string. She wore a dark green dress and simple black flats. "Hello, I'm Saje. We're waiting for two more people, so just sit tight."

She went off to another section of the library and returned with a large white writing board that rolled on wheels. *Controlling Your Urges* was written on it in blue marker.

A tall, muscular blond man entered the room and took a seat

beside Charlotte. He looked worn and rugged in his stained white T-shirt. A cigarette was placed behind his right ear. After him came a small, very pale, rather lugubrious looking girl dressed in black. Her leather jacket was zipped up to her neck, just below a choker adorned with long, metal spikes. The girl took a seat close to Catherine and began to look through her bag. Catherine saw that the girl's eyes were heavily lined with thick black makeup.

"Good, everyone's here," said Saje, taking a seat in front of Catherine. "If you don't already know, my name is Saje, and I'll be teaching this class. Now, we all know that you're here because you've been having some trouble controlling your urges for blood. I'm going to be giving you some pointers on how to deal with your cravings. I want this to be a safe place for everyone, a place where you can all speak your mind. I want you all to come out of class feeling like a stronger person, a happier person. Now, let's introduce ourselves, shall we? Please tell us your name and why you think you are here. You could talk about something you regret, for example. Okay, how about you start."

Saje pointed to Charlotte. Charlotte smiled a cat-like smile and took in a deep breath.

"All right. Hello, my name is Charlotte," she said, giving a little wave. "I guess I'm here because I've been getting into some trouble back home. My parents think I need…assistance."

"Would you like to explain what kind of trouble you've been getting into?" asked Saje.

"I've been, uh, going out with guys and drinking their blood. I've been using people, I guess," she said, grinning a little.

"Do any of the guys know about each other?" asked Saje, making notes on her clipboard.

"No. I never speak to them either, after I've finished with them."

"Aren't you afraid that one day one of them will run into you," asked Saje, looking up from her notes, "or another one of your victims?"

"No. I don't think any of them will admit to being turned off by a girl sucking on them."

A few chuckles arose in the room.

"Thank you, Charlotte," said Saje. She pointed at the blond guy.

"Hey," the man said. "I'm Jimmy. I hurt some people bad."

"How so?" asked Saje.

"I don't really want to talk about it," he said, fiddling with his cigarette.

"All right," said Saje. "Thank you, Jimmy." She nodded to Morgan next.

"Hi, my name is Morgan. I guess I'm here because I hurt a few people. I let my needs take over. I took blood from people without asking first."

"Care to elaborate?" asked Saje, making more notes.

"Well, I put someone in the hospital."

"That's not true," said Catherine. "We both put a boy in the hospital. We attacked him together."

"No way," said the little goth girl beside Catherine. "You're the Blood Villains. Wicked."

Charlotte and Jimmy stared at Catherine and Morgan, their eyes widening.

"Please introduce yourself," said Saje, nodding to Catherine.

"I'm Catherine. I hurt people. I attacked people. I'm sorry."

"Thank you, Morgan and Catherine," Saje said, making another note.

"I'm Amy," said the girl in black. She bit her dark, purple lips for a moment before speaking. "One of the worst things I've done was steal blood from a hospital."

"How did that make you feel?" asked Saje.

"At the time, exhilarated, but afterwards I felt pretty low. I know others need that blood more than I do."

"Thank you, Amy," said Saje, tucking her clipboard inside her binder.

She rose, walked over to the writing board, and picked up a marker off the ledge beneath it. Facing the class, pen uncapped, she asked, "So why do you think you need more than other vampires? Anyone?"

After a moment of silence, Jimmy said, "I don't think we need it more. I think we like it more. We abuse it."

"Good point," said Saje, writing *Abuse Equals Need* on the board.

"I think we've realized what it can do," said Catherine.

"What do you mean?" asked Saje.

Catherine swallowed hard. "Blood makes us feel powerful. It... changes us."

"Yes," said Saje. "You've all probably felt what it's like to have an excess amount of life energy. For some, this is an addicting feeling, and for some, this state of being brings a new sense of awareness that sometimes has permanent effects. I think you're all trying to deal with the fact that what people are getting mad at you for is also what makes you feel so good."

"What's so bad about drinking a lot of blood, anyway?" asked Amy, raising her thin black eyebrows.

"Well, for one thing, your energy levels will become off balance. You'll need more and more energy to get high or even to feel normal. It will become increasingly more difficult to balance out your levels and you will become very unhappy, or even suicidal. This happens over time, so don't laugh and tell yourself that this won't happen to you. If you abuse blood, it will. On top of that, when you do have too much energy, your mind is altered. Your thought patterns change, and you could end up doing things that could harm you, possibly even kill you. When you have that elated feeling that comes from having too much energy, you could make decisions that you will later regret."

Catherine sighed. She didn't regret anything, but she did feel terrible about some things. She had drunk to the point when she didn't care about consequences. She had endangered herself and others. She had messed up her energy levels even more than they had been before she ever tasted blood.

"I hope my speech has changed your minds about over drinking," said Saje.

She wrote down some of the consequences of over drinking on the board and then sat back down. She smiled sweetly, her eyes wide and alert, and asked the class if they had any more questions.

"Yeah, I do," said Charlotte, looking slightly annoyed. "What if I don't over drink, but I do drink more than most vampires? Isn't that okay? I still want that feeling I get from blood. I still want the effects."

Catherine was running her hands over the smooth wooden surface of the table, staring at the patterns in the wood grain. Suddenly, she felt an impulse to look up at Charlotte. Charlotte winked at her. *I have it too.* Catherine heard Charlotte's voice clearly in her mind. She gasped, alarmed, and focused on the table.

"Eventually, Charlotte," Saje began, "you'll need more and more blood to get that feeling you want. You're putting yourself at risk. Even though you think you have things under control, you probably don't."

"So what's the proper amount of blood to drink?" asked Jimmy.

"That depends," answered Saje, "on the person. When you do consume blood, which should usually be only about once a week or less, normally you only need about a glass full. It should make you feel more comfortable with yourself, if that makes sense. You should feel at ease with your surroundings, feel ready to face life head on."

Catherine pursed her lips. *I have been greedy. Could I handle just feeling...okay?*

For the remainder of the class, each student described how it made them feel to drink too much blood. They then described how it probably made others feel. When it was time for Catherine to speak about how her actions affected those around her, her heart sped up.

"I've noticed that people react to me differently," she said quietly. "Some people ignore me now because they think I'm dangerous."

"Do you think you're dangerous?" asked Saje.

"Yeah. I guess I do. I have hurt people."

"Does it make you feel guilty to know that you've hurt people?" asked Saje.

Catherine nodded.

"How do you think you could get rid of that guilt?"

"I really don't know."

"Have you ever talked to one of your victims?" asked Saje, listening carefully.

"Yeah, I have. Not for a long time though," said Catherine, remembering Lilly.

"Give it a try," said Saje. "Ask a victim how it made him or her feel when you attacked."

Catherine nodded and sagged tiredly against Morgan.

Saje told the class that their homework was to speak with a former victim, to find out how their actions affected that person.

It was nine o'clock. Catherine and Morgan went up to Catherine's place to talk about the class. Catherine sat by the fire looking perturbed.

"What's wrong?" asked Morgan.

"Charlotte. She spoke to me in my mind."

"Really? She has it too, then."

"We aren't the only ones. It's cool, but I feel...violated somehow."

"I don't think people can read your mind if you don't want them to," said Morgan. "Well, not clearly anyway."

"That's good to know." Catherine stretched out on the floor and beckoned Morgan to her. "Class was all right. I guess we should really try to control ourselves. I don't ever want to feel like we did a few days ago. I felt so pathetic. Everything felt so pointless and hard. I kept thinking about blood and how I was going to get it. I didn't even care about anything Amber or Zach had to say."

"I think we can do it, Cat," said Morgan, lying down beside her.

Catherine closed her eyes. She thought of Morgan. She thought of life.

This is all I need for now and for always.

13

"Every living thing has energy," River said Tuesday afternoon. "It is harder to get energy from, say, trees, than it is to get from people. Today, we'll be going outside to practice receiving energy from nature. It takes a lot more focus and concentration."

The class left the castle to venture into the forest. The leaves on the trees, where there were any at all, had bright hues of orange and yellow. Large fir trees with their needles still intact emitted a fresh welcoming scent. Catherine breathed it in. She looked at the sky. It was luminous blue with no clouds in sight.

The class gathered around River, dressed in coats and scarves. Alex wore bright red mittens that matched her boots. Everyone was happy to be outdoors.

"I want everyone to go off and find a tree. When you've found a tree, I would like you to sit under it, facing it, and meditate for at least ten minutes," River began. "When you feel prepared, stand and place your hands on your tree. Close your eyes and concentrate. Do exactly as you did when you practiced taking energy from a person in class a while ago. Imagine a white light flowing from the tree into your hands. Imagine that energy filling your body, making you feel warm and complete. You were all born with the ability to extract energy. This should feel natural to you. In half an hour, return to this spot."

Catherine kissed Morgan before walking away from him in a different direction. She made sure not to step on any rotting logs as she continued into the forest, trying to get as far away as possible from the other students. She had to push a few branches out of her way and her legs got scratched by prickly bushes. She was not on any path and it got darker as she went deeper and deeper into the woods. She finally stopped at a grassy area with a large pine tree in the centre. It was as tall as a house, but not very wide. Catherine walked up to the tree and placed her hands on the bark. It was cold and rough and had mossy patches. She looked up. The tree trunk seemed to go on forever. The branches looked like arms reaching out for something. Only a few cracks of sky could be seen from below. Pine needles were scattered all about her feet. She sat down, picked up a single needle, and sniffed it. She smiled and placed the needle in her pocket. Then she closed her eyes.

After telling each part of her body to relax, Catherine took herself on a journey to a forest in her mind, practising her visualization skills and calming herself. She was walking alone in the woods and took a seat beneath a tree, much like the one she was sitting in front of. She stared at the green all around her. She listened to a babbling brook off in the distance. She smelled the air. She felt the grass beneath her. Then she heard a voice—Charlotte's voice.

Catherine's eyes shot open.

She stood up, still relaxed, though a bit shaken by the voice. She inhaled deeply and focused on her breathing for a moment before placing her hand on the tree. Then she set to work, imagining energy flowing into her and coursing though her entire body. She could feel it entering her, but it wasn't as powerful as a human's energy. It was nothing compared to the power of blood.

"Hey," whispered Charlotte, stepping out from behind the pine tree.

"What are you doing here?" Catherine whispered angrily.

"I need to talk to you."

"About what?" asked Catherine, her heart beating quickly. "You scared me."

"You knew I was coming," said Charlotte, turning to face Catherine. "I know you have...powers. I do too. I haven't met anyone else who has them yet."

Catherine, though annoyed, became interested. Charlotte brushed her hair from her eyes and took a seat on the ground. Catherine joined her.

"When did you get it?" asked Catherine.

"Not that long ago. Maybe a month or so."

"I only found out a few days ago. I've been practicing with—" She stopped herself suddenly, afraid that she had said too much.

"Morgan, I know," said Charlotte. She leaned in closer and took Catherine's hands. "Let's practice."

Catherine was a little taken aback by how forward Charlotte was being, but she wanted to practice just as much as Charlotte did.

"Close your eyes," said Charlotte. "Clear your mind. Do whatever you have to do to think of nothing. Imagine a black screen, a dark well that never ends, anything. Then focus on me. My mind. I'm going to send you something."

Catherine did as she was told. She imagined a deep stone well. She looked inside and saw darkness. She stared deeper into the well until she could only see black. Her mind went clear. That's when an image of a dog flashed into her consciousness. Without opening her eyes or losing her focus, Catherine told Charlotte what she had seen.

"That's my dog," said Charlotte. "Now you go."

Catherine cleared her mind and then, deciding to try something more difficult, she framed a sentence in her mind.

Thank you, Charlotte sent back.

The girls opened their eyes and smiled at each other. They tried speaking telepathically with their eyes open, but they couldn't focus and receive as well. Catherine remembered how clearly she had received even with her eyes open when she had drunk blood the other day.

A cold, strong wind whipped past, making the girls' hair fly about their faces. They shrieked and giggled and stood up to leave.

"I have to get back to class," said Catherine. "Thanks for practicing with me, but don't *ever* scare me like that again."

Charlotte laughed and waved goodbye.

Catherine walked back to River, her mind racing with excitement. She was the last of the students to arrive. River greeted her with a disappointed stare and told the students that they would each be describing their experience to the rest of the class. For the entire time, Catherine stood bubbling with joy. She felt confident in her skills and tried to send Morgan a message. *I want you.* Morgan looked over at her, his eyes wide. *Me too,* he sent back. *Not now. Class.* Catherine laughed out loud at how amazing her life was becoming. The rest of the students stared at her like she was crazy, but she didn't care. River, on the other hand, sighed strangely and gave Catherine a grin. *Please pay attention.* She heard River's voice clearly in her head, and gulped.

At lunch, Catherine told Morgan about what River had done.

"He's probably really good at it. Do you think he could hear us?" asked Morgan.

"No. I was only sending it to you. I was shielding. I think he could just tell, by the way we were acting, by the way we were looking at each other."

Morgan was silent. Suddenly, Catherine remembered Charlotte and she started to explain what had happened during class. When Amber and Zach strolled up to the table, Morgan and Catherine stopped talking.

"Why so quiet?" asked Amber, setting down a bowl of soup. "Zach told me."

Zach shrugged. Catherine and Morgan glanced at Zach and then at each other.

"We've only known for two days," said Morgan. "We're not used to it yet."

"Can you actually read minds?" said Amber.

"Sometimes," said Catherine, sighing with relief now that Amber knew. "If the person has it too, and they're open. If the person doesn't, I can only get a feeling, usually."

"What about you, Morgan? Are you strong like Zach?"

"Zach's strong, too?" said Catherine.

"You're not, then? I'm not, either. I wonder why the guys got it. I didn't get anything."

"You haven't drunk as much blood," said Catherine.

"Zach hasn't, either," said Amber, confused.

No one said a word. Zach and Morgan just shrugged at each other.

Maggie taught class the next day instead of River. She told the students that stones and crystals contained special qualities that could be used with meditation and energy transfer. She showed the class an array of shiny, colourful crystals. Each student was told to choose one crystal they felt drawn to, which they could keep. Maggie then walked about the back tables describing the properties that each crystal possessed.

Catherine had chosen a light pink crystal. It was quite small and light. She could hold it in her palm easily. She liked the jagged edges that jutted out in all directions. The imperfections made the crystal beautiful and unique. She fingered the rough surface and studied it as if something new and magical would appear the harder she stared at it. She rolled the crystal in her palm as Maggie told the class what the different crystals meant. When Maggie came to Catherine, she smiled and held out her palm. Catherine placed the crystal into Maggie's smooth hand.

"Kunzite," Maggie said, holding the crystal up to catch the light from the nearby windows. "This crystal is beneficial to people who are dealing with addiction." She paused and grinned, though at no one in particular. "It also strengthens your heart. It balances out emotional, mental, and physical bodies and it enhances self esteem. It allows the user to accept what is. It's associated with the Heart Chakra."

Maggie placed the jagged chunk of pink back into Catherine's palm. Catherine squeezed it tight. It was slightly warm from Maggie's grip. She liked her choice. It fit her well and would definitely be useful.

Morgan had chosen Aquamarine. Maggie explained to the class that it calms nerves and balances, purifies and allows for creative self expression, and banishes fears. She told the students that it is associated with the third and fifth chakras.

After Maggie had described each crystal, she taught the students how to use crystals with meditation. Then the students were free to go.

At lunch, Catherine and Morgan sat alone together. Amber and Zach had gone to town to go shopping and eat at a seafood restaurant. The atmosphere in the ballroom was the same as it had been the day before. Alex, Emily, Tyler, and Kevin kept to themselves, ignoring Catherine and Morgan completely. It saddened Catherine, but she knew that in a way, she deserved the isolation. She kept her mind on Morgan to keep happy. She liked the way his nose crinkled when he tasted something bitter. She liked when his lips parted ever so slightly when he was thinking. She liked the way his dark eyes could ease the sadness from her soul.

Catherine could feel the freezing wind nipping at her cheeks the next afternoon. The sky was all white. Snow would be falling soon. Although the weather called for a heavy coat, scarf, and toque, Catherine had chosen not to don warm apparel. She stood outside the castle in a sweater and shorts, shivering. For class today, the students were to go on a jog. River explained that exercise could make one feel energized, not in the same way blood did, but it could help to ease the cravings. He stood in front of the class in a grey sweat suit. Catherine could hardly recognize him—she had only ever seen him in black. He looked friendlier. Catherine could sense that he was happy.

"All right, kids. Follow me. We're going to run west along the path. It will take us through the forest. Once we're deep enough, it will fork off in different directions. There should be maps along the way. Keep up and don't get lost," River shouted, already starting to pick up pace.

Catherine felt alive and energetic. The air was keeping her alert. She ran at the front of the group with Morgan, the rest of the class following behind. She could feel her heart pumping as she pushed on. She breathed in through her nose and out through her mouth. The cold air hurt her throat slightly, but as she continued to run, she got used to the pain. The farther she ran, the warmer she got. She could feel sweat trickling down her forehead, running down her nape and back. Her arms swung with the rhythm of her breath. Her stomach was quite empty and she felt light and bouncy. Beside her, Morgan looked determined, his cheeks red, beads of sweat collecting on his face.

When the class came to a fork in the path, River slowed down to a stop. Panting, he told the students that they would be taking the right side path. He consulted a huge map in a plastic case that hung on a tree before instructing the class to start moving again. Catherine and Morgan let the other students run ahead of them, allowing themselves to slip to the back of the group. They were tired from running full speed and needed a break. They slowed down and watched the other students. Alex was struggling, her face as red as her mittens, her arms flailing awkwardly. She looked like she was punching the air. She whined and slurped back water from a pink plastic bottle. Kevin kept nagging at her to share the bottle with him. Emily and Tyler ran beside each other silently, focusing on the forest around them. Zach and Amber chatted and giggled as they ran, keeping a steady pace in front of Morgan and Catherine.

The students ran for an hour in all. By the time they had reached Blacklune, everyone was exhausted. Catherine felt great, though she was tired. She and Morgan sucked back water like air before showering in their own bathrooms.

Catherine welcomed the food at lunch. The jog had made her extremely hungry. Her stomach growled for nourishment. She ate quickly, staring out the windows, her body and mind content.

In front of the castle after lunch, Catherine, Morgan, Amber, and Zach stood smoking, dressed in scarves and toques. The air had grown even cooler, though there was no wind. The sky was so bright it was hard to look at. Even without the exhalation of smoke, Catherine could see her breath before her.

"Is that snow?" asked Amber, squinting up at the sky.

Catherine looked up and took in a breath of winter. Large, white flakes had started to fall from the sky. She tried to follow one flake's path to the ground, but her eyes kept getting distracted by all the other flakes. The air was filled with white dots. The snow was sticking to the earth and soon the ground would be covered in a blanket of powder. The four of them stood staring out at the forest, watching as it transformed into a winter wonderland.

"I want to have a snowball fight when it gets thick enough to play in," said Catherine.

They went up to Catherine's room to sit with Charmer, who had never seen snow before, and stare out the window, warm and delighted. Charmer's eyes were wide with wonder. The kitten looked curious, but afraid, and he made everyone laugh as he batted at the glass, trying to catch the snowflakes.

After a warm supper, they got dressed in whatever they could find that would keep them dry. They went out the front doors and stepped into a foot of snow. Catherine squealed with joy and scooped up some powder with her mitten-covered hands. She could feel the wetness seep through her mittens to greet her palms. She raised her face to the sky and felt the flakes tickle her with icy kisses. The familiar smell of snow made her think of happy times: Christmas, winter breaks, sledding, drinking cocoa. She felt like a child again, catching snowflakes on her tongue, feeling them melt into water. She ran over to Morgan, and he greeted her with a snowball to the face. Laughing, Catherine threw a snowball at Morgan and then flopped to the ground to make a snow angel.

Alex and Kevin had come outside to stare at the snow. They

watched Catherine waving her arms in the snow, her eyes closed and her mouth open wide. Alex started to laugh. Catherine looked ridiculous, but she did look like she was having fun. Alex knelt down and scooped up a handful of snow. She carefully shaped a ball with her hands and then looked at Kevin and grinned. She stepped forward and aimed the snowball right at Catherine. It hit Catherine square in the nose.

Catherine's eyes shot open. "Hey! Who did that?" she shouted, scrambling to her feet. She was soaking wet and covered in snow. Her hair was poking out of her toque in all directions. She looked rather like the abominable snowman. She shook herself off, adjusting her hat, and looked around. She heard a familiar laugh, turned around, and spotted Alex. Her heart sank. She could feel her cheeks flushing.

"Can I join you?" Alex asked, another snowball in her hands.

Catherine glanced behind her. Amber, Morgan, and Zach had stopped goofing around. They were silent, staring at Alex and Catherine. Catherine nodded.

"What the hell?" Kevin whispered to Alex.

"We can't stay mad at them forever," Alex whispered back. "I know they really messed up, but I think they're different now." She paused and looked down at her perfect ball of white. "I think we've all changed for the better."

Kevin shrugged and followed Alex into the fight. Soon Emily and Tyler joined in and two teams of four were established. The snowball fight continued until eight o'clock. Afterwards, everyone went inside to warm up in Amber's suite. Since they were all there, Amber called an Animal Kingdom meeting. Everyone called out their nicknames. No one drank blood. They talked and apologized to one another. The snow, clean and pure, had given everyone a chance to start anew.

On Friday, River told the class that they were to prepare a presentation for Monday about what they learned from their time at Blacklune. It could be presented in any form: a speech, a skit, a poster, and so forth. There had to be an oral portion and the students were to work in pairs that River had assigned: Emily and Morgan, Tyler and Zach, Amber and Kevin, and finally, Alex and Catherine.

"For the rest of today's class, work on the project with your partner. I've provided you with some poster supplies. You have the weekend to prepare. Monday is our last class. I'll be talking about your final ceremony, which will happen Tuesday at midnight. Your parents will be here to pick you up."

Catherine was happy that she was going home, but a part of her wanted to stay at the castle. At Blacklune, she could be alone with Morgan. She had her own place, new friends, a new life. She was sad that it would soon be all over.

Catherine and Alex sat in one of the bay window seats to brainstorm for their presentation. After talking for ten minutes, they decided that making a poster and explaining it would be the best way to approach the project. They made two lists: advantages of being a vampire, and disadvantages of being a vampire. They wrote up a rough draft of each and then made good copies on two separate pieces of paper. They cut out the text boxes and set them aside to work on the paragraph that would explain the lists. Catherine drew pictures of fangs and blood to accompany the text. The girls glued everything down on a piece of white poster board and wrote the title *What Blacklune Taught Us* in red marker at the top. They decorated their drawings and text boxes with borders of red marker. When they were complete, they started to practice presenting.

After class, Catherine and Morgan went up to talk in Catherine's room, cozy on the bed. Morgan stared out the window, mesmerized. The snow had picked up again. He was glad to be indoors with Catherine.

"What are we going to do?" asked Catherine.

Morgan knew what she was talking about. He could feel what Catherine felt. He knew she was worrying about them, about what they would do when they had to part.

"We'll write to each other. We'll call each other. We don't live that far away. Silverslate is only a three hour drive from Stoneysea. You've been there before. We'll visit each other. I'd like to see your cottage. I want to meet your friends."

"Silverslate is so big and busy. There are so many places to shop. There are so many things to do. I want to see your apartment. I want to meet your friends. I even want to meet your parents."

"I'll introduce you on Tuesday," said Morgan. "They'll love you."

"My parents will love you," said Catherine, curling into Morgan's chest. "Who wouldn't?"

Morgan smiled and hugged Catherine tight.

On Saturday, Catherine went to practise presenting with Alex and Morgan practised with Emily. The day went by quickly and after sunset, everyone went for a walk in the snow.

Sunday was a rather depressing day. It was raining heavily, washing away all the snow. Morgan went with Catherine to talk to River about making an important call to the hospital. They had chosen to speak with Peter for their homework assignment. River gave them the number and told them to be polite. He smiled at them. Catherine was happy that River was in a better mood now.

Catherine and Morgan stood huddled around the phone in the library. Catherine had been brave enough to talk first. She called the hospital and was put on hold for five minutes. When a shaky male voice answered, she gulped, unsure of what to say.

"Uh, hi," said Catherine. "I wanted to say that I'm sorry for what I did. I was the one who attacked you." She spoke quickly and then paused, her heart racing, waiting for a reply. Peter didn't speak, so she continued. "My name is Catherine. I'm a vampire."

"I knew it," the boyish voice said. "I told everybody, but they wouldn't believe me. The doctors think I'm crazy. They made me speak with a psychiatrist. I was under suicide watch for a while. They thought I did this to myself." Peter paused. When he spoke again, Catherine could hear anger rising in his voice. "You could've killed me. Why did you do this to me?"

"I'm sorry," Catherine said, sighing. "We didn't know what we were doing. We've changed."

"Who's we?" asked Peter.

Catherine passed the phone to Morgan and nudged him with her elbow. Morgan placed the phone to his ear and introduced himself. He explained to Peter what blood did to them and why they attacked him. He asked Peter how he was doing.

"My wounds have healed," he said quietly. "I'm being let out on Monday. You guys really scared me, you know. I thought I was going to die. You really messed me up. I kept telling myself that you really attacked me, but then everyone kept telling me I was delusional. I started to doubt myself. Now at least, I know the truth."

After the conversation ended, Catherine and Morgan realized just how much in the wrong they had been. They felt proud that they had confronted Peter and had cleared things up, but Peter's voice had disheartened them both. Catherine felt like a monster. For the rest of the day, she didn't laugh, not even once.

Catherine drank three cups of coffee Monday morning. She walked to class feeling prepared and energetic. She was excited to give her speech, but also a little nervous.

Everyone sat at the same table. Catherine sat next to Alex, chatting quietly. When River entered, he smiled at the class and clapped his hands together. He took a seat with the students, pointed to Kevin and Amber, and told them they were up first. Amber jumped up enthusiastically with a bag filled with props at her side. She set the bag down to the left side of the "stage" and began taking out objects one by one. She lined up her props for easy access and then joined Kevin at the front of the class. She told her audience that she and Kevin would be doing a skit for their presentation. When she felt ready to begin, she whispered to Kevin. Kevin rushed over to the props and picked up a thin, black scarf. He nodded to Amber and they began.

"Are you ready to fully become one with the night?" Kevin asked in a deep voice, trying his best to imitate River.

Amber nodded as Kevin proceeded to run around Amber with the fabric. They acted out the initiation ceremony and then the scene switched to a classroom setting. Side by side, Kevin and Amber took turns introducing themselves as the students watching.

"I'm Alex," said Amber, flicking her hair behind her and jutting her hips out to one side.

The class laughed. River was greatly amused. Alex smiled as she rolled her eyes.

Kevin impersonated River again and taught Amber, who had taken the role of the entire class. Kevin told Amber that being a vampire was a blessing that she had to accept. Then Kevin started to speak very quickly, cramming every lesson into one long speech. He taught Amber about energy centres, chakras, yoga, meditation, energy transfer, controlling urges, blood letting, and acceptance. Amber nodded fervently, every once and a while shooting up her hand to ask a question. The skit ended with Amber telling Kevin thank you.

"Blacklune has changed my life forever," Amber said. "I'll never forget it. I'll never forget the people here. Thank you."

"And scene!" Kevin shouted, miming the snap of a movie director's slate.

He and Amber rushed together to the front of the class and took a bow. River stood and started to clap wildly. The rest of the class joined in. Everyone cheered. River even gave a whistle.

Amber and Zach laughed and hugged each other. Amber looked like she was trying not to cry. She shook her head and took a seat next to Zach. Kevin skipped back to the table to sit with Alex.

"Thank you so much," said River. "Emily and Morgan. You're up next."

Emily shot Morgan a look of fright. She was visibly shaking. Morgan told her things were going to be okay. Emily nodded and stood up, trying to find her inner strength. They walked to the front together, their speeches in hand. Morgan began first.

"When I first came to Blacklune, I didn't know what to expect. I was scared and excited and confused. The first time I drank blood, everything became clear. I experienced what it felt like to be happy, to be alive. I was thankful to be alive. I enjoyed the lessons I was taught. I learned that energy could be attained in many ways: through blood, through nature, through meditation. I enjoyed the feeling that energy gave me and I wanted that feeling all the time. I became greedy. I thought I had everything under control, but I was wrong. When I over drank, my mind was altered. There were no consequences, and I hurt people. But then everything changed. After drinking large amounts of blood for days in a row, after being in that state of bliss, I realized that my body was changing. It was trying to adjust to make those amounts the normal amount. I realized I needed more and more blood to even feel okay. After attacking Peter and drinking from Cindy, I felt awful. Everything became pointless. I almost wanted to die. I never want to feel like that again, so the most important thing I've learned here is to listen to River and drink the proper amount of blood. My levels are finally adjusting and it feels good not to need. I'm no longer going to attack people. I'm going to live a healthy and happy life. I'm sorry to those I hurt. Thanks for putting up with me."

The class clapped. The speech had been straight from Morgan's heart. It had taken a lot of courage for him to speak those words aloud. When Emily began, the class quieted down and listened intently. She started off by thanking each person who sat at the table before her, and Morgan. Then she reviewed the lessons taught by River and described the ones she'd most enjoyed in detail. She was especially glad for the opportunity to try out everyone's favourite activity. She told the class that she had grown to love things that she had never known she liked. She gave a curtsy at the end of her speech and let out a quiet sigh of relief. The class rose to applaud, and stood for a long time before sitting again.

Tyler and Zach presented next. They had elected to show the class a slideshow of pictures. The class gathered around Zach's laptop and watched as pictures of Blacklune appeared on the screen. Tyler and Zach took turns narrating a story that went along with the photographs. Catherine smiled at how creative and clever the boys had been. They had even managed to snap a photo of her without her noticing. There was a photograph of every student working on the project during Friday's class. Zach had managed to catch a snapshot of River wearing a smile. River chuckled when he saw the picture. The show ended with beautiful shots of the beach and sky. The boys took a bow each and everyone clapped. River patted the boys on the back, surprised and pleased by how much effort they had put into the project.

Catherine and Alex stood in front of the class holding their poster together, smiling nervously. Catherine began by listing the advantages of being a vampire.

"You get to see the world like no one else does," she said, gazing at the class before her, her heart racing. "You get to be unique. You get to be one with nature. You get to feel what others feel. You get to appreciate life more. You get in touch with yourself more. You get to experience perfect happiness and balance."

She went on like that for a while before Alex listed the disadvantages.

"You're different from everyone else. You can become dependant on blood. Your energy levels can get out of balance and cause you to feel sad. You could be isolated. You could frighten people and be called a freak. You could drain people without knowing it. You could attract unwanted attention or people. You could get yourself into dangerous situations."

The girls took turns describing what the advantages and disadvantages meant and how they affected people. They pointed to the drawings and diagrams to illustrate their words, and finished by giving each other a high five. The class clapped and cheered, happy that everyone had done such a good job.

River quieted his students down, and smiling, he began to talk about the upcoming ceremony. He told the class that tomorrow they would wear the black outfits that they first wore for the initiation ceremony. The event was to recognize the fact that each student had finished the course and was ready to go out into the world as a vampire. Each student would be entitled to sign their name in the official Vampires United book that held a record of all the vampires in the area. That way, River explained, he would be able to keep track of the students and invite them to meetings. He would be able to introduce them to other vampires. Together, he promised, they would learn more about their gifts. He went on to explain that there were vampires all over the world and that teachers like River kept track of them and had private meetings of their own. Of course, it was a personal choice if a vampire wanted to become part of Vampires United. Some chose to stay secluded. Sometimes vampires visited Blacklune. Exchanges all over the world were taking place as River spoke.

Catherine listened eagerly, her heart singing with a sense of accomplishment. She had finished the course at Blacklune and had made up with her friends. She knew now that she had a whole world of mysteries to discover.

River took the class to the ballroom to show them what they would be doing tomorrow night. They did several run-throughs to make sure nothing would go wrong for the ceremony.

That night, Morgan and Catherine sat together in the urges class, completely contented by their half glasses of blood. Saje encouraged each student to talk about their homework assignment. Jimmy went first.

"I talked to my old friend Rick," he said, shifting in his seat. "After I bit him, he wasn't my friend anymore. I said I was sorry. He didn't forgive me, but I least I said it, right?"

"Right," said Saje. "Did it feel good to talk to him?"

Jimmy nodded, his eyes somewhere else. He refused to say any more about the situation.

Charlotte spoke next. She had called up an old boy-toy and had apologized for the pain she had given him. She told the class that the boy had yelled at her over the phone. He had cursed at her and not forgiven her. He hung up before Charlotte even had a chance to explain herself.

Saje nodded her approval, saying that Charlotte had tried her best.

Amy had emailed an old friend and had explained to her that she was a vampire. The friend replied with a number to a local psych ward. Saje sighed and patted Amy on the back.

Catherine and Morgan told the class that they had called Peter together.

"He was shocked at first, I think," began Catherine, looking to Morgan for encouragement, "but he was happy that he had been right about us...about what we are. He told us that everyone thought he was crazy. I felt really bad for him."

"Ho told me he was doing better though," said Morgan, eyeing Saje. "He said we scared him, but he was surprisingly calm when he spoke to us. He was happy that he knew the truth. I think we fascinate him."

Saje nodded, making a note on her clipboard. She stared out the window, lost in thought.

"That does happen," she said, returning her focus to the class. "I'm glad everyone made an effort and I'm sure you all feel better about yourselves because of it. You should all be very proud."

For the remainder of the class, the students talked about some of the things they were ashamed of. Near the end of class, a student asked a question that made Morgan's heart speed up.

"Can you turn someone into a vampire?" asked Amy, a crooked smile stuck on her face.

Saje took a deep breath before answering. "Yes. If a vampire drains a person near death, if a vampire feeds on all that energy and leaves the person empty, the victim will crave that energy. If the victim then drinks the blood of a vampire, he too, will become one. He will never be completely balanced again. I'm sure some of you knew that already. Am I correct?"

Charlotte nodded. The rest of the class stayed still and silent. Catherine was very intrigued indeed. Morgan was petrified, sweat running down the back of his neck.

"Of course, I'm sure none of you have ever made someone into a vampire," said Saje, eyeing the students before her.

Morgan took in a deep breath, trying to calm his nerves. Catherine looked at him. She could sense his fear. She closed her eyes and tuned into his mind. What she saw made her stand and flee the library.

"Catherine?" Saje called out, alarmed at Catherine's sudden departure.

"I think she's ill," said Morgan. "I have to go help her. Bye."

He ran from the library. Amy and Jimmy shook their heads in confusion, as did Saje. Charlotte, however, slapped her hand to her mouth to keep herself from saying anything.

Morgan found Catherine on the balcony, sucking back a cigarette. He knew she had found out the one thing he had been keeping from her.

"How could you?" she asked, staring out at the sky.

Morgan walked toward her. He laid a hand on her back, but she shook it off. "You don't understand, Cat. I made a deal with him."

"How could you make a deal with *that*?" Catherine snapped, exhaling through her nose. "He tricked me, and you! He's an awful person."

"I know," said Morgan, frustrated. "He asked me and Zach to do it. We didn't even know if it was going to work. Anyway, I said that if I was going to turn him, he had to leave you alone in exchange. I only did it to protect you, Catherine."

Catherine turned her head to face Morgan. She inhaled her cigarette and exhaled slowly, her thoughts running rampant. "You trust him?"

"He hasn't shown up since. Like you said, you can't change the past."

"I guess," Catherine said quietly, thinking back to her own past. *Xavier was so persuasive.* "I wish you'd told me though. He's a dangerous guy." She paused when a new thought popped into her head. "That's why you and Zach are so strong!"

Morgan nodded, relieved that Catherine had taken the news so well.

"A vampire witch," said Catherine. "A vamitch? A witpire?"

Morgan grinned and took the cigarette from Catherine's fingers. Catherine sighed. She was upset that Morgan had kept the secret from her for so long, but she was glad she now knew. She hoped it would be the last secret revealed. She punched his arm and took the cigarette back from him to kill.

14

Catherine and Morgan stayed up late talking, alone in the library. They sat crossed legged, facing each other, on a bay window seat. Only a few of the lamps along the walls were lit. In the darkness, the shelves of books and the shadowy aisles looked eerie. Catherine gazed out the window at the moon, which was dogged by two bright stars. Morgan gazed at Catherine, her exquisitely beautiful profile washed with twilight. He closed his eyes for a moment, cleared his mind, and sent her an image of himself pressed up against her. Catherine snapped out of her daydream and put a hand to her mouth, giggling.

"So that's what's on your mind," she whispered, leaning forward for a kiss.

Morgan parted his lips, leaned in, and met Catherine's mouth. Eyes closed, he allowed himself to dive deep into the moment, to think of nothing else. He listened to his body; he felt her warmth, her heartbeat, her love. When he paused, Catherine was smiling, exhilarated, her cheeks rosy. She exhaled loudly and waved her hand before her face like a fan. Morgan laughed, but not too loudly. He didn't want them to get kicked out of the library, not when things were getting so steaming hot.

They kissed again and allowed their bodies to relax against each other, twin souls bathed in white moonlight.

"There's something I didn't say in my speech today," said Morgan, red-faced and slightly out of breath. "I forgot to say what the absolute best part about coming to the castle was."

"And what was that?"

"Meeting you," said Morgan, grinning.

Catherine laughed and kissed Morgan hard. She didn't have to explain what the best part for her was. Morgan already knew.

Fortunately, it was sunny the following morning. Catherine woke up extra early. She wanted to walk around the entire castle, every nook and cranny, before leaving. She wanted to say goodbye to the grounds and to all her new friends. She started the day by talking a walk in the courtyard. She smoked and let her mind wander freely over the last thirty-seven days.

Breakfast was loud and lively. The food was delicious and everyone was bubbling with excitement. Catherine could feel the anticipation rising like a physical being in the centre of her table. Everyone exchanged phone numbers and e-mail addresses. Alex began to cry and she and Kevin started hugging everyone, which caught on, and soon breakfast had turned into a soap opera-worthy farewell session. Even the boys let a few tears roll from their eyes.

Since there was no class, everyone cleaned and packed and went off in different directions. Alex and Kevin went to town to pick out souvenirs for family and friends. Emily and Tyler went for a walk in the forest. Zach and Amber made out in Zach's bedroom and tried on their ceremony outfits together. It was after lunch when Catherine was finally finished putting all her things away and tidying her suite. She always liked to leave her mark wherever she went. She decided that writing *Catherine + Morgan* in permanent marker beneath a window ledge would be perfect. She could come back to the castle, look at the names, and instantly be flooded with happy memories of the past. After she finished writing, she slipped the pen back into her suitcase, and went to pick up Charmer. "We're going back to my home, kitty!"

Charmer meowed softly. Catherine hugged the kitten and

sighed blissfully. She set him down and took a final look around the suite, nodding with approval. Then she ran to see Morgan.

Morgan had showered and his hair was still slightly wet. Catherine ran up to him and breathed in deeply, intoxicated by his manly and familiar scent. He smelt extraordinarily delicious and she told him so.

River, Maggie, Saje, and Delores joined the students for dinner that evening in the ballroom. Charlotte, who was staying at the castle, joined Catherine's table. She and Catherine made sure to exchange information so they could keep in touch.

Delores had cooked an especially excellent farewell dinner. Plates filled with fancy hors d'oeuvres were set out on tables along with trays filled with rich cheeses and a colourful array of fresh fruit and vegetables. There were so many main course meals to choose from, Catherine had a hard time deciding what to eat. Everything looked so delectable. She decided to have salmon baked with lemon accompanied by wild rice and salad. She made sure to save plenty of room for dessert. Cakes, pies, cookies, brownies, tarts and cream-puffs were displayed on shiny silver trays like art pieces.

Flowers had been arranged on every table along with candles and a goodbye gift for each student. In the middle of dessert, Amber raised her strawberry milkshake, exploding with whipped cream, to the centre of the table.

"A toast to friends," she said, smiling.

Catherine, Zach, Morgan, and Charlotte all raised their glasses high and took sips.

"Now let's open our presents!" Amber squealed.

Catherine took a bite of moist chocolate cake before picking up a rectangular box wrapped in blue and gold paper. She carefully peeled back the paper to reveal a gold cardboard box. She opened the box and immediately smiled; all her friends, with their jack-o-lanterns, were smiling back at her. She picked up the photograph and studied each person before inspecting the next item, a personal note from River. She read it without speaking. It was about how proud River was of Catherine. She laughed softly when she came to a part about how he was slightly relieved that he would be getting a break from her. The last present in the box was a silver bracelet. It was a delicate chain with a flat, rectangular piece in the centre. Engraved on the surface of the rectangle was Catherine's name in beautiful cursive. Next to the name was a smile: a set of grinning teeth with fangs. Catherine wrapped the bracelet around her left wrist and had Amber do the clasp for her.

Everyone had received a bracelet along with a picture and note. The guys' bracelets were thicker with heavier links.

Catherine finished her dessert and went back up to her suite with Morgan. They talked and played with Charmer while River and Maggie began to set up the ballroom below.

Catherine and Morgan, both extremely excited, decided to change into their outfits two hours before the ceremony which, of course, was to be held at midnight. They were told not to enter the ballroom until that time, so they snuck about the upper hall quietly, hoping to catch a glimpse of the action. At eleven, Catherine could hear faint whispers and footsteps coming from the entranceway and ballroom. She saw vampires clad in the traditional black entering the castle doors. One woman wore a large, frilly black hat with dotted netting draped from the front of it, concealing her identity. She held the arm of a man wearing a black cape lined with fur.

At ten to midnight, the students gathered in the upper hall. Amber, the leader, led them down the staircase and into the entranceway. Catherine was the last in line. The students ahead of her were gasping in awe. When her eyes finally fell upon the ballroom, she knew why. The beautiful chandelier hanging from the ceiling was glowing with the light of at least one hundred candles. Candles were lit along the walls as well. There was no other light. The room was filled with chairs facing the front of the castle. In those chairs sat the friends and families of the students, all in black. At the front of the ballroom, where the buffet tables usually were, a space was cleared. River stood there, holding a stack of papers. He was beaming a triumphant smile. Catherine had never seen him looking so proud.

"Can you see your parents?" Catherine whispered to Morgan, eyeing the silent crowd as she entered the ballroom.

Morgan quickly pointed to the woman with the large black hat. Catherine grinned. The man with the cape was her husband, Morgan's father. They were sitting together in the first row of chairs. Catherine stared at them as she followed the students to the west side of the ballroom. They were all supposed to line up along the wall with the secret door that led to the kitchen. Suddenly, something caught her eye: a pale, waving hand. She looked at the owner of the hand and recognized her mother. She laughed out loud and waved back. She waved to her father and then shook Morgan to get his attention.

"Our parents are sitting next to each other," Catherine whispered to Morgan. "Weird."

Morgan smiled and took Catherine's hand. He squeezed it tight. "This is it," he squeaked out, smiling with fangs showing.

Catherine's heart was beating rapidly. She giggled and closed her eyes and took in a deep breath. When she opened her eyes, the mysterious beauty of the ballroom filled her with enchantment, and her stomach stopped fluttering.

River started the ceremony by introducing himself. He talked a little about the castle and what the students had been doing for the last five weeks. The room warmed with quiet applause. Then, one by one, River called the students to his side.

"Amber Blakestone."

Amber happily strode up to greet River. She shook his hand enthusiastically and then stood quietly adjusting her sparkly black skirt.

River then placed a certificate in Amber's hands. Amber took it and carefully examined it. It was a black certificate bordered with a red floral pattern. Red calligraphy scrolled across the centre. It read, *This certificate shows that Amber Blakestone has successfully completed* her schooling at Blacklune and officially declares her a member of Vampires United. It was signed at the bottom by River. Next to his signature, River had added a personal note: *Thank you, Amber, for being so earnest and outgoing.* Amber rolled her eyes. She had always been called "outgoing." She thanked River, then walked over to where Maggie stood smiling at her. Maggie helped Amber, one arm at a time, into a sleek black robe. It was thick, yet comfortable and light. Amber shook hands with Maggie before walking over to a table covered with a red cloth. On the table was the Vampires United book. Amber signed the book with her name, address, and telephone number. Then she proceeded to the east wall of the ballroom to wait silently for the others to finish.

The ceremony went on with River calling out names and handing out certificates, and Maggie swathing students in darkness. Catherine smiled when she read River's personal note on her certificate: *Thank you Catherine for being so strong and intuitive.* When she received her robe, she hugged Maggie and thanked her for all the help and advice she had given her.

"Congratulations, class. You are now members of Vampires United," River said loudly, raising his hands to the ceiling. "A round of applause, please!"

The room exploded into a paroxysm of clapping and the entire audience rose to their feet. Catherine could see her parents beaming at her, proud and overwhelmed. When the clapping died down, River thanked everyone for coming and told the students to go find their parents.

Catherine walked over to her mother and father. She stopped in front of them and smiled, showing off her fangs.

"Oh honey!" cried Aneese, pulling her daughter into a hug.

"We're so proud of you," John said, wrapping his arms around his wife and Catherine.

"Thanks," said Catherine, genuinely happy to see her parents.

"Are you excited to be going home?" asked Aneese, letting Catherine loose.

Catherine looked to the left of her. Morgan was hugging his parents, talking excitedly, adding to the cacophony in the room. Aneese smiled understandingly.

"I'm glad you get along so well with Morgan. We haven't seen him in ages," Aneese said, looking over at him.

Catherine choked out a laugh. "What?"

"Your mother and I have been friends with the Silverwoods since before you were born," John said. "We all met at Blacklune a long time ago. In fact, before we had our children, we used to vacation together. Wolf and Marie came by the cottage once for a visit when you and Morgan were just babies. You two actually met about seventeen years ago."

Catherine's mouth was agape. She couldn't speak. All she could do was stare in amazement at her parents. While she stood open mouthed and bewildered, Wolf and Marie made their way over to greet John and Aneese. They even hugged Catherine.

"You probably don't remember us, Catherine," Marie said, her hat bobbing up and down. "What a beautiful woman you've become."

Catherine shook her head. Morgan had just been informed of the situation as well, and was slowly making his way to Catherine's side, shocked.

"What a handsome man you've grown into," Aneese said to Morgan.

"We moved around a lot when you and Morgan were growing up," Wolf said to Catherine. "Of course, we always kept in touch with your parents. I'm so happy that you and Morgan finally have gotten to spend some time together. You'll be seeing a lot more of each other now that we've moved back to the area."

Morgan stared at Catherine in disbelief. He started to laugh. Catherine joined in, relieved that she would not have to introduce Morgan to her parents. After all, they already knew him.

"Cat, we're all heading back to the cottage," said Aneese, indicating that "all" meant Morgan's family too with a wave of her arm.

"Are you serious?" Catherine felt like she was almost drowning in her own joy.

"We're all getting together to celebrate. We have so much catching up to do," said Aneese. "Now both of you go and get your things and say your final goodbyes. We're leaving in twenty minutes."

Catherine and Morgan walked off to retrieve their suitcases. Morgan was still looking completely shocked. Catherine grinned at him, and they both laughed and laughed at the amazing absurdity of life.

LaVergne, TN USA
08 February 2010
172435LV00006B/64/P